ATTENT

This is not a finished book.

This galley proof has not been corrected by the author, publisher, or printer.

The design, artwork, page length, and format are subject to change, and typographical errors will be corrected during the course of production.

If you quote from this galley, please refer to the final printed book.

Thank you.

THE ONE WHERE THE KID NEARLY JUMPS
TO HIS DEATH AND LANDS IN CALIFORNIA

Mary Hershey

Publication date: March 2007
U.S. $15.99 (Canada $20.00)
Ages 10 up * Grades 5 up
288 pages
ISBN 1-59514-150-2
ISBN-13 978-1-59514-150-7

Razorbill
Published by Penguin Group
Penguin Young Readers Group
345 Hudson Street
New York, NY 10014
www.penguin.com/teens

THE ONE WHERE THE KID NEARLY JUMPS TO HIS DEATH AND LANDS IN

CALIFORNIA

A NOVEL BY

MARY HERSHEY

razOr
bill

The One Where the Kid Nearly Falls to His Death and Lands in California

RAZORBILL

Published by the Penguin Group
Penguin Young Readers Group
345 Hudson Street, New York, New York 10014, U.S.A.
Penguin Group (USA) Inc., 375 Hudson Street, New York, New York 10014, U.S.A.
Penguin Group (Canada), 90 Eglinton Avenue East, Suite 700, Toronto, Ontario,
Canada M4P 2Y3 (a division of Pearson Penguin Canada Inc.)
Penguin Books Ltd, 80 Strand, London WC2R 0RL, England
Penguin Ireland, 25 St Stephen's Green, Dublin 2, Ireland
(a division of Penguin Books Ltd)
Penguin Group (Australia), 250 Camberwell Road, Camberwell,
Victoria 3124, Australia (a division of Pearson Australia Group Pty Ltd)
Penguin Books India Pvt Ltd, 11 Community Centre, Panchsheel Park,
New Delhi – 110 017, India
Penguin Group (NZ), Cnr Airborne and Rosedale Roads, Albany,
Auckland 1310, New Zealand (a division of Pearson New Zealand Ltd)
Penguin Books (South Africa) (Pty) Ltd, 24 Sturdee Avenue, Rosebank,
Johannesburg 2196, South Africa

Penguin Books Ltd, Registered Offices: 80 Strand, London WC2R 0RL, England

10 9 8 7 6 5 4 3 2 1

Library of Congress Cataloging-in-Publication Data is available

Printed in the United States of America

FOR jill WITH THE OCEAN COLORED EYES WHO
DROPPED FROM THE SKY AND STOLE MY HEART

THE ONE WHERE THE KiD NEARLY JUMPS TO HiS DEATH AND LANDS IN

CALIFORNIA

CHAPTER ONE

I FIRST BECAME FAMOUS WHEN I was eight years old and my dad took me skiing at Lake Rochester with his old-lady boss. My picture was on the front page of all the newspapers for miles around. Heck, Aunt Clem said she even caught me on the national news. And it wasn't because I was such a hotdog skier. The real story was that I took a dive out of the ski lift chair. Broke my right leg so bad they had to cut it off.

It wouldn't have been such big freakin' news if it was just some poor kid falling out of a lift. But I didn't just fall. The newspaper said I laid a hundred-dollar bill on the kid next to me, lifted the safety bar, and then bailed right out. From forty feet.

Funny thing is, I don't remember jumping—I only remember the landing. Man, I thought snow would be way softer.

I spent a lot of days in Sacred Heart Hospital near Lake Rochester. My mom flew in and stormed around the hospital with a look on her face that made the security guards nervous. And the patrol dogs kept their eyes glued to her. They could smell the Mama Bear rage that burned off her like a fever.

After that day, The Jump became the main event in our lives. And no matter what anyone said to Mom—Aunt Clem, the shrink, the family court judge—it was always and would ever be HIS FAULT: Richard Hudson III, my ex-father, her ex-husband.

Even though they'd doped me up pretty good at Sacred Heart, I remembered the big fight Mom and Dad had outside my room. Mom grabbed him by the shirt and screamed at him that I was just a little boy and not a goddamn jock for him to show off. She shook him like a rag doll and he kept just trying to hug her when any idiot could see she was not in the mood to cuddle.

And now, five years later, my mother the traitor was sending me to go stay with the jerk who ruined our lives. I swore at the suitcase that sat next to my bed. Then kicked it over with my fake foot on a stick. As far as prosthetics go, it was the cheapest model on the planet. I picked it out myself. Mom and pretty much everyone else wanted to buy me a better one, but I wouldn't let them. What's the point? You can dress it up all you want, but a stump is a stump is a stump. I hated even putting it on, but Mom insisted. And she didn't think it was funny at all when I took off my leg at school, put it in my locker, and then tied a rag around my stump with fake blood on it.

After that, though, the kids at school pretty much knew if anyone was going to be cracking jokes about my leg, it was gonna be me.

I heard Aunt Clem clomp up the stairs in her hiking boots and pause at my door. After a moment she knocked.

"Hey! You decent?" she asked.

"Oh, like that would stop you," I said as she swung open the door.

"Always the big wise guy," she said, coming over and plopping down next to me. She crooked an elbow around my neck, pulled me next to her, and laid her face in the top of my hair.

I unhooked myself from her arm. "I'm not going," I said.

"Yes, you are," she said matter-of-factly. "It's the deal."

"I won't like it. I won't like California, and I won't like Skylight or whatever her name is. Mom can send me, but I'm coming back."

She pulled off her glasses and started cleaning them nice and slow with the front of her T-shirt. The shirt had a big rainbow on it—not like a *Wizard of Oz* rainbow, but the gay people kind of rainbow. When she took her glasses off to clean them, it usually meant I was in for a lecture. There's nothing worse than getting a lecture from a lesbian who never had any kids of her own.

Aunt Clem was not my real aunt, but she was a real lesbian and a big-shot professor. She was my mom's first AA sponsor, but a few years back she decided Mom needed a tougher one than her. She resigned and took the job as Mom's best friend instead and a stunt-double mom for me. She jumped in when something needed to be done that Mom couldn't handle. Aunt Clem had been sober for ten years. My mom had been sober about ten days this time.

"Alastair—" she started.

"Why can't I go with you two for the summer? I could help cook and carry stuff—"

"Because you are a guy," she said, sighing. "Even if you're only thirteen. And the whole point of the Wild Women in Recovery Project is for us to get in touch with our personal power. That seems to work best for most in a man-free zone."

"I think it's a big scam for all the lesbians to hit on the straight ladies," I snapped. "You've got the whole summer to try to convert them. I swear, Aunt Clem, if Mom comes back gay, you're going to have to answer to me."

"I just want your mom coming back healthy, sober, and excited about her work, okay? If she doesn't get her act together with her business, she's going to lose all her biggest clients."

"No kidding," I said. "I saw the letter from the Hallmark company. It was in her trash. They said her valentines for next season were 'late, sloppy, and depressing.' They're about ready to can her."

Which would be terrible. Next to me, my mom loved her art best. She could draw anything and was bust-a-gut funny. Since Dad left us, she'd pretty much supported us by making cards. Dad sent money because the court made him, but she always squirreled every cent of that into a college fund for me.

"Did you see the birthday cards she wrote for the 'other woman'?" I asked. "Man, those were mean."

"Yep, they were," she said, pulling me to my feet. "Though the sad thing is that they'll probably sell off the shelf."

She smacked me on the rear. "You've got five minutes to say goodbye to her. She's in her room trying not to cry. And I mean it about the five minutes, and then we're out of here. Otherwise you'll miss your plane."

I looked at her, hopeful, with a grin that grew.

"Don't even think about it. I swear to God, Alastair, I'll put you on Greyhound. If you want to sit on a bus for three days, fine by me. Maybe we can even get you next to some hormonally toxic teenage girl that can LIKE tell you LIKE how LIKE she LIKE *totally* understands LIKE what it's LIKE *totally* to be an amputee."

"You play dirty," I said.

"Yep. Now LIKE go!"

Mom was lying on her side on the bed resting—at least I hoped to God that was what she was doing. Every time I saw her with her eyes closed, my heart started pumping like I'd just run a four-minute mile. I'd be scared to death that she'd jumped off the wagon and was passed out drunk. Or, worse yet, tried to kill herself because she couldn't be a better mother to me. Even though she blamed Dad for what happened in Lake Rochester, I knew she blamed herself for not being there on the trip. And for being the kind of mom that nobody asked to drive on school field trip day.

"Mom?" I whispered, scrootching down next to her on the bed. I touched a wavy piece of her hair lying on the pillow.

A blast of cold water shot me right in the face, blinding me. "Whaa—! Hey, no fair!" I said, grabbing my Super Soaker water gun from her.

She giggled, which sounded like her old laugh, just kinda more tired. "Got ya!"

I jumped off the bed, gave the Soaker a few quick pumps, and popped off a fast load at her, being careful to mostly miss.

"Stop! Stop!" she said, waving her arms. "I surrender."

"Good," I said, blowing imaginary smoke off the gun's end. "God, where'd you find this old thing?" I sat down next to her.

"I was out in the storage shed and I found it in a box of your old toys." She reached under the pillow and pulled out a stuffed white cat. "Look what else I found, Alastair! Remember Boo-Boo Kitty? Do you want to pack her for the trip?"

I grabbed it and gave Mom a soft thump on the head with it. "No!" I felt around on Boo-Boo Kitty's stomach for the button to press that made her purr. I smiled as she began to vibrate.

"Hey, wait a second!" I said, narrowing my eyes. "I thought you told me that you tried to wash Kitty and she fell apart during the spin cycle."

Mom pulled her back from me. "I know, sweetie, sorry! You wouldn't go to kindergarten without her, and the kids were teasing you. It seemed the kindest thing at the time."

She tried to move the hair out of my face and I jerked back like I always did. "Oh, Alastair. Let your poor old mom see that face of yours before you go, huh? I forget what you look like. Well, that's not entirely true," she said. "I do recall that you are bodaciously handsome."

"I look like a girl," I said, my tone flat. "Bo-da-cious-ly?" I repeated, rolling my eyes. "Is that a real word?"

"Isn't it great? It's from the sixties. It's such a robust little sucker, don't you think?"

"Totally groovy," I said.

Mom pulled my hands toward hers. "And you do not look like a girl. You are extremely pleasing to the eye."

"Right," I said. "*P-r-e-t-t-y*," I spelled.

"Not pretty—*handsome*," she said. "You look a lot like your dad."

"Oh, great!" I said. "That cheers me right up."

"Alastair." She shook her head. "Let's give the guy a chance, huh? He says he's got a good job now, and his wife sounds nice on the phone. Your dad seems to think you and Skyla are really going to hit it off for some reason."

"Hit it off?" I said, feeling my lip curl. "If the two of you are so hot that he and I play father and son this summer, he should at least send *her* off to camp or something."

"Honey, this has nothing to do with her. She's not a home wrecker, you know. Your dad was single. She had every right to marry him."

"But she's barely old enough to be my big sister," I said. "What? She's like eighteen and a half?"

Mom chewed on her thumbnail. "I might have been exaggerating just a teensy bit on that. She's in her mid-twenties, I think."

"Well, whatever she is, this is not a good time for me to be leaving.

Could we put this on hold for a year or two? I want to be with you, Mom. You need me, you just won't admit it."

She unballed the fist in my lap, then ironed out my fingers. "What I need right now is some time for me. And my counselor says you deserve a chance to get to know your dad so you can make up your own mind about him."

"What's there to know? He's a loser. End of story. He left us without a word. What kind of guy leaves a wife with a crippled kid? The jerk still probably thinks I stole that hundred bucks I supposedly gave the kid on the ski lift. I can't believe he told the cop at the hospital that."

Mom sighed. "Well, he didn't exactly say that, Alastair. He just couldn't figure out where the money came from. He said he hadn't given it to you."

I took back my hand and looked away. Mom didn't say anything else, but I could hear the quiet plop of the imaginary welcome mat being put out. Like, "I'm ready to listen whenever you're ready to tell me." It had always been the same way with the shrink.

I decided it was time to change tracks.

"I think I'm right on the brink of puberty. Do you really want to miss this? I'll probably come back with a mustache and a very deep voice."

She laughed. "The mustache I can handle. You come home with hair on your back, though, and we're headed right over to Salon Patine for electrolysis."

"You can send me, but I'm won't stay," I threatened.

"Well, if you come back to Taombi Springs, you're not going to have a place to live," Aunt Clem butted in from the doorway.

"What do you mean?" I said, looking at Mom to Aunt Clem and back.

"God, Clem, you can't hold water, can you?" Mom said, an edge to her voice.

"I just like to live in the land of truth," she replied, folding her arms across her chest.

"What's going on?" I asked.

Mom put her hand on me. "I can't afford to pay rent for three months if we're not here. We're going to pack up and move out this weekend. But I'll get another place before you even get back, and your room will be all ready for you. You'll hardly notice the difference."

Just what I needed. Another move. But at least that explained why she'd been out rummaging around in our storage shed. I'd had a flash of panic that she'd been out there hooking up with a bottle.

"Cool!" I lied, not wanting her to feel bad. "Just make sure I get the big bedroom next time." I swallowed hard.

"Please behave with your dad and Skyla," she said.

"Why?" I asked.

"For me, will you? And if you really don't like him—"

"We'll simply rent another ex-husband. LA is full of them, I hear," Aunt Clem said. "Look, I hate to break up the party, but I've got to get this guy on a plane, Nan. I'll go throw the stuff in the car and meet you there. You two have sixty seconds, got it?" She backed up toward the door. "Fifty-nine—I mean it, you two—fifty-eight," she said, her voice fading as she went down the stairs.

Mom propped herself way up on her pillows. "Come here," she said, pulling me toward her.

I laid my head in my regular place right under her chin. We didn't say much. We hadn't been apart for more than a couple of days since I went to space camp in fifth grade. Since Dad moved out five years ago, we'd been the center of each other's world.

"Did you remember to pack your bathing suit?" she asked.

"I dunno—I just dumped the dirty clothes hamper into my suitcase. If it was in there, I got it."

"Smarty-pants!" she hissed right next to my ear. "That's not what good mothers like to hear."

"Okay, Alastair," Aunt Clem shouted up the stairs. "I'm calling Greyhound!"

Mom gave me a quick and fierce hug. "Have a bodacious summer, sweetie!" she said, her voice choking at the end.

I nodded and pulled myself off the bed. Gave her one long last look. Stored her up behind my eyeballs, which were already pretty busy trying to hold back a flood of little boy tears.

"Right on, Mom," I whispered.

CHAPTER TWO

¡ STUDIED MYSELF iN THE small airplane bathroom mirror. Moved my hair back off my face where it usually stayed closed like a curtain. I checked to see if any boy hormones had made a recent visit since I'd last looked—a big manly, oozy zit of any kind or, even better, any sign of facial hair. I checked all sides, close and careful. Not one thing new. Same old perfect baby boy skin. I resolved to eat a ton more cheesy jalapeño fries to see if I could harvest up a really bad crop of acne. Chances were I wasn't going to see a lot of facial hair anytime soon. I wasn't a very hairy guy.

I bared my teeth in the mirror. I should start playing ice hockey and get a couple of teeth knocked out. Then I wouldn't look like such a pretty boy. Or have so many girls chasing after me.

I liked girls all right, or I did until around last year, when they all turned thirteen and went completely insane. Started treating me like some kind of celebrity, sending me weird notes with hearts all over them, whispering and pointing at me when I'd walk by them at school. Like they hadn't seen me every day since kindergarten. At first I didn't mind the attention too much, until the guys got wind of it. Believe me, there was nothing that was worth getting on their bad side. They started making kissy noises when I walked by, or they'd sock me on the arm so hard I thought the pain might give me a brain hemorrhage.

I tried to stop showering and washing my hair to add some gross points. Mom got wind of that and put her foot down hard. I patted my Buddha-like gut, which I was quite proud of. It took a lot of work to keep it on. Plenty of ice cream helped—the full-fat kind with double-double hot fudge.

The plane wobbled, then bucked a good one. I grabbed the safety bar just before the plane dropped fast and hard. I sucked in my breath and held it until we leveled out. I wasn't a huge fan of flying, particularly since planes liked to occasionally dive like that. I'd done enough falling through the air at warp speed to last one lifetime.

The pilot's voice broke through a small loudspeaker in the bathroom. "Ladies and gentlemen, please fasten your seat belts and put your seat in the upright position. We're encountering some Santa Ana winds."

There was a sharp rap on the restroom door. "Excuse me! Please return to your seat now!"

I pulled open the narrow door and came nose to nose with what looked like a walking, talking window mannequin in a flight attendant's uniform.

"Back to your seat, honey," she said with wintergreen breath, and then took my arm and propelled me right to it. Which wasn't too far. I was sitting in first class for the first time ever. Dad had sent the tickets. Big deal. Leather seats. The extra leg room was kinda cool, though. My fake leg liked it.

I clicked my seat belt and darted a quick look at my seatmate, an older girl who so far the whole trip had been buried beneath a baseball cap, an earphone, a small laptop, and a partially hidden bag of licorice—which I had noticed right off because it's like my favorite thing in the whole world. But now she was sitting upright, staring straight ahead, and doing some serious white knuckling of the armrests. She was looking pretty green around the gills, as Aunt Clem would say.

The plane reared up and jumped like a horse in a steeplechase. The girl moaned and caught her breath.

"You okay?" I asked.

"No," she said in a tight voice, then quickly pressed her lips back together. Maybe she thought if she could just hold on to *that*, it might keep the plane in the air.

The plane shimmied, then dropped down a story or two before bouncing back up. She grabbed my arm hard and dug her fingers into my sweatshirt, squeezing her eyes shut.

I was a total sucker for a damsel in distress. Hardwired for it.

"Don't!" I said, turning in my seat to face her. "Don't do that. Open your eyes. You'll just make it worse."

Her eyes snapped open and she looked at me, her lips still sealed shut.

"Singing helps," I said.

Her eyes grew wider, and she stared at me as if she'd just added Sitting Next to a Lunatic Boy on her list of things you don't need right before a plane crash.

"Trust me," I said, "it will help. Come on—*Jingle bells, jingle bells, jingle all the way*—" Man, I couldn't believe that was the first song that came to my mind. I was such a dork.

She shook her head, closed her eyes, and dug down another half inch in my arm's flesh.

"C'mon, c'mon! *Oh, what fun it is to ride*—"

The plane banked hard right, spilling her into my seat. She muffled a small cry.

"Hey, do you *want* to be freaked out or something?" I said.

She shook her head, her eyes bright with fear.

"Then sing with me. I promise this will work. My aunt taught me this."

"Jingle bells, jingle bells, jingle bells—" I started.

"—jingle all the wa-a-aayyy," she chimed in, her voice shaky as the plane.

I gave her an encouraging smile. *"Oh, what fun it is to ride in a one-horse open sleigh—"* we sang together, not likely to win a recording contract but getting the job done.

"Again," I said, "but louder this time."

She drew in a breath. *"Jingle BELLS, jingle BELLS, jingle all the WAY. Oh, what FUN it is to ride in a one-horse open sleigh!"*

The plane took a deep plunge down as one mean mama Santa Ana blew over the top of the plane. She squeezed her eyes shut.

"Don't stop! C'mon! *Jingle bells, jingle bells,* c'mon, sing, sing! Now bounce!"

"Do *what*?" she said, in her first full sentence to me.

"Bounce, c'mon!" I grabbed her hands. "You've bounced before." I dug her hands from the armrests and coaxed her into a bounce with me.

". . . all the WAY. Oh, what FUN it is to ride in a one-horse open sleigh! Hey!"

"Again! But you lead this time. And bigger bouncing!" I said.

"Jingle bells, jingle bells, jingle bells all the WAY," she sang. We bounced as high as we could from under our seat belts. *"Oh, what FUN it is to ride in a one-horse open sleigh . . . hey!"*

That verse won me a small smile.

Next round the man and woman across the aisle harmonized with us, then a little boy and his big sister two rows up bounced and sang along.

My seatmate totally missed the next wave of turbulence and the one after that, and I sure wasn't going to bring it to her attention.

I studied her a moment as we worked our way through another verse. The girl was—to borrow a phrase from my mother's collection of weird slang—a fox, a total *f-o-x*. She wasn't that fluffy kind of pretty like some girls—you know, like a pink frosted cupcake—sticky sweet and just full of air. This girl was like a hearty bundt cake with chocolate chips and nuts. Make a boy drool all over himself.

I was starting to hope the trip could last a lot longer, though, but then the stupid plane settled itself and got down to the business of descending into Los Angeles.

She collapsed against the back of her seat and drew a deep breath. She looked over and studied me.

I studied right back. Her eyes were bright now, and her cheeks flushed like the rosé wine Mom loved.

"Wow, thanks, I almost lost it back there," she said. "Thank God it's over. So—do you live in LA?"

"Nah, I'm just visiting."

She yanked the now-smashed bag of licorice from under her leg. "Want a piece?"

"Sure," I said. "I'm an addict."

She grinned. "Hey, me too—red or black?"

When I hesitated, she said, "Ah, wise choice. Both, huh?"

"Where do you go to school?" I asked, really meaning what *grade*, but since I didn't want to answer the same question, I couldn't ask it. I didn't want her to know that I was only going into the ninth grade. She was probably a junior or senior.

"Well, um—" She hesitated, chewing over her licorice. "I don't really go to school with other kids."

"Your mom homeschool you?" I asked.

"Kinda."

The lights clicked overhead and little bells announced that we could take off our seat belts.

"I really hate flying," she said, with a big sigh as she unlocked her belt and pulled her things together. "Sorry you had to put up with me freaking out."

"You should have seen me on the teacup ride at Disneyland a few years back," I said. "Talk about your freak-outs. My mom had to hide all our cups and saucers at home for a couple of months after that."

She laughed. This girl was more than a fox. She was a major babe-a-licious. I sucked in my gut. Just a bit. Even though she was way out of my league. Even though I needed a hot older woman in my life like I needed a whack on the head.

She leaned over, gave me a quick kiss on the cheek. "Have a good summer, Jingle Boy."

CHAPTER THREE

THE AIRPORT IN LOS ANGELES looked like all the other airports I'd been in, except it was very sunny, even inside. It was huge and smelled like pizza, Tidi-Bowl, and really strong coffee. Mom had told me to go right to the baggage claim area and Dad would meet me there. He hadn't seen me in a while, so he might not recognize me. I was sure I'd be able to recognize him, though.

I moved through crowds of tan, thin people. Nothing but happy reunions. Everybody had somebody really glad to see them. I found my bag claim area and waited for the giant chute to spit out my suitcase. I peered out of my hair to see if I could glimpse him coming yet, but nothing. Wished I had a secret periscope so I could see all around me without looking too pitiful or eager.

I plunked myself down on the armrest of a chair and dumped my backpack. Tried to blend in. Tried not to look like a minor in distress. I definitely did not want some airline person to come nab me and take me into protective custody.

To heck with him. It wasn't my job to find him. He was supposed to find me. Besides, I was starved. I didn't eat the boring snack Aunt Clem had packed me. A slice or two of pizza sure sounded good right now.

I hitched up my backpack, tipped my suitcase up on its wheels, and followed my nose across the terminal. Everyone looked like they were going to a luau. Shorts, sunglasses, and flip-flops seemed to be the dress du jour. Guess I shouldn't make fun, though. In Colorado, everyone dressed like a park ranger. Lots of green-and-tan outfits with boots.

I moved left to avoid a woman sprinting through the airport. On two prosthetic legs.

"S'cuse me!" she called out as she whizzed past.

My head whipped around in amazement to watch her and saw as she came to a fast stop. She twirled in her tracks on two small metal feet that looked like the landing gear on a spacecraft.

She eyeballed me. "Alastair?" she said in a winded voice.

I stared back, puzzled.

She smiled big then and said, "Oh, yeah, it's gotta be you. Definitely you!"

She stepped over to me and I could hardly stop staring at her legs and feet, even though I knew better than anyone that I shouldn't.

"Welcome to LA, Alastair! I'm Skyla."

"You're—" I started.

"Yep, that's me. Your dad's wife—and, well, as things go, I guess that makes me your stepmom." She moved in toward me looking like she was about to give me a big old hug. I stepped back and moved my suitcase in front of me. An awkward silence pulled up and parked its ugly self right in front of us. I willed myself to stop staring at her legs.

I couldn't compute this. Skyla was a double gimp? What the hell was going on? Was this supposed to make me feel better?

It finally blurted itself out. "What happened to your legs?"

"Accident. Drunk driver," she said matter-of-factly. "Hey, like my new feet? I just got them. I can run on the track and on the treadmill and sprint through airports." She smiled and did a little jig. "They're called Renegades. They're great! Maybe you'd be interested in trying one this summer."

We both looked down at my leg, which compared to hers looked like a tree trunk planted in a big brown shoe box.

I couldn't figure out what I was brewing inside, but it was hot and combustible. "Where's Dick?" I asked, my voice low.

One eyebrow shot up a second. She opened her mouth, then closed it. Then started again. "We got stuck in some bad terminal traffic and your father was ready to stroke about being late. I told him I could hoof it faster, so I jumped out. I had a feeling I'd be able to pick you out of a crowd. And I did. God, you look just like him!"

"No, I don't, really." I bit my lip and looked around. Where were those magic portals when you needed one to swallow you up? This whole scene was just too weird.

Skyla looped an arm around my shoulders and pulled me with her. "C'mon, I told your dad we'd wait for him at the food court. You probably haven't had anything to eat but airplane peanuts for the last few hours, huh?"

I shrugged and managed to Houdini myself out from under her arm.

"I'm not really hungry," I lied.

"Well, I'm hungry enough for both us," she said. "I'll eat and you can tell me all about yourself—what you like to do, what you are dying to see in California—you know, that kind of stuff." She threw me a sideways look. "If you feel like it," she added.

Jeez, do I look like the dinner show or something?

"Not much to know," I said. "Mostly, I like to be alone," I lied again. Five minutes into the game and I was two for two.

Twenty minutes later, I was sitting behind a Sundowner, which is a jumbo banana-wheat-berry protein shake with real grass mixed in it. They grew it in little pans behind the counter. At first I thought it was for decoration—like instead of plants—but then the guy fixing my shake lopped off a chunk of it and threw it in my drink. It actually cost more to have it added. I could have made a killing if I'd stayed home this summer. I could have mowed lawns, then set up a street booth and sold shakes with the clippings.

Skyla peered at me over her drink, which I think was basically a raw omelet with some mulch thrown in. She wasn't at all like I pictured she'd be. Besides the having-no-legs part. Well, she had legs. Just no knees or calves. I had my knee, which everyone always said was "lucky." Yeah, that's me. Mr. Lucky.

I'd figured Dad would have married a girl version of himself, an airhead that would be the Malibu Barbie to his Malibu Ken. Someone tall with long bleached-white hair and tan boob tops. Instead, she had shiny reddish hair, a lot of freckles, and the bluest eyes I'd ever seen. She had some serious girl biceps on her, too. I made a mental note not to wear any tank tops around her. My arms were long and skinny like a chimpanzee's.

"So, Alastair, do you like it?" she asked, motioning to my drink.

I took a tiny sip from my straw. "It's okay." I stirred it around and around with the straw, hoping it might start evaporating. It tasted like pond scum.

"It's so important to keep your system flushed and clean. These shakes are full of antioxidants."

Great, I was drinking Liquid Plumber.

"I love your name," she said. "Your dad tells me it belonged to your great-great-grandfather."

"No one calls me that anymore," I lied. Number three. I was on a roll.

"Oh, sorry! I didn't know. What do they call you?"

"Stump," I said, a total mouth fart if there ever was one. Just popped out before I knew it and left me to deal with it.

"Oh!" she said, taken back. "You like being called that?"

"Yep," I said.

Skyla glanced at her watch. It was one of those big sports watches that does everything but hurl javelins for you. "Your dad should be here pretty quick. He sure can't wait to see you! It's been a long time, Stump, huh?"

I cocked my head and shrugged like it didn't much matter whether it had been last week or several years ago. But I knew exactly how long it had been. To the day.

It was the day we'd gone to our last family counseling session together. Before my dad bolted and moved to California. In the middle of the night like a coward.

"How's your mom doing?" she asked, in the careful voice people use when talking to me about Mom. What they really meant was, was she on the wagon or doing the backstroke through a wineglass somewhere?

"Mom? Oh, she's great!" I said. "She and my aunt Clem are going to have a seriously radical summer. They'll be rock climbing, mountain bike riding, hiking, you name it. Mom will probably come back so fit and cut that she'll have to beat the men off her." I gave Skyla a very pointed look. "All my friends say I have a very sexy mother, you know."

She nodded and gave me a warm smile. "Yes, I've seen pictures of her. She's beautiful. And I'm glad to hear she's doing so well!" She put her hand over mine, but I slipped it out from under so I could scratch my nose.

"Um, I need to use the restroom," I said.

"See? It's working already!"

"Huh?" I asked.

"Your Sundowner," she said nodding toward my shake. "It's ready to take out the trash, as they say."

She laughed at what must have been a blank stare on my face. I knew what she meant but couldn't quite believe this was normal table conversation with a new stepperson.

"Sorry! I'm a bit obsessed right now with the lower intestines. I'm studying the art of high colonics. It's fascinating. When we get back to the house, I'll show you some charts. It's an absolute miracle the way our bodies move our by-products." She waved me away. "Don't get me started. Go! We've got the whole summer to talk."

Don't count on it, Skywalker, or whatever your name is, I thought as I hurried away.

Just don't count on it.

After all that, Dick's wife would have been mighty disappointed if she'd known that it wasn't my bladder or my miracle intestines that were calling on me. I just needed to get away. "Find a back door" as my shrink used to say. It was about the only decent piece of advice he had ever given me.

Get-me-out-of-here. Back home when I felt this way, I would jump on my skateboard and take off. I was pretty good at it. I had great balance on my good leg. Hell, paint me pink and I could probably get a gig at a zoo as a flamingo.

I loved to ride through all the different neighborhoods and look at houses. Old ones in particular. I had a thing for them. When I found one I liked, I'd stop and find a private place to sit and check it out. Study the lines of it, mostly. I usually had my notebook and I'd make some sketches. Then when I'd get home, I'd finish it and imagine the floor plans and draw those, too. I liked to think about what colors would work best inside. Lately, I'd even been drawing the landscaping in.

But the LA airport was not inspiring me to want to sit and draw. And when I'd gotten out of Aunt Clem's car, she'd made me leave my skateboard behind because it was old and the wheels fell off about once a week. She was tired of trying to fix it. Told me to have my dad buy me a new one. I told her to bite me. She gave me a big old kiss instead and blew her nose.

I ducked out of the way of the airport hordes and pulled out the cell phone that she'd made me promise under the threat of torture that I would only use in an emergency. Mom didn't have a cell phone. She'd lost three, so she decided she couldn't afford them anymore. Aunt Clem bought me this one for the trip. I poked in her number and ducked into a corner of a gift shop. Her voice mail came on. Damn.

"Hi! It's Clem—leave a message after the beep. If this is Alastair, leave a message ONLY if the plane has crashed, you've been hijacked by the Hare Krishna, or you can't stop the bleeding. Or if you are standing in front of Angelina Jolie. You can put her right on the line."

Very funny, Aunt Clem. I was tempted to leave a message, but she might cut my service off completely. At least I could talk to Mom on Sunday. They promised. I stabbed the end button and flipped it shut.

I had a terrible taste in my mouth from the evil shake Skywalker had made me drink.

I went over to the counter and picked out three packs of bubble gum in the smelliest flavors possible. Mom never let me chew gum in front of her. Got on her nerves.

I slid my money across the front counter and dug in my pocket for some change. A crisp fifty-dollar bill and then some Gummy Bears slid up next to mine.

"He'll take these too," a man's voice said.

I looked up quickly, my heart drumming.

My ex-father looked down at me—at least I think he was looking at me. I couldn't really tell through his orange-mirrored sunglasses. He smiled and patted me hard on the back, like maybe he was trying to dislodge a piece of meat stuck in my throat.

"I—I—I—" I tried to speak, but my voice was broken by his continued thwacking on my back.

I was hoping that after five years, he wouldn't look as good as I remembered. That maybe I'd see he was just some guy, some kid's regular old father. But the man just got better with age. He was still grossly handsome, but now he was tan and had golden highlights in his hair. I'd bet money he had gone to one of those fancy man salons and had them artificially put in. They were just too perfect.

He stopped whacking me and said, "Good to see you, Alastair." I could tell he thought maybe he should give me a hug, so I glared at him from behind my hair. He took his change and handed me the Gummy Bears. "Here, I got these for you. I remember they're your favorite."

"When I was like four," I said. But all the same I grabbed them and shoved them into my back pocket. I didn't want to take the chance of running into Cute Plane Girl while I was walking through the airport with my daddy, carrying a bag of Gummy Bears. Not that she'd notice me if I was walking next to God's Gift to the Female Species.

"Hey, I'm sorry I was a little late—the traffic on the 405 was terrible. I sent Skyla in after you. Did she—"

I cut him off. "Is she supposed to be some kind of *joke*?"

He pulled his sunglasses off then and looked down at me. "A joke?"

"You know, like I'm not supposed to feel bad that I've only got one leg because she doesn't have any? Where'd you find her?" I said, my voice getting louder. "Gimps R Us?"

"Knock it off, Alastair! That's my wife."

"Yeah? Well, if you think the fact that your *wife* doesn't have legs squares something between us, you're crazy. You know that?"

"Skyla doesn't have anything to do with you!" he said.

I shoved two pieces of gum into my mouth. "That's right, *Dad*. And don't you forget that." I chewed up my gum as fast as I could and blew a giant bubble, which popped.

Right into all the hair on my face.

I tried to pull it out, but it stuck. He reached over to help, but I turned from him.

"Let's go," I said. "Skywalker is waiting."

"Sky-*la*," Dad hissed, his voice low.

My laugh was empty and as mean as I could muster with a face full of hair and gum. "Yeah, Dad, that's much better."

CHAPTER FOUR

IF YOU EVER WAKE UP on another planet after being abducted by aliens that could pass for humans, then you'll know exactly how I felt the next morning when I woke up in a giant, fluffy bed in Skyla's beach house in Lumina Beach. Which is not to be confused with her mountain chalet in Vail, her ranch in Idaho, or her island pad in Maui. Apparently, Skyla was loaded.

Which cleared up the whole mystery for me about how two grown-ups could afford to spend so much of their time sailing, snorkeling, shopping, spa hopping, and paying people to hose water up their rear ends. Over dinner last night, I learned more than I would ever want to know about colon hydrotherapy. Man. Back when my mom was working full-time, she barely had time to fit in an occasional pedicure. And in a pinch, she'd talk me into painting her toenails for her. What can I say? She paid me a buck a toe if I did a really good job.

I dug myself out from under a big fancy bedspread. I sat up, gave my eyes a good fist massage, and sucked in a deep breath.

The whole friggin' Pacific Ocean was sitting at the foot of my bed.

Miles of it. As far as you could see. Which was quite a bit because one whole end of my bedroom was floor-to-ceiling windows. I got up, dazed, and hopped over to the sliding glass door. And leaned out onto a private balcony. A cool breeze riffled through my pajama bottoms. I wrapped my arms around myself and sniffed in the salty air.

I shook my head. Unbelievable. I'd seen the Atlantic once before and even some pictures of the Indian Ocean. But never the Pacific. I remembered from Ms. Cameron's science class that the Latin root for its name meant "peace." It was a good name for it. It looked like God had pulled a big blue blanket up to tuck in the West Coast. Still, there were some reasonable waves coming in and a surfer out there catching a good ride. God, I'd love to try that.

I looked over the railing of the balcony and saw a large deck below. There were a bunch of palm trees in pots and a whole jungle of flowers. And there was an outdoor breakfast table already set and loaded with enough juice and water to float an armada. Below that was a small deserted beach with a couple of kayaks set out. Aunt Clem and I had rented kayaks once at Henley Lake near my house. But I'd never tried it in the ocean.

I pulled back when I heard footsteps on the deck and slunk back into the bedroom. I wasn't ready to see anyone yet. Unless it was Mom or Aunt Clem. Dad and Skyla were total strangers to me. I still couldn't believe I was stuck here for the next three months.

I looked around the bedroom, which was huge. You could have parked four Suburbans in it. A giant gift basket sat on the dresser, with a card sticking out that said, *Welcome!* Under that someone, probably Skyla, had written, *Alastair, here's your California survival kit!* She'd signed it for both of them. Figures.

I pulled out a thick beach towel, some magazines, a large bottle of sunscreen, and a fairly cool-looking pair of sunglasses.

I slipped on the sunglasses, then checked myself out in the mirror, lowering my pajama bottoms a couple of inches and giving my belly a pat. I tried to shake out the serious guy stiffness in my shoulders. "Hey, *dude*. What's goin' on?" I asked my reflection.

Jeez, I looked like my dad. I yanked off the sunglasses and pulled my pants back up.

I finished pawing through the basket. There was a map of Lumina Beach, a few packs of vitamins that smelled funny even through the wrapping, some postcards with stamps already licked on, organic chocolate, and an iPod. Oh, man, it was the kind that played movies and everything. I'd been wanting one of these forever.

There was a quiet rap on the bedroom door and I froze. Like I'd been caught snooping in someone else's room, for pete's sake. I shoved everything back into the basket.

"Stump? Are you awake?" Skyla asked through the door.

I grabbed the T-shirt I'd had on yesterday and threw it over my head. "Yeah," I said, still rooted to the spot.

She edged open the door and poked her head in. "You ready for some breakfast? Your dad's already eaten, but I haven't."

"Okay," I said, though breakfast with the step sounded gross. I was relieved, though, that my dad had already eaten. I wasn't quite ready for a "family breakfast" on my first day.

"Great! Come on down, okay? I'll be on the deck." Her eyes dropped down to the floor next to my bed where my fake leg was propped up. Looking like something out of the Gimp Museum. "Is that comfortable?" she asked.

"Yeah, fits like a dream," I said sarcastically.

She started to say something and then held it back. Gave me a smile. "Hope you're hungry. See you in a minute, Alastair."

"Stump," I said. "I don't go by Alastair anymore." Well, not since yesterday, anyway.

"Right, *Stump*," she said, closing the door softly.

Skyla was tucked behind the business page when I joined her for breakfast twenty-seven minutes later. Her plate was still empty, and I knew she'd waited for me to eat. I felt a moment's guilt about that but choked it down. Being a real jerk was a new gig I'd have to work on.

She folded up the paper and nodded toward the covered silver dishes on the table. "Help yourself, Stump," she said.

I spooned up some eggs and potatoes and closed the lid quickly on something that looked like it could bite me right back.

Skyla held up the pitcher of juice toward my glass. "OJ? Fresh-squeezed this morning—"

"No, thanks," I said. "You got any Coke?"

She raised her brow at me. "You want Coke for breakfast?"

"Yeah, it's what me and Mom always have for breakfast," I lied. "Well, she drinks diet and I drink regular."

Now this was straight out of the Driving your Stepmom to Drink 101 manual—pure kid stuff—but I couldn't help myself. And judging by the look on her face, as old as the bit was, I could tell she was taking the bait.

After a moment, though, she lifted her shoulders and dropped them gracefully. "Sure, why not? Be right back. I think we've got some in the bar."

I shoveled some eggs down quickly before she got back. I was ravenous all of a sudden but for some reason didn't want her to know.

She plopped the can in front of me. "I'm betting you like it straight out of the can, right?"

"Yep," I said, and took a long, big guzzle to prove it. "Thanks. And thanks for the basket and stuff," I said before I could stop myself. That was way too polite. Jeez, next I'd be hugging her and planning our day together. "I mean, I already have *all* that stuff, but it's good to have some backups in case your regular stuff gets lost."

She looked down at her plate, but I could still see the redness in her cheeks in between all the freckles. I studied her a quick second in the bright morning light and decided that Mom was way, way prettier. When she wasn't drinking, that is.

"Well, you're welcome," she said with a funny smile.

"Where's your husband?" I asked. Man, it was scary how fast I'd gotten good at this game.

She nodded over to the water. "He's right there."

I scrootched up in my seat to see over the railing. "On the beach?" I asked. "Where? I don't see him."

"No, in the water. Surfing."

I plopped down back in my seat, quickly shifted gears to Totally Bored Kid. I made a sea of mashed potatoes across my plate with my fried potatoes, then built a cantaloupe boat—an ark, actually—and filled it with two blueberries, two strawberries, two bananas, and two wheat flakes.

"Do you surf?" Skyla asked after a moment. "I told him to wake you up and take you with him, but he wanted you to sleep in this first morning."

"I live in Colorado," I explained as if I was talking to a preschooler. "Nobody surfs there."

"Of course, I just thought maybe you'd learned somewhere on vacation. Do you like sports?"

"Oh, yeah—love 'em. You should see me play ice hockey. I skate one-legged and use my fake leg as a stick." I glared at her.

Skyla pulled off her sunglasses and looked at me dead-on. "Lots of amputees play sports. You just need a different prosthetic. I'm involved with a wonderful organization called the Challenged Athletes Foundation. The kids compete in track events, skiing, all sort of different sports. It's where I met your dad, in fact."

"Cool for them. I'm not interested," I said.

"So what do you like to do?" she asked. "We really want you to have a fun summer with us. Your dad has been looking forward to this for weeks. It's *all* he's talked about."

"I like to do stuff by myself," I blurted. "I'm kind of a loner, like my mom. I like to read, listen to music, go for walks." I stopped myself. I sounded like a middle-aged woman. "I'm into hunting."

"Really?" she asked, sitting back, looking a bit stunned.

"Mostly targets," I added. "I'm not into killing things."

"Well, I bet you're great at it."

I overturned my cantaloupe ark and slowly hacked it to pieces. "I'm okay at it. It's my mom, though, who's *really* good at it."

Skyla took a long drink of juice, never taking her eyes off me.

I paused in my ark mutilation. "You wouldn't want to get on her bad side, that's for sure."

"I'll keep that in mind," she said. "Thanks for the warning."

A body appeared like a ghost next to me and I nearly vaulted out of my seat.

"Oh—Ian, great!" Skyla said. " I'm glad you're here. I want you to meet Rick's son. Stump, this is Ian, my personal assistant. Ian, meet Stump."

I started to stand up like my mom taught me when you meet people but stopped myself just in time. I quickly grabbed my fork and took a bit bite of eggs. "H'lo," I mumbled through them.

"Very nice to meet you," he said. But I could tell I wouldn't be added to his Christmas card list anytime soon.

"Ian, sit down with us," Skyla said, pulling out a chair for him. He did, but not before he refilled both of our water glasses, checked the temperature of the serving dishes, and moved the flower vase a quarter turn.

I gave him a good once-over as I mashed through my eggs. Thin. Tall. Pale. Too pale to be living in California. Not bad to look at. Potential member of Aunt Clem's Rainbow Club.

"Ian is the more organized half of my brain," Skyla explained. She laid a hand on his arm and gave him a warm smile. "This family couldn't run without him. He manages all the household staff, keeps my calendar, does all the grocery shopping—"

"I wouldn't have it any other way," he interrupted. And the way he looked at her when he said it made me doubt he was gay. He was crazy about her.

I eyed them both.

"And he takes care of the house and our cars, plans all our parties, gets us tickets to all the best shows, knows absolutely everything about *every*thing!" she gushed.

"Oh, stop! Really, Sky!" He turned to me shaking his head, then dove headfirst into the flattery orgy. "Your stepmother is the most brilliant, creative person I've ever met."

I burped up some Coke and didn't excuse myself.

"Well," he said, jumping to his feet. "Let me leave the two of you to your breakfasts. Stump, if there's anything I can do to make your summer more enjoyable, please don't hesitate to ask. If you're interested in any concert tickets, I've got some excellent connections."

As he hurried away, I turned to Skyla. "So is a 'personal assistant' like the new way to say butler?" I asked.

"Oh, no—well, not in the way you're probably thinking of a butler. He doesn't wear a tux around the house and doesn't open the door for guests." She smiled. "But he is here most of the time, and I rely on him to keep the house and staff running."

"So how many servants do you have?' I asked.

"I don't have any servants, Stump, but I do have a number of staff employed here. Ian is the only one here around the clock. He lives in the guesthouse, which is over thataway," she said, pointing over her shoulder. "You can't really see it from here because of the trees. The rest of the staff are scheduled depending on what's going on at the house. We have people that come to cook, clean the house, do the laundry, clean the pool, keep the garden going—there's lots to contend with," she said with a big sigh.

"So what do you and my—er, your husband do?"

She raised an eyebrow. "Us? Well, our businesses keep us very busy. I spend most of my time on my family's business. It's a philanthropic organization that provides funding to nonprofits. I have a home office so I can telecommute quite a bit. Your dad spends most of his time with our health and fitness clubs. He goes to the downtown office—meets with our clients and works pretty intently with our marketing department. He's shooting a video this week for some new equipment we have coming out. He's very good at that and a real natural in front of the camera."

"So, you're like his boss and give him a paycheck for that?" I asked, knowing full well it was none of my business. I could almost feel Mom kicking me under the table for that one.

"We're more like partners," she clarified.

"But he does work and earns money for it, right?" I asked.

"Yes, we have a financial arrangement about the work he does for the company." She cocked her head. "Why do you ask?"

I shrugged. "I dunno. Just making conversation, I guess." And trying to figure out where the child support had been coming from for mom and me. From my dad working or from the loose change in the bottom of Skyla's purse.

"May I be excused?" I asked, again forgetting my resolve to be Psycho Kid with Bad Manners. I really was going to have to practice this.

"Sure. Is there anything else I can get you, or—?"

"Naw, I'm done. I think I'm going to go hang out and stuff."

"Oh!" she said, clearly surprised. "Well, do you want to go out with me for a while? I have some errands in town and can show you around a bit. I could give you a quick tour of Lumina Beach and the best places."

I looked down at her legs. "So, do you drive?"

"Of course. I do pretty much everything, except get pedicures."

"Hellooo! Hello-hellooooo!" A distant voice came up from the beach.

Skyla pushed back her seat and smiled. "It's your dad." She moved over to the railing and leaned over, shouting, "Hey, you! Get any good rides yet?"

Dad yelled back something that got lost in the sound of a crashing wave.

I eased my chair back with warrior stealth.

"Me and Stump are just finishing breakfast. Come on up!" she shouted, then waved him in with big gestures, like she was directing a herd of elephants.

I took my cue and bolted. You can bring a boy to his father, but you cannot make him stay.

CHAPTER FIVE

You CAN'T REALLY GET LOST in a town like Lumina Beach, even though I wished I could have. I eased open the massive front door and closed it behind me as quietly as I could. Like some kind of burglar—only I wanted out, not in.

I zipped up my hoodie and hurried away from the house. Looked left, looked right—tried to get the lay of the land. Pretty simple. Ocean on the right, mountains on the left. And everyone—well, at least all the richies—seemed to live on this one same street called Blue Coast Way that ran alongside the ocean. I passed mansion after mansion and driveways stuffed with BMWs and SUVs made by companies like Mercedes and Cadillac. Yeah, right, like they're experts on all-terrain vehicles.

It made you think about the families behind all the fancy gates. I wondered how many were real families still together and how many were what they called in social studies "blended families." Every time Mrs. Cronkel used that phrase in class, I kept imagining new stepparents stuffing poor kids in a giant blender and pulverizing the snot out of them. I got a vile taste in my mouth just thinking about it. I tried to hock up a good one so I could spit a big manly wad on Blue Coast Way but ended up kinda just drooling on myself.

Mental note—learn how to spit this summer.

I got tired pretty quickly of looking at houses that my mom and I could never afford in a million years. I wished I could get down to the beach, but I didn't see any more staircases down to the water like the one Skyla had right next to her house. How the heck did all the richies get down to the beach? Maybe they had special rock-climbing butlers—I mean rock-climbing *personal assistants*—that piggybacked them over the cliffs. I bet Ian would jump at the chance to carry Skyla around. Man, my dad better watch out. I didn't trust that guy far as I could throw him. And I threw like a total girl.

After a while, the big houses started to thin out, and it began to look more like a real town. Lumina Beach had gas stations, mini-marts, yoga and yogurt, and a lot of people with dark tans even though the summer had barely begun. They probably stayed tan all year. And they were probably brown all over, even on their butts and stuff. Aunt Clem said people in California and Europe, too, like to nude-sunbathe and they have special beaches where they go to do that. I bet my dad and Skyla just got naked right out on their deck.

Oh, man. I hoped to hell they weren't planning on doing that in front of me. If they did, I was checking right out of Villa Skyla, let me tell you. I did not want to see my dad in the buff. Didn't want to see him period.

I checked my watch—it wasn't even noon yet. I still had the whole day to kill. I pulled off my sweatshirt and wrapped it around my waist. A piece of paper dropped out of my pocket and fluttered to the sidewalk.

Uh-oh.

It was the note that I'd scribbled off in my room to Dad and Skyla. I meant to leave it on the table by the door, but I guess I'd forgotten to when I hurried out.

Went to check things out. Back at four. Stump.

Five hours was probably a long time to be away my first day, but there was no way I was going to hang around with them. I could tell Skyla was just itching to fill up my days with some serious family-bonding activities—windsurfing, hiking, parasailing, shopping for the perfect California Boy outfits to match California Dad. And though she hadn't mentioned it yet, I was betting there was a trip to Disneyland tucked in there somewhere. And she had made some mention of a niece she was dying for me to meet. Save me, please.

I guess I should stop and call them, I thought as I passed by a pay phone outside a real estate office. I hadn't brought my cell phone. Still wasn't used to having one. I shoved my hands into my pockets. I had a wad of crumpled one-dollar bills but no change. I stopped and cruised through my options.

One, I could turn around now and hightail back to Skyla's before they got too worried. Apologize all over the place and explain about the note in my pocket.

Two, I could ask someone in one of the stores to let me use their phones. Adults will always let you use the phone to call your parents. I could tell them where I was and ask politely if I could stay out a while longer.

Or, option *three,* I could do neither and just see what happened.

My reflection in the window of the real estate office was staring back at me, waiting to see what I was going to do. I mean I couldn't just stay out all day without letting them know where I was, could I? They'd freak.

The me in the window staring back shrugged and said, "So what?" And then right before my very eyes, he took the note I'd written—*Back at four*—and tore it into a million tiny pieces. Then tossed it into the air, where it came raining down on me like some kind of liberation party. I hate a litterbug, but I liked his attitude.

Looked like we were going with option three.

Two Blast-Caff Colas later, I was perched on top of a picnic table staring out over acres of white sand, watching the waves roll in. And setting an all-new personal record for the junkiest lunch ever. It was an all-plastic food festival—crackers and cheese with tiny slick brown slices called ham, two chocolate puddings with stirred in peanuts and M&Ms, and a grande-size bag of chili chips. I was also working through a dozen or so candy bars. But after two of them, I knew I'd never make it through them all, so I was just taking the heads off the end of each of them. I could take them home with me for later. They didn't have much junk food at Skyla's, and it was going to take some work to keep my pudge rolls fat and happy this summer with all the lousy low-fat food they liked to eat. I'd noticed Dad eyeballing my rolls a couple of times and I could tell he was just itching to say something or drop down and demonstrate some sit-ups. Dream on, Dick! I took a big, happy bite.

"Trying out for a zit commercial?" a man's voice asked from behind me.

I whirled around. An old guy stood behind me, stuffing his head into a swimming cap. He had one of those tiny men's bathing suits on that make you feel like you want to look away. You know, in case something comes poking out of their suit unexpectedly. But maybe old guys don't worry about that too much. For me, it was the stuff of nightmares.

I crammed my junk into my bag, "Uh, no. I mean, yeah—I was just having a snack. I don't get zits," I said.

"I never did either, when I was a kid," he said. "Could eat anything." He patted his stomach. "Now I've got to watch everything I put in the old tank."

I doubted that. His "tank" was tight and trim. In fact, he was pretty much a stud for an old man. He looked like he could be Popeye's grandfather. I wasn't ever any good guessing old people's ages—

"Seventy-two," he said, reading my mind and freaking me out a bit.

"Wha-at?" I asked, unnerved.

"I'm seventy-two, just last month," he said. "That's what you were wondering, right?"

I shrugged, kinda embarrassed.

"It's okay. People see an old fart like me swimming and it makes them wonder. We're all curious about growing old." He pulled a pair of goggles over his head and then parked them up on top of his cap. "You ever think about it?" he asked.

I lifted my shoulders. "Yeah, sometimes. I wonder what it will be like to be eighteen."

The man's eyes squinted up like he was going to laugh, but then he just grunted. "Ahhh, yes—to be an old man of eighteen."

He put his leg up on the table and stretched out his hamstrings, looking over the remains of my lunch. "So, who did the dumping? You or her?"

I stared at him, wondering what the heck he was talking about.

"You broke up with someone, right, kid?"

"Oh!" I finally caught his drift. "Nah," I said. "I don't even live here. I'm just visiting for the summer. Today's my first day. I didn't know where to go for lunch, so I just got a bunch of stuff over at the gas station."

"Hmmmph. You keep eating like that and you won't make it to eighteen. If you're interested, I can recommend a few places better than the gas station around here to eat."

"So how far do you swim?" I asked, wanting to change the subject before I got a whole nutrition lecture from Old Man Speedo. Nothing like spending an entire summer surrounded by a bunch of health freaks.

"Just a mile—I'm working this afternoon, so I need to cut it a little short today."

"You have a job?" I asked, surprised.

He bent over at the waist and touched his nose to his knees. "Well, I called the cemetery this morning and the grave diggers hadn't finished shoveling out my plot, so I thought I'd at least work a while longer." He straightened up and then bent over to one side.

"Uh, sorry! I didn't mean you were too old, I just—"

He bared his teeth, but I wasn't sure if it was a grin or not. "It's okay, kid. I am old. And retired. But I like to work now and then. It keeps me fresh. "

"What kind of work do you do?"

"Coaching, mostly," he said.

"Like sports, you mean?"

"Yeah—I worked at the high school for a few hundred years. I still give them a hand now and then." He cocked his head at me and checked out my leg. "You do any sports?" he asked.

"Nah. I could if I wanted to. Just not interested."

He kept looking at my legs, and I wished I'd worn long pants. My good leg looked like a girl's. I could pretty much be a leg double for Barbie. It was long and smooth and hairless. Not the kind of leg I'd want to show off in front of a guy that swims with sharks.

"What happened?" he asked.

I shrugged. Started stuffing my candy bars in my bag. "I had an accident a few years ago. Double fracture of the femur," I recited. "It got infected, so they had to cut it off."

"You get any physical therapy after the accident?" he asked.

"Sure. But I dunno, the guy that was my PT, Bert, he was pretty much a jerk. He was always pushing me around. Trying to make me do stuff I couldn't do."

"Hmmm," was all he said. But something about the way he said it made me want to explain some more.

"So did you finish your therapy, or did you quit?" he asked.

I felt my cheeks heat up. "*Bert* didn't think I was done. But man, I went for a few months. Seemed like it should be enough. Mom finally said I didn't have to go anymore. Of course, Bert wanted me to keep coming. Wanted to get me back on the slopes, too. Like it was his life calling or something. Kept telling my mom it would be good 'closure' for me."

The old guy cocked up an eyebrow at me.

"Well, that's how I broke my leg and stuff—learning to ski. So, you know, he thought it would be totally 'happily ever after' if he could get me back on the slopes."

"Must have been some fall," he said, stuffing a key in a little tiny pocket in his tiny bathing suit.

A car horn blared from behind us in the parking lot and I jumped nearly out of my skin. Boy, I'd had way too much caffeine. Skyla waved to me from a green convertible. And it wasn't a "Well, hi, how great to run into you here" kind of wave either. I recognized the Mad Lady Look.

I gathered up my trash quickly. "Gotta go," I said. "It's my dad's wife."

He put out his hand and I gave him the manliest handshake I could muster up. "S'nice talking to you," I said. "Have a good swim and all."

"Thanks, and welcome to town. Maybe I'll see you around, kid. And go easy on the sweets."

I turned to wave again before I got to the car, but he was already jogging across the sand toward the water.

"Um, hi!" I said. "Are you looking for me?" I asked, clearly the dumbest question in the world.

"Yep, I'm looking for you," she said. "Please get in."

I started brushing the sand off my foot and then remembered my new gig as Kid Rude. If I'd known how to jump over the door and into the seat like cool guys do, *man*, this would have been the perfect time to do it. But I wasn't quite sure I could pull it off and didn't want to humiliate myself by doing a big belly flop into Skyla's lap. I made sure I gave the door a good slam when I sat down, and gave her my best very annoyed teenager sigh.

I put on my sunglasses so she couldn't see I was nervous. "So what's up?" I said, resting one very sandy foot up on the dashboard.

Skyla shoved the car into reverse, peeled out about four feet, stopped, and took a deep breath. She put the car into drive then slowly moved back into the parking space.

I reached over and started fiddling with her sound system. She was wired for satellite radio, and I punched through about ten stations before she cut the engine so the music went off.

She turned in her seat and stared full-on at me. "Stump, I'm pretty flexible about most things. But when someone gives me a big responsibility—like your mother did when she let you come visit us—well, I take that very seriously. And I am pretty sure that even in Colorado, thirteen-year-old boys—"

"I'm almost fourteen," I interrupted. Well, five months isn't really almost, but I doubted she knew when my birthday was.

She gripped the steering wheel even tighter. She was nearly choking it to death. I was pretty grateful it wasn't my neck. "O-kay, 'almost-fourteen'-year-old boys don't take off for hours on a Saturday without letting anyone know where they are."

"You never said I had to tell you before I went anywhere," I said.

"I also didn't tell you this morning not to put your head in the oven!" she said. "I assumed some things went without saying."

I wanted to throw out a great comeback to this, but my mind got fixated on the image of my head in a roasting pan. "Well, if there's gonna be a bunch of rules this summer, it might be nice if you clued me in to them!"

"Okay, rule number one—" she started.

"But I don't mean from *you*," I said. "You're not a real parent. If there's gonna be rules, they have to come from my dad."

The air between us went quiet and crypt-like.

She raked her fingers through her hair. "Stump," she said, her voice quieter and sort of ragged around the edges.

"Could we go now?" I said.

She continued to stare at me. I couldn't hold the stare, so I started cleaning out the sand between my toes onto the dashboard.

"Oh, you bet," she said, sounding as if dumping me off the end of the pier might be our first stop.

CHAPTER SIX

i HAD THREE WOMEN MAD as hell at me—Skyla, Aunt Clem, and Mom. I don't know if my dad was mad at me or not. He wasn't even home when we got back to the house. This didn't look good for his Father of the Year competition. Must be present to win.

Skyla told me to call my mom right away as soon as we started back. Apparently, she had called when I was out and Skyla had to confess she didn't know where I was. She'd told Mom she was just getting ready to go looking for me in the car, which Mom said was a really excellent idea. Then she asked to speak to my dad and found out he was at the spa getting a mud bath.

I had a better idea now why Skyla was so ticked off about the whole thing. She'd been a stepparent for less than twenty-fours hours and had already been on the receiving end of my smart mouth and Mom's wrath. Not to mention having the bejezus scared out of her when she thought she'd lost me, and all the while the real responsible party was out surfing and playing Beauty Boy in the mud.

Aunt Clem answered the phone mid–first ring.

I licked my lips. "Hi, Aunt Clem! So how's it going?"

"Just tell me you're all right," she said.

"I'm fine! I just went for a walk in the neighborhood. Man, you should see how pretty it is—"

"Al-a-*stair*!" she hissed, cutting me off. "Do you have any idea how worried your mother has been?"

"Well, it's a very long beach," I said lamely.

"Honey?" Mom came on the line. My heart started hammering.

"Mom, I'm sorry! I didn't mean to worry you. I did write a note," I said, all the cool guy gone from my voice now. I turned my shoulder away from Skyla so she couldn't hear me. "I just forgot to leave it, and then when I realized I had it in my pocket—I dunno, I just got stupid. I should have called them. I don't really know why I didn't."

"You owe Skyla a huge apology," she said. "Do you have any idea how much you scared her?"

"Well, Dad must not be too worried. He's not even here!"

"Alastair, misbehaving is not your ticket home, if that's your game plan. Though after today, I wouldn't blame Skyla if she put you on the first plane east."

I caught my breath as hope soared a moment—

". . . but she really wants to have you with them this summer."

Hope crashed.

"I'm going to hang up now because you need to apologize to Skyla. And I'm in big trouble with Clem for even calling you today." She took a big breath. "I'm glad you're okay, but I'm very pissed at you."

"Well, I'm pissed too. I *hate* it here."

"You just got there," Mom said. "How can you hate it already?"

"Because our ex is here, and he makes me want to puke. Like he's Man of the Year all of a sudden because he married a cripple. You could have warned me, Mom, that Skyla didn't have any legs. Is this supposed to be a valuable life lesson that you and Dad cooked up for me?"

"What do you *mean* she doesn't have legs?" Mom said.

"You didn't know?" I asked, suspicious.

"She doesn't have LEGS?" Mom asked again.

"No!" I shouted.

"For God's sake," Mom said. "Your father should have told me. Is she in a wheelchair?"

"Hell, no!" I said. "She's got these fancy high-tech knees and feet. She cruises around like some kind of gimpy supermodel."

"I'm going to kill your father," she said.

"Get in line."

It's hard as hell to be in big trouble in a strange house with a couple of people you really don't know very well. When I'm in trouble with Mom, I know exactly what's going to happen. She'll yell, cry, get quiet as a reptile, or a combo of two or more of those items. All of which last twenty minutes or less. If I've really screwed up, there will be a consequence, usually involving household labor of some sort. Which she says is supposed to help develop my character. The last time I got in trouble and was sentenced to leaf raking, I suggested that maybe I could go develop my character across the street for the Linds, who didn't have any kids to rake for them. (They also had a lot less leaves in their yard, but I was hoping she wouldn't notice that.) Mom gave me a high eyebrow and told me to take my character outside and get busy in our yard.

I had no idea what was going to happen at Casa de Skyla. When we got back, the aforementioned dropped off her purse and picked up a remote control from a giant glass coffee table. With just a couple of swift clicks she turned on soft green lights in the living room, released a waterfall cascade from a towering wall, and filled the house with eerie whale sounds. Then, without a word, she went upstairs and disappeared. She reappeared for a moment a second later with a cell phone stuck to the side of her head. "Your father will be home shortly," was all she said.

I wasn't sure what to do, but I got the feeling I was supposed to stay put. Which I did for close to a half hour, even though the whale CD and the living room waterfall was making me have to go to the bathroom something fierce. But it was about half a mile to my bedroom from here and somebody was bound to come looking for me the minute I'd get up to go.

I sighed hard. Waiting for the ax to fall this long was nearly child abuse.

It did give me some time to prepare some good verbal ammo. I didn't want my dad to think he could up and leave Mom and me and then step back in and play major-league father whenever the mood struck him. Despite what I'd said to Skyla, I wasn't in any frame of mind to listen to a bunch of rules from him either.

He sure as hell wasn't in any position to talk to me about leaving without a note. That's pretty much what he had done to Mom five years ago.

The *Amazon Rain Forest* CD started. Oh God, no. I recognized it from school. Our science teacher had it and was always playing it. Rain began to fall by the tons, drumming through the treetops, splashing across rocks and feeding tiny rivers that joined with big rushing torrents—my bladder started to howl. I couldn't take it anymore and jumped up.

Just as the front door slammed.

"Alastair?" My dad came into the living room behind me. I whirled around and stopped dead in my tracks. I folded my arms across my chest. "Yeah?" I said.

He tossed his keys from one hand to the other and looked at me.

I looked back.

The man was damn radiant. His skin was aglow, perfectly tanned but not too much, and every sun-kissed hair on his head was in place. I steeled myself against him.

"You and I should discuss things. Let's go for a walk," he said.

I did a quick sort on possible replies. There was always the direct and defiant, "No." Too basic, I thought.

Or, "Sorry, your father permit has expired. Please reapply at the next counter." Too clever.

Maybe, "Bite me, Dad." Too harsh?

"I gotta go to the bathroom first," I blurted, with all the sophistication of a kindergartner.

Fifteen minutes later, we climbed down a steep wooden stairway that ran next to their property and led right down to the beach below their house. A No Trespassing—Private Property sign was posted at the top, middle, and bottom of the stairs.

We didn't talk for a long time. Just walked.

And then, finally, he started talking in a rush, like someone had just replaced his batteries. I couldn't get a word in edgewise. He started telling me all about his job, the kind of boring adult stuff that nearly causes a brain bleed in a kid. I could tell he was trying to convince me of something, I'm just not sure what. Like maybe he deserved his fancy new life because he worked so hard. Even if it was his wife's company. And maybe he had to spend a lot of time at the spa because the way he looked sold the equipment. What-ever.

"I don't want to see you and Sky get off on the wrong foot together," he said.

A dry laugh escaped me. "That's a good one, Dad. No chance of that, huh? Yuk-yuk."

"Sorry, I didn't—" He shoved his hands in his pockets.

"Did she have legs when you met her?" I asked. "Or did you marry her like that on purpose?"

He stopped walking then, and turned to face me. "Look, I know you're really mad at me and probably think you hate me. But Skyla has nothing to do with us."

"Oh, yeah? Gee, what a funny coincidence, then."

He sighed and ran his fingers through his hair. Careful, don't muss, I thought.

"It's not like that. I was concerned about the prosthetic leg your mom told me you picked. You can't do much with it. I wanted you to be able to do all the things the other kids could. I started looking into higher-tech models and got hooked up with the Challenged Athlete Foundation. I went to one of their fund-raisers to meet some of the kids and Skyla was there. We started talking and—"

"You fell madly in love with the legless woman. You're a regular Prince Charming, Dad. And gee, I guess you can just skip right through the glass slipper part with Skyla, huh?"

"She's the most amazing person I've ever met. You'll see."

"No, I won't. *Mom* is the most amazing person I've ever met," I said, turning and heading back toward the house.

He grabbed my arm and stopped me. "Go ahead and be as mad at me as you want. I'm warning you, though, Alastair. I won't put up with you taking it out on Skyla."

I tried to wrench away and stumbled over a big piece of driftwood. He grabbed me tighter and I shook him off. "Look! I'll apologize to her. Let's just drop it. I'm sick of this stupid conversation. I want to go back."

He took off his sunglasses and put them in his shirt pocket. Didn't say a word. Just looked at me.

"So are you gonna bawl me out or not? Okay, I blew it! Tell me off, ground me, whatever. I'm sorry, all right? It was really rotten of me to leave without telling you." I took a deep breath and then blew it out in a big gust.

"I really want us to get to know each other better this summer."

"So I'm not in trouble? I'm not grounded or anything?" I asked, shaking my head, stunned.

"No, of course not. But, we probably should go over a few guidelines with you for the summer." He reached into his shorts pocket and pulled out some Chapstick. He rolled it over his top lip, then his bottom lip with great care. Jeez, he took more time than Mom did putting on her lipstick.

He handed the Chapstick my way. I looked at him like he was trying to hand me a dead fish. He seemed more concerned with the state of his lips than the fact that his kid had been AWOL for hours and had come back with a nasty attitude.

"We'll see about getting you a cell phone right away. That should clear up any future misunderstandings, and we'll be able to keep track of you."

Yeah, that's definitely what we need here. Some electronics. He was a piece of work.

"No thanks," I said. "I already have one and I promised Aunt Clem I wouldn't use it except in an emergency. And, I'm not allowed to give out the number. She said it would be very expensive if anyone called me outside our roaming zone." And I wouldn't take a cell phone from Dad if it printed out twenty-dollar bills on demand.

He looked at me and I could guess he was weighing how hard he should push this with me right now. He folded.

Score one for the champ!

He looked at his watch. "C'mon," he said, "let's get back to the house. Jesse should be there by now and I know Skyla has a big dinner planned for all of us."

"Who's Jesse?" I asked.

"Skyla's niece," he said. "We told you about her last night."

"Please don't try to fix me up with other kids," I said. "Especially not girls."

"Don't you like girls?"

"No, I'm pretty sure I'm gay." Good one, I thought, giving myself a mental high five. That will keep him up a few nights.

He gave me a sidelong glance. "Oh!"

"I'll race you back," I said.

"Really?" he said.

"Yeah, I can book on this thing. Ready?"

"Ready!" he said with a big smile.

"Set!" I said, and flashed then on the two of us playing this game about a hundred times when I was little. The memory stuck me like a hot poker somewhere in the gut.

"Go!" I shouted.

He took off with a burst.

I strolled behind him. What a moron. And I couldn't believe he invited a little playdate over for me.

He looked back in a few seconds and saw me walking, then circled back.

"I forgot!" I said, slapping my head. "I don't run."

"You could if you wanted to," he said, his voice winded.

"Don't want to."

We walked in silence after that, and I watched the waves roll in. Before I knew it, the house came in sight, and I stopped and studied its outline. From this view, it looked different, and I had a sudden itch to draw it.

"Jess!" Dad shouted. "Come on down and meet my son."

Oh, swell, the niece. I looked up and made her out next to Skyla and Ian.

No.

No *way.*

It couldn't be, I thought. The world isn't that small.

LA, however, apparently was.

The gorgeous girl from the plane looked down at me. Shoved her baseball cap back and stared. "Jingle Boy?" she called. "Is that you?"

CHAPTER SEVEN

iT WAS AN iNCREDiBLE DiNNER. Like something out of a movie. If I were a girl, I'd have written several pages in my diary about the night—about the way the red sun sizzled down into the water, which we could see through the floor-to-ceiling glass walls of the dining room. Above us was an enormous chandelier lit by what seemed like a hundred tiny white candles. The candles smelled really good, like this stuff Mom rubbed on my chest once when I was sick. Dad said the candles were eucalyptus. And Skyla's staff served us plateful after plateful of food that was so good you just didn't want to stop eating. Apparently, when Dad and Skyla had guests come over, the low-fat regime went right out the window. Thank God.

And then there was Jesse sitting across from me. She kept shaking her head and saying, "This is so weird! Don't you think it's *weird?*" But she was smiling at me like she thought it was a nice weird.

Skyla beamed through it all as if she had personally given birth to Jesse just hours before. She laughed and then shrugged at me. "I can't keep up with this girl. I didn't even know she was in Denver. If I'd known, I would have tried like the dickens to get you two kids on the same flight. And look how marvelously it all worked out by itself!"

I could barely keep my eyes off Jesse. But I tried. I know how much I hated it when girls stared at me. But she had this amazing mess of wavy brown hair that was the color of maple syrup and all shiny. I knew I'd never be able to eat pancakes again without thinking of her. I tried to get a grip. All the good food, the great smells, and amazing scenery were screwing with my head big time. It was like I'd been drugged.

Not that it really mattered to me, but I quickly discovered that Jesse was so far out of my league she was nearly on another planet. Not only was she fifteen years old, she was a freaking soap opera star. And for some reason, she really liked it that I'd never heard of her or seen her on television before.

"Jesse has quite a devoted following," Skyla said, polishing off about her fourth glass of water. She pretty much needed one whole staff person to stand by and keep her glass full.

"Young guys, old women, and everyone in between," Dad said. "*Splendor Town* is a very hot show, particularly on the West Coast."

"So what's your character like?" I asked.

She sighed. "Bo-ring, really, completely boring."

"She is not," Skyla interrupted, turning to me. "She's a great character. The nicest one in the bunch if you ask me. Her name is Savannah."

"How long have you been on the show?" I asked.

Jesse looked at her watch, then over at Skyla. "Let's see, well, that would be, um, gee, fifteen years. Right, Auntie Skyla?"

Dad shook his finger at Jesse. "Don't you mock, missy. That show is one gourmet meal ticket. And it's going to pay for the finest college education anywhere you want."

Skyla leaned over toward me. "Jesse has never quite forgiven me about the show."

"You might as well have sold me to the carnival!"

"As I was saying," Skyla went on, "I was babysitting her one day when she was about six months old and had to go by the studio where they were filming *Splendor Town*. One of the set decorators was working on a fund-raiser with me and I needed to have a meeting with him. Anyway, I was standing in the back of the set waiting for Leonard. They were trying to film a scene with this poor baby who would not stop crying. They were getting very behind and the director was about to have a stroke. One of the cameramen spotted me in the back with Jesse and asked if he could just borrow her—"

"So she sold me right there on the spot!" Jesse jumped in.

"I didn't sell you; I just lent you for one scene. Your mother is responsible for the rest. And most days you love it," she reminded her.

Jesse snorted.

Even that was sexy.

"Can't you just quit?" I asked.

"Who would keep my mother in designer gowns then?" she said, grinning toward the adult end of the table. She grabbed her hair in both hands and pulled it into a tight fistful on the top of her head. She smoothed up the sides with her free hand. I was mesmerized. She looked over at me and smiled, then tied it up in a knot. I looked away, feeling my face heat up.

"Hey, can we change the channel here?" she said. "I'm sick to death of talking about work. Stump—" she said, and then stopped herself. "Are you sure you don't mind being called that?"

From her mouth, it sounded like music. "Nope—all the kids at school call me that." Not true, but not completely a lie. After the accident first happened, a couple of sixth graders started calling me that, but the principal suspended them.

"I want to hear all about you and what you're going to do with yourself all summer. Maybe shoot some waves with the old man, huh?" she asked. "Oh! I mean—God, I'm sorry. You probably can't— duh!" Her face turned red.

"It's okay," I said. "Don't worry. I probably could surf. I have stellar balance. It's one of the perks of being an amputee."

"There's actually a number of perks," Skyla said, smiling down my way. "I save a ton of money on shoes and don't have to worry about losing my socks in the dryer. "And I've got five less toenails to cut—I did the math on the time-saving once, and I think it ends up being a whole extra year added to my life," I added.

"I never have to spend time shaving my legs," Skyla added.

"And my chances of getting athlete's foot are reduced by half," I said.

Skyla gave me a big smile and I turned away from her. Forget it, lady, I thought. We're not going to be friends and start a Happy Gimp Club. I know Mom said she didn't have anything against Skyla, but I still felt like a traitor.

"Wow!" Jesse giggled. She leaned in closer to me, and now I could smell her beautiful hair. "So, if you're not surfing this summer, what are you going to do? Just lie around the beach and break all the hearts out here? The girls are going to just eat you up," she said combing my hair behind my ear.

And I let it stay that way. For at least a whole sixty seconds.

"I love the water," I said. "Just not surfing. I'm not into using boards or skis. They're just props, you know. Swimming is the only real water sport, in my mind." I stole a quick look at my dad, Mr. Sports Equipment USA. If the sport didn't have at least one piece of expensive equipment to go with it, he wasn't interested.

"Ooh," Jesse cooed. "A natural man. I like it."

I shrugged. "It's kinda my thing back home," I said, shoving an asparagus spear into my mouth. What a crock.

All eyes were on me, apparently waiting for me to go on. I took my time chewing, hoping they'd get bored waiting and start talking about something else. Wouldn't you know it? They were all pretty much riveted. All six eyeballs stuck on me like I was going to deliver the State of the Union any moment.

I chewed on that bite of asparagus until there was just nothing left of it but a fine green slime. Then I took a big slow drink of milk to pass some more time and hoped I didn't come up belching, which long drinks of milk tend to make a kid do.

Jesse reached over and jiggled my arm. "Details, please. So do you swim on a team or play water polo?"

I lifted my shoulders and then dropped them. "A little this, a little that," I said, which was true. I'd played in two different water parks. Raging Falls and Kowabunga Beach. "I started swimming back when I was just a kid, well, after you left," I said, nodding in Dad's direction. Ten lessons at the Y courtesy of Aunt Clem. His eyes looked away from mine. For once, Dad's exodus from my life was going to come in handy. He had no idea if I was lying or not. And I seriously doubted Mom had kept him clued in. She wasn't exactly the newsletter kind of mom.

"Well, if you like to swim, you've sure come to the right place!" Jesse said, motioning behind her. "Behold! The world's largest swimming pool."

"Pool swimming and ocean swimming are two different animals," Dad said. He looked over my way. "You know, we've got a great lap pool down at our downtown office. I'll get you a key to the whole fitness center. We've got some excellent new equipment in our gym. I could help you set up a training program."

"No, thanks," I said, cutting him off. "I met a guy today. He used to be the coach over at the high school. I'm thinking about swimming with him this summer. The guy's a regular dolphin."

"Omigod! I bet I know who you mean—Coach Witsak! Old guy about ninety? Swims every day down by the pier?" Jesse asked.

I nodded and held my breath, afraid of what might come next. Please, please, please, don't let him be like the local crazy person who thinks he's a coach on Mondays and George Washington all the other days of the week.

"My friend Sierra had an older brother who went to Lumina Beach High School, where Coach Witsak worked. Well, I was complaining in ballet one day about how masochistic Madame Rinaldi was and saying someone ought to call the authorities on her for child abuse. Then Sierra starts telling me about this kid that was on the swim team with her brother who actually did call Child Protective Services on their coach."

Jesse's eyes grew big. "Well, you'll never guess what Coach did when the social worker came over to the pool and tried to talk to him."

"What?" all three of us asked in unison.

"He picked her up like an old sack of dog food and threw her right into—"

A crashing noise sounded outside the window and the glass shook. I jumped in my seat. Loud voices shouted from the rear of the house.

Dad leapt from the table and flew from the room, cursing up a blue streak.

And then a load of firecrackers popped off near the windows. Sounded like a war zone.

"Rick! Don't! Ian can handle it," Skyla shouted after him.

"What's happening?" I asked, gripping the edge of the table.

Jesse had her hands over her ears. "Surfers, probably!" she yelled, her voice nearly lost in the banging of another round of firecrackers.

"Surfers?"

"Long story!" she said, wincing at the continued crackling outside the window. "It's about the beach stairs!"

"Damn!" Skyla said as the voices and shouting outside grew louder. "I forgot Ian is off tonight. I better go help him." She scooted out from her chair next to me.

"No!" I said. "I'll go—you two stay here."

"You two are crazy!" Jesse said. She reached into her jeans and pulled out a small cell phone. "I'm calling the cops."

"Don't, Jess!" Skyla warned her. "Please! That will just make it worse."

The shouting outside grew, and there was another big crash, like things were being thrown.

I jumped up as Skyla headed toward the noise. I ran after her. "Don't! It's not safe out there! I'll go!" Just before we got to the glass door to the back, my stick leg hooked one of her landing gear. I pulled her right down, landing flat on top of her. Our heads crashed against the glass and against each other's. Hard.

"Oh God!" Jesse yelled. "Are you two okay?"

I rolled off Skyla, or tried to, but our legs were hooked somehow. We couldn't get apart.

She had her hand over her eye and groaned.

Jesse crouched over us both. "I got it! Hold on. Stump, don't pull. You two are stuck together right at this metal piece." She struggled with it a sec. "Okay—there!" She separated our legs and I rolled to my side, rubbed my head where it hurt.

She helped Skyla to a sitting position and pulled her hand away from her face.

"Oh, man," Jesse said. *"Felipe! Somebody!"* she shouted over her shoulder. "I need ice!"

Jesse looked over at me. "Stump, you all right?"

I nodded, mortified. I was used to falling. It was part of the gig of being one-legged. But taking down my stepmother in front of Jesse was a new all-time low.

"Skyla, I'm sorry!" I said, sitting up.

"It's fine," she said. "Are you okay, Stump?"

"Yeah," I said, feeling stunned.

Several staff materialized out of nowhere finally and pressed ice over Skyla's eye and helped her up.

"Let me get you up," Jesse said to me, in that special voice people have reserved for hurt animals, old ladies, and gimps. Hearing that from her felt worse than the fall. I didn't want her to put me in that category.

I shook her off. "I can do it!"

She sat back on her heels and frowned. She pulled her phone out again, started stabbing in numbers.

I grabbed it from her. "Skyla said *don't!*" I tried to pull myself to my feet and slipped back down again.

Jesse's eyes were full of pity for me.

I looked away, jumped up on my good foot. Banged out the door into the night.

CHAPTER EIGHT

DAD WAS STANDING NEAR THE beach stairs where they ran next to the pool deck. He was holding a couple of the No Trespassing—Private Property signs. I could see the shadows of some people moving down the stairs: one of them carried a torch; the others had surfboards. Dad turned as I approached him. "Alastair! Get in the house. This doesn't concern you."

One of the people turned back to us and shouted, "You can't stop us, man. We'll be back!"

"Get out of here! *Now!*" Dad growled at them.

"What is going on?" I asked.

"Damn trespassers," he said. "They took down the signs and threw them onto the deck. Almost broke the window."

"So, why don't you call the cops on them?"

"Won't do any good," Dad said.

"But if it's private property, they're breaking the law. The police can arrest them." Not that I cared if the surfers ran through the house naked, but I didn't get why everyone was acting so helpless about the whole thing.

Dad sighed and planted his hands on his hips. "It's complicated. Let's go inside."

Jesse and Skyla were sitting at the table when we got back. Skyla had an ice pack over her eye.

"Sky!" he exploded. "What happened!" Did one of those jerks—"

She shook her head, "No! Of course not!"

"I did it," I said, and all eyes turned on me. "I tripped her." I stared at Dad. "It was an accident," I added, like an afterthought.

Dad took a deep breath. Gave me a long, hard look.

Jesse rushed over and put her arm around my shoulders. "He was trying to keep Skyla from going outside to help you! That's twice in one week you've saved a poor damsel in distress, Stump. First me on the plane and now Aunt Skyla. You're a regular Lancelot."

Dad just stared at me. I couldn't read him. But I could smell something coming off him. The faint scent of suspicion. Like I'd seen an opportunity to knock his wife around and I took it. Yeah, right.

I glared back. It was gonna be a long summer.

It figures. In my whole life, I've never given anyone a black eye. That is, until I met my new step-whatever, and in the first week I'd given her the biggest shiner I ever saw. I couldn't stand to look at her. It made me physically sick. Skyla tried to make me feel better about it, though. Told me right off that when she was first learning to run on her new feet, she'd fallen and given herself an even bigger one.

All the same, I decided to retreat to my room and lay low for a few days. I drew a big DO NOT DISTURB sign and posted it outside my door. Then I rehearsed what I was going to say to Dad when he came and tried to get me to come out of my room. Figured he'd have some Dodger game tickets or something lined up for us, and I couldn't wait to blow him off.

I dug out the sack of candy bars I'd beheaded at the beach and made my meals out of those. I called Ian and asked if he had a computer I could use in my room. Within two hours, at my doorstep, I had a brand-new wireless laptop with enough brainpower to launch the space shuttle. And a thank-you note from Skyla saying she appreciated me trying to protect her and the laptop was mine to keep. I sent her a note back and said I'd give it back when I was done with it.

I still had a couple of days I had to wait until my phone call to Mom, but nobody said I couldn't e-mail. Aunt Clem was addicted to her BlackBerry, and no matter how crazy and woolly those women were going to get, I knew she wasn't going to leave it at home.

Friday, 1.15 p.m.

Dear Aunt Clem and Mom,

This was a very bad idea to send me here. I'm getting my character ruined by living with rich people. I just got a free computer by snapping my fingers at the butler. If you let me come on your trip, I will be very helpful and quiet. I could dress up like a girl and no one would know. I could come as a teenage DIT (that's a Dyke in Training, Mom). Please let me be with you guys. If you don't, I'm going to hitchhike all the way home in cars with strangers. I'll live in the storage shed until September. You don't want me to do that, do you??

Love always,
Alastair

Saturday, 8:40 a.m.

Dear Mom,

Dad and I had a nice long father-son talk yesterday and worked it all out. I finally remembered why I jumped out of the ski lift. Turns out I had just dropped a glove and was trying to go after it! Isn't that funny? Everything was a big misunderstanding. So, since we worked things out, I can come on your trip, okay? Okay, Mom?

> Love always,
> Alastair

> Saturday, 11:00 p.m.

Dear Aunt Clem,

Are you showing Mom my e-mails?? She wouldn't want me to be this unhappy. You have NO idea how wacko these people are.

Come GET me, please!!!!!!!!

> Alastair

PS I gave Skyla a black eye—swear to God!!

> Sunday morning, 9:45 a.m.

Dear Alastair,

Skyla assures me the black eye was an accident—a chivalrous one at that. She thinks you're quite the gentleman. She is worried, however, that you've been holed up in your room for three days calling "room service" for junk food delivery. I ordered you an omelet for breakfast and a spinach salad for lunch. Eat them or I'll paint a giant rainbow on your bedroom wall before you come home.

After you eat, go outside and play. That's what your mom needs right now so she can focus on her sobriety. She is picturing you surfing, going to Knott's Berry Farm, and making new friends.

I will save all your e-mails for her to read after you
come home. Right now she needs your love, laughter, and
support.
    Send jokes.

              Love,
              Aunt Clem

There was a rap on my door—finally, and I bolted off the bed ready
to rumble with Dad. If he thought he could square things between us
by treating me to a fancy summer in his richie house, he had another
thing coming. But it was just my breakfast. To hell with him.

I was ravenous. I parked the tray down on the bed and wolfed
down the omelet, fruit, and enormous glass of milk. I flicked through
the channels on the TV, but nothing interested me.

I lay back on the bed and belched. I ran my hands over the mountain
that was my gut. It was hard, like I'd just swallowed a bowling ball
whole. I burped again. Then tried to burp my whole name out like
I used to be able to when was a kid. Gee, that would surely impress
Jesse. I gave myself a quick mental kick. God, I was pathetic. Why did
I care what she thought of me?

I rolled off the bed and threw open the door to the balcony, letting
the fresh air blow over me. I sniffed under one armpit and decided I
should probably take a shower, even though I didn't smell too bad yet.
I hadn't had one in two—whoops, no, three days.

Then maybe I'd go out on the beach for a while. Maybe take a
good book to get my mind off things.

Skyla had told me they had a library upstairs if I ever needed
any books or anything. I was hungry for a big fat mental escape and
I'd already watched all the DVDs in the room. Plus two really lame

exercise videos starring my dad and one CPR training video he'd done, probably when he was a poor bachelor. I actually watched it three times for some reason. Sick, I know.

I took a quick shower and then snuck out of my room. The library was on the second level of the house and it was open—kind of like a big giant loft above the living room. The top of the glass-enclosed waterfall that fell down through the living room started here. I had to admit it was the coolest library ever. Mom would have killed for it. It had floor-to-ceiling built-in bookshelves and a large hammock hanging across one corner, right next to a window with a giant ocean view. Across the room was a big fireplace with a soft overstuffed couch. The ceiling was spectacular. It was vaulted and had these really interesting planes and angles. The very top was a pyramid-shaped skylight with that kind of glass that was cut to reflect light. I grabbed a pen from a table and sketched it out on the back of my hand. Imagined how the structure under the plaster worked.

I would have loved to flop into the hammock and hang out, catch some z's, or even just watch the lights move around the room. But I didn't want anyone to catch me looking like I was having a good time or anything. I scanned the rows of bookshelves searching for something that might interest me. There was a framed picture of Dad and me on one shelf. From about a hundred years ago. We were hiking in the Garden of the Gods in Colorado Springs. Dad had me on his shoulders and I had a big old kid grin on my face. I remembered that day. We'd stopped afterward and had giant root beer Slurpees that were so cold they made my teeth ache. I turned the picture to face backward.

Underneath the picture was a section of books that would have made my English teacher weep. Jeez, Skyla, or maybe Ian must have called her before I came. I ran my fingers over the bindings, tracing the titles. Mrs. Henselton's entire recommended summer reading list was here. Plus some. *Sabriel. Sonny's War. Speak. Stoner and Spaz.* It was pretty nice of Skyla to do that—probably set her back a few hundred bucks. I was betting it was Ian that put it all in alphabetical order. I mixed them all up, just to give the man some meaningful work.

One of the bookcases near the hammock had sliding doors over it. Like maybe it was rated X—and not for visiting kids. I looked around to make sure none of the staff was lurking nearby. Then I eased the doors back as quietly as I could.

I stared at the rows and rows of black plastic cases. Oh, man. Welcome to *Splendor Town*—years of it. Someone had taped Jesse's entire career. Hours and hours of her on-screen. I could think of a few worse ways to spend my time as long as I was stuck here. Or like Mom would say, it was better than a poke in the eye.

I grabbed as many cases as I could fit in the waistband of my shorts, front and back—then stuck a couple in each of my pockets.

For the next forty-eight hours, I had a Savannah marathon. But to keep the elders off my back, I ate dutiful meals and took a daily walk on the beach. I snuck back into the library every few hours to load up on a new supply.

I called had Aunt Clem on Sunday and had a short conversation with her and Mom. The reception was bad. They were in the middle of an electrical storm, so I had to shout, but I did what Aunt Clem had asked and acted like I was having a pretty good time. Guess I faked her out because Mom didn't send me a plane ticket after the call.

I dove headfirst back into *Splendor Town*, where I wished I could live. Anywhere but here. I watched Jesse grow up on-screen. She was a cute kid and even went through a chubby phase with braces. I jumped ahead a few years to the episodes where she had morphed into teenage Savannah. Despite the fact that I'd pretty much sworn off girls since they'd all gone psycho on me, Jesse had really gotten under my skin. I fast-forwarded through any scene she wasn't in and slow-mo'ed through the scenes with her lame boyfriend, Tye.

I couldn't seem to get a grip on myself. I did not want to like this girl, or any girl. I was determined to sail through puberty without having my hormones take over my brain. It ruined perfectly good kids. It had ruined my dad. Girls complicated everything. Turned you stupid.

But Jesse haunted me even though I knew better. I didn't want to think about her, but I couldn't seem to stop myself. Must be how Mom felt about booze—even though she could see how it ruined her life, it would sneak up on her and take over her thoughts.

When I wasn't watching the show, I'd catch myself replaying each second I'd spent with Jesse and reinterpret every single thing she'd ever said to me. Tried to erase the memory of her pulling me off Aunt Skyla and the look she gave me afterward. I vowed that she'd never look at me that way again—like she felt embarrassed and bad for me.

I found her private phone number on Skyla's speed dial and called her throughout the day, when I knew she wasn't home, just to listen to her voice message before I hung up.

Oh, great. Now I was a phone stalker.

Even, still, I began rethinking my potbelly that I'd worked so hard for and started a flurry of sit-ups, hundreds of them, push-ups too. Anything to change my young boy bod into something that might turn the head of a fifteen-year-old girl who could probably have any boy in America.

What—was I completely *crazy*?

And when Jesse called me on the sixth day of my exile and asked me
I wanted to do a Celebrity Adventure Race with her that included an
ocean swim, *me*—who hadn't swum in over three years, *me*—whose
last race was the three-legged kind with Aunt Clem at the Durango
Gay Pride Festival, well, I was not all that surprised to hear myself
say—

"Sure! Why not?"

CHAPTER NINE

JESSE SQUEALED INTO THE PHONE, nearly rupturing the tympanic membrane in my ear.

"You will? You really will? Stump, I'm so glad! I told your dad you would."

"He didn't think I would do it?" I asked, feeling my blood heat up.

She rushed to cover. "Well, he just wasn't sure you'd be up for the training and all. There's a swim, a mountain bike ride, and an obstacle course. A little kayaking too. Your dad thought maybe you just wanted to kick back this summer and stuff."

"He doesn't know what I want."

"I know! That's what I told him, so this is just great! There will be three of us on the team—you, me, and Sergio. He's the guy that plays my boyfriend Tye on the show, and most days he's a conceited jerk, but he's a good athlete. The rules say we just have to have two celebs on the team and the rest can be whoever we pick. And I pick you!"

Note to self—object of desire, aka Jesse, doesn't like conceited jerks. Don't ever be one. Not a problem. I think Dad got all the family DNA on that.

"When is it?" I asked.

"Not until the last week of August," she said. "You have plenty of time to get ready."

Oh, man, was I crazy? Eight weeks? It would take me more like eight years. "Well, is it just kids racing?"

"There's two categories," she explained. "Adult and teen. There are two other teen teams racing, *Miami Loves* and *Chicago Central*. *Miami Loves* have beat everyone for the past three years. They just can't get over themselves. It's really sickening. Sergio and I are dying to do some serious whoop ass on them. Oh, we also get to pick an alternate, but it has to be an adult. They stay with us the whole time. It's kind of lame, but it's an insurance requirement for the race. They'll be our alternate racer in case one of us needs to drop out but also our course babysitter. Sergio's older brother, Phil, will be our backup man, since he's over twenty-one. But we won't need him," she said confidently. "And guess what? The winning team gets fifty thousand dollars donated by the sponsors to their favorite charity. Isn't that cool?"

I was still stuck on the "serious whoop ass" that I would be expected to perform, but I tried to sound fairly enthusiastic. "Excellent!"

"Sergio and I will have to work out late after the show, but you're lucky, you can train whenever you want. I've got to do some work on my swimming. I've never done a half mile in the ocean before."

I coughed and hoped that the blood would return to my legs sometime in the near future. "A half mile?" I squeaked like Minnie Mouse. I cleared my throat and then tried to bring it down several octaves. "I mean—just a half—not a whole mile?"

"Yeah, that's okay for you, isn't it?" she asked. "I know you haven't done much ocean swimming, but since you're already a kick-ass swimmer, you'll be fine. For the race, we go out in this big boat into the channel, and they drop us off. From there, we swim the rest of the way to Santa Therese Island, where the bike course is. It's supposed to be a total blast! Thank God we've got the summer to—

"I'm *coming*!" she said, to whoever was trying to get her attention. "Sorry, Stump. It's my mother. I better go. We're having what she called a mother-daughter spa day, but it's actually a torture your daughter day."

"What do you mean?"

"She's very worried about the five pounds I gained this year, which she said are all in my ass. First, they're going to wrap my butt in giant leaves and try to sweat it off. After that, they'll scrub it with a cellulite brush until I can't sit for a week. Then she's scheduled me for eyebrow electrolysis, which is nearly child abuse. After that, we'll celebrate with a jicama-and-honey sundae and then go buy clothes that are too small for me. Fun, huh?"

"I think you look perfect the way you are," I said.

"Thanks, Stump, you're a love. Why can't all guys be as nice as you? Mother worries that I'll get dumped from the show for hairy eyebrows or something and she'll have to get a job." She turned her head and shouted, "I'm *coming*!"

"You gotta go—"

"Yeah, she's about to implode. Anyway, I'm so glad you're going to do the race. I'll sign the three of us up today. Then there's no backing out!" she said, laughing. "I *heard* you already!"

"Bye, handsome!" she added, and clicked off.

I fell back onto the bed, holding the phone over my heart, which was pounding like it was trying to break out of my chest. From what, I wasn't entirely sure. From having talked to Jess or from having just agreed to a physical feat better suited to someone with gills and fins?

I picked up a pillow and covered my face, only slightly smothering a very, very bad cussword.

For the next four days, I traipsed up and down Lumina Beach, sweat running down my legs and my fingernails raw from being chewed on.

I stalked the picnic table where I'd first seen Coach, my eyes fixed on the water, straining to see his white swim cap. Man, he just had to show. I was dead if he didn't. There weren't any Witsaks in the phone book. I couldn't catch a break.

On the fifth day, with less than eight weeks left until the Adventure Race and a potential major life humiliation hanging like a noose over my head, I decided it was time. I had to get into the water.

I knew how to swim, for pete's sake. There couldn't be that much difference between lake water and ocean water. Well, except for the salt part. I mean the basic rules of flotation and cold and wetness would all still apply, whether you were in Henley Lake or the Pacific Ocean.

Skyla had been dropping hints like mad about my dad taking me out to do some workouts. Yeah, that was going to happen. Unless there was a female audience involved, Dad couldn't be bothered. Or maybe he just didn't ever want to be alone with me because he was a coward. Afraid that he might actually have to have a real conversation with me about how he ruined Mom's life. And mine. He was still acting funny around me since I gave Skyla that shiner. He was probably worried there was one coming with his name on it. This whole summer vacation with Dad was a scam. I was stupid to think he might actually want to work things out. Not that I would have let him. But you'd think he'd at least have tried.

There was no way I was going to do any training with him. He probably swam like a merman, or whatever the male counterpart of a mermaid was. I was betting he had a whole special outfit with a matching swim cap and state–of–the–art goggles to go with it. I had some cutoffs and only one-and-a-half legs.

I waited until Dad and Skyla headed into town to the office. They had a big lunch scheduled with a new client. They invited me, but I passed. I'd had enough fresh fish, tofu chunks, and long stringy green things to last me a while.

Even so, I snuck down the steps from the house to the beach. I wasn't entirely sure that Ian or some of the other house staff weren't filming my comings and goings these days. They were nice, but sneaky. Like no matter where I hid my dirty underwear, by the time I'd get back to my bedroom, it would be washed, pressed, and folded into perfect triangles in my drawer. Trying to outsmart them had become a little game I'd started to keep myself sharp. Yesterday I'd hidden my underwear inside a Scrabble game on the highest shelf in my closet. I was betting it would take at least a week for them to track those down.

The sun was out technically but was blocked by a big fog bank. As usual, the beach was pretty deserted out in front of the house. An occasional neighbor would come by on a walk with dogs, but your regular summer beachgoers were down farther south near the public access stairways. And near the lifeguards.

I wrapped my arms around my puny boy bones and tried to chase the chill away. Up close, the ocean didn't look all that peaceful or inviting. I tried to calculate how far out I'd have to swim to get past all the waves. When I was looking for Coach Witsak, I noticed that all the swimmers went out as far as the buoys, which looked like they were halfway to Maui. It seemed way far out, but I didn't want to look like a big goober by swimming too close to the shore. Maybe there was a rule about it or something.

I took off my leg and stowed it under a towel on the beach. I hopped over to the shoreline and let the water rush over my toes and foot. It was seriously cold. A shiver worked its way down my front. This was painful. I either needed to get in quick or get the heck out. I looked back at the house for a moment and imagined crawling back into my sweats and spending the afternoon with Savannah and another few episodes of *Splendor Town*.

Being a lovesick fan was not going to win me any points with Jesse. She probably had moon-faced kids all over the country moping over her. I had a chance to really get her attention. I had the whole summer with nothing else to do but devote myself to being a major-league swimmer. Technically, she was too old for me, but you never know. She did say she thought I was a hunk.

I took a deep bracing breath, hopped ahead into the waves, put my head down, and dove right in. And forgot to close my mouth.

A ton of icy salt water hit the back of my throat, and I coughed and sputtered and struggled to get to the surface. I took a big gulp of air just in time to have a wave crash over the top of my head. My foot scrambled for the bottom, but I couldn't find it. I bobbed up again, choking and spitting

Swim, stupid! My legs paddled like crazy under me and my arms dug into a breaststroke. I chased down the last big wave and managed to ride right over the top just seconds before it crashed over.

I slid down the other side and coughed up the rest of the water I'd swallowed. Treading water, I tried to catch my breath. It looked like I'd managed to get onto the other side of the waves. Behind me the shoreline was starting to look pretty far away. But the buoy was looking even farther away. I peered down into the water to check if I could see bottom, but it was too murky. I'm guessing it was pretty deep under me.

Keep going, keep going. Back home at Henley Lake, I could swim out to the floating dock half asleep. I trained my eye on the buoy and lined it up on my sites as my target. Managed to do about twenty decent strokes before I got tired. Okay, I was a little out of shape. No problem. I flipped over on my back and went into torpedo mode, churning up some serious wake.

Awesome! I was cutting my way through the water. *Vrrrrrr—o-o-oom!*

I kept looking behind me to see if I was out to the buoy yet. For as fast as I was going, it was taking a very long time. I was hoping it was going to be like the thing they print on your car side windows: Objects in the mirror are closer than they appear.

Two weeks later, I finally hit the buoy. I was tired, but I was feeling pretty dang good. Well, now what? Now I was supposed to swim a half mile? I had no idea how far that would be.

I started doing the sidestroke just to keep moving. Checked myself against the shoreline to make sure I was swimming parallel and not farther out to sea. Just nice and easy. I glanced at my watch and hoped it was waterproof. Since I didn't have any distance markers, I could at least swim for time. Maybe go out fifteen minutes and then back fifteen minutes, catch a wave, and cruise in. Piece of cake.

The water was still freezing cold, but at least it was calm, and the sun had poked through some clouds and was shining down on my head. This really wasn't too bad, I thought. I flipped over to my other side when my arm got tired but then quickly flipped back. I couldn't see the beach facing that way, and I knew I'd better keep myself oriented to the land.

I was getting into the groove of it but could tell I was moving pretty slowly. I kicked harder to get myself really going. Having only a leg and a half was a handicap, but I remembered my old PT, Bert, telling me I could use my stump as a "power tool." I turned my head to watch the wake I was making behind me. Better. I put my head back down again and could feel the water skimming under the side of my face, felt myself cutting through the water. Man, I was a regular dolphin boy.

Kick—glide. Kick harder—glide farther. Kick faster—whoosh!

Kick! Kick! *Kick!* Man! If Jesse could see me now—

A fiery pain shot though my leg like a bullet. The pain pulled me under.

I clawed my way back to the surface. Shark! I yelled and spun and slapped the water looking for the sharp triangle fin.

Oh-God-oh-God! The pain was intense. It was hot and burning and it wouldn't let up.

"Help! Somebody help me!" I screamed. I slapped at the water and made as much noise as I could. Then I tried to make myself look big and mean and yelled some more. *"I've got a gun!"* Oh God. This couldn't be happening to me! I waited with dread for the water to turn red with my blood.

And I waited for whoever bit me to come back and finish me off.

CHAPTER TEN

THE PAIN WAS FURIOUS. I howled like a mad dog. Oh, man, I didn't want to die today. I did not want to drown in front of my dad's house. Mom's face flashed in front of me, and I screamed for her.

I circled around and around in the water, but I couldn't see anything. Maybe it wasn't a shark—maybe it was a man-o'-war, or a giant swordfish sawing away at the rest of my leg, or—

Down again I went. It pulled at me. I came back up hacking and gasping. Oh God! It must still have its fangs on my leg. I tried to shake it, and the pain burned like a blowtorch.

I dug down through the cold green water. All I could see was seaweed and one white leg.

I surfaced for a breath and saw it before it saw me. A giant paddle came down and whacked me right across the head.

BAM! The impact sent me under. I came back up spitting seawater. "HE-E-E-EYYY!" I yelled, coughing. I tried to grab the paddle.

A guy in headphones looked down and then swore like he'd just seen Shamu.

"Damn! I'm *sorry*, I didn't see you!"

I grabbed the front of his kayak and clung to it. My head throbbed and bright drops of blood fell onto the blue plastic.

"You're bleeding!" He scrambled to the front toward me. "Let's get you up!"

I shook my head, which was the easy part. Every part of me was shaking. "I—don't think I can—can—lift—my—leg—I—I'm bit!"

The guy's head whipped around and he did a quick search of the water. "Get in!" he barked. He grabbed the back of my shorts and dragged me up over the top. Then shoved my butt over. "Oh, shit! Oh, man! Your *leg*!"

I grabbed my stump and squeezed it. "S'kay, I'm an amputee!"

I wasn't bit! It was all there. No jagged teeth marks. No bloody meat hanging from me.

I tried to bend my leg toward me and the white-hot sword stabbed me again. "Ooo-o-h-HH!" I yelled. I cursed and grabbed at my calf. It was a friggin' leg cramp.

He shoved the paddle next to me. "Hold this and don't drop it!"

Leaning around me, he ran his hand over my legs. "It's okay! You're not bit! You're fine. You've just got a whale of a—"

"A-aa-AA-HHHH!" I yelled as the pain stabbed me again.

The guy headlocked me from behind, and then grabbed the skin under my nose between two fingers and squeezed. Hard. Really hard.

"Oohh—ahhahhhh—aaaAAachhh!"

"Hold on! Hold on! I know it hurts!" He squeezed harder.

I yelped like a kicked dog and he tightened his hold.

"Hang on!" he said. "Come on—just breathe into it. Tell me when it lets up."

Whaaat? My leg? The hole he was tearing into my face?

He leaned over my shoulder to look at me. "Better?"

"*No!*" I shouted. But then in the next second, like a bloody miracle my leg went soft, and the pain vanished.

I nodded dumbly.

"Cool," he said, and let the death pinch go.

"Now move up a little, kid," he said. "Careful of the paddle."

I scrootched up and tried to keep from shaking, but I couldn't seem to stop. My teeth were clattering like a pair of castanets.

"How'd you d-d-do that?" I asked, amazed.

"Old lifeguard trick. Works every time. It's some kind of acupressure thing."

I rubbed my leg where I'd expected to find giant bloody teeth marks.

Not even a fleabite. I'd almost drowned in front of Skyla's house from a leg cramp.

I was such a wuss.

"Man! You freaked me out! When I pulled you up and saw you were missing part of your leg—*whoa!*" he said, settling in behind me. "You just took about a year off my life there, kid!"

I wrapped my arms tight around myself and tried to stop shivering.

"Man! That's why you should always swim with a buddy," he said. "Get a cramp out here and you could be a goner."

My vision went dark pink and I wiped away blood that was falling into my eye from the cut on my head.

"Here, let me see that," he said. He leaned around me and peered at it. "It's not deep. I just grazed you. Head cuts just bleed a lot." He grabbed a T-shirt from behind him, turned it inside out, and pressed it against the cut on my head. "Hold this a minute—good and hard." He dug a Chapstick from his shorts and wiped the rest of the blood from my head and face. He rubbed the Chapstick over my cut. "That should get it to stop bleeding a bit. I don't think you'll need stitches."

He reached around me and pulled on a small compartment in the bottom of the kayak.

"Hey, help me open that, will you? There's a life jacket in there. Put it on."

"S'okay. I don't n-n-need a life jacket," I said, embarrassed. "I can swim. I just—"

"It's not for safety. You gotta warm up. It'll help."

I pulled it out and fumbled with the armholes. Like trying to put a dress on an iceberg.

He reached around me from behind, and cinched it up tight, then pulled me next to him. "Promise I'm not trying to hit on you, man—but this will warm you up. How long you been in the water?" he asked, scrubbing my arms with the heels of his hands.

"I—dunno—f-feels like a long t-t-time."

He looked over my shoulder. "You got a watch on—what time did you start?"

I couldn't answer. I was too busy trying to stop my teeth from clattering. Afraid they might start breaking.

"You from around here?"

I shook my head. "C-Color-a-a-do."

"Okay, look. Here's the rules for swimming out here. Number one: wear a wet suit, even just a shortie. Number two: swim with a buddy. And number three: keep track of your time."

Okay, so I'm a total idiot.

"You feeling any better yet, kid?"

"Ye-ee-a-ah," I lied.

"What's your name anyway?"

"Ala—well, j-j-just call me Stump," I said.

"I'm Kiki—s'nice to run into you! Man, bad joke, sorry! So

where'd you start from? I'll take you back. You really need to get in a hot shower."

I looked to the shore and tried to pick out Skyla's place. I couldn't see it from where we were. Looked like I had drifted out a ways. At this distance, all the houses looked the same.

"I s-s-started out from my house—I mean, my dad's house. It's sorta pinkish." A violent shudder ripped through me and I shook hard. "S'got stairs next to it."

"I know where it is. I've gotten chased off those stairs a few times by the guy that lives there. What a jerk. Oh, sorry! He's your—"

I shrugged. "My dad," I said. "He doesn't like people on his property." Even me, I thought.

"Those stairs aren't his property. They're public stairs, but he tries to make you think they're private by putting all those bogus signs up. City hall keeps making him take them down. You should talk to him about it. I live up this way, and I have to drive all the way down near town to put my kayak in the water. I gave up hassling with him a couple of years ago. Life is too short for that kind of mojo."

"They're public stairs?" I asked. I tried to process this. "Oh, yeah, he's in the local paper at least once a month. Raises hell at city hall. A few years back, he hired some guy to come in with a big bulldozer and pull the stairs down. He got fined a hunk of change for doing that. So now he's trying to buy the stairs. He's offered a ton of money for them. But the locals don't take kindly to rich people trying to limit our access to the beach."

He picked up his paddle. I tried to get out of his way, but there wasn't anywhere to go. "You're cool," he said. "I can do it like this. It's not that far." He dipped one end in and stirred the water. It turned us around a bit. I watched him, got a sense of his stroke and how lightly he held the paddle. Stuff I'd need to know for the Adventure Race. If I still wanted to do it, that is.

"Maybe you could talk to him for us? I mean, what's the big deal about us using the stairs? I don't get it."

"I c-c-can try. I don't know if he'd listen to me. We're not exactly close or anything."

"I know how that goes. I've got one just like that myself."

I rubbed my hands back and forth over the tops of my legs. "So did you use to be a lifeguard?" I asked.

"Yeah, back when I was a kid. Why?"

"You must be a good swimmer."

"I do all right. Why?"

"Do you think maybe you could you teach me how to swim out here?" I turned to look at him. "For money, I mean."

"I don't really have the time, kid. I run a hamburger joint in town, and that keeps me pretty busy. It's hard for me to even slip away for a short time like this. But I'm sure you can take a class over at the Y."

I shook my head. "I need private lessons. Mega-lessons. I'm in a race at the end of the summer, and I need to be able to swim a half mile out here by then." I hesitated a second and then confessed. "This was my first ocean swim."

"Wow! Well, then that's a serious goal."

"Do you know anybody that could teach me? I want to be a *really* good swimmer in less than eight weeks."

"Well, I know somebody that could do it, but he's tough. He'd work your tail off. You'd have to be some kind of masochist to voluntarily work with him. He used to be the coach down at the local high school."

"Is it Coach Witsak?" I asked excitedly.

"Yeah, why?"

"I've been trying to find him! I've heard he's kind of tough, but I want someone really good."

"Well, he's good, all right. But he's the meanest sonofabitch I've ever met. If you're looking for some punishment, you could pay me to beat you with a stick all summer." He laughed and dipped the paddle deep on the left, turning the nose toward shore.

"Almost there, Stump," he said. "You warming up at all?"

I nodded and swiped at my nose, which had begun to run like the water slide. We skimmed across the top of the water. His blue plastic tub was a swimming machine. That's how I wanted to be in the water. The kayak cut across the surface with just the smallest flicks of his wrists on the paddles. It was all about the right stroke. That's why I needed Coach Witsak.

"Do you know how I can get ahold of him? His phone number is unlisted."

"Who—the Swiminator?"

"Yeah—"

"Well, besides out here in the water, he hangs out at one of the local shake shops. You know, where they make smoothies out of compost. It's over by the pier. It's called the Grass Shack. He usually goes there after his swim.

"Okay, hold on, kid!" he said. "We're going to catch some waves in."

CHAPTER ELEVEN

THE WHiR OF DUELiNG BLENDERS almost blew out my eardrums before I spied Coach Witsak in the Grass Shack camped out behind an *LA Times*. I was pretty nervous now that I knew he wasn't just some old guy in Speedos I'd met last week. He was legendary B-A-D in these parts. I hadn't forgotten what Jesse had told me about him throwing that social worker lady in the pool.

"Um, sir? Uh, excuse me?"

He gave me a quick glance over the top of his paper. "Hey, it's the human candy machine. How goes it?"

"Fine, sir! I mean—Coach!"

"Glad to see you've acquainted yourself with a better eating establishment than the gas station." He took a quick swig of some grassy green and suspiciously thick beverage in a tall glass.

"Oh, yeah!" I crackled as my voice took a quick trip to puberty. I cleared my voice hard. "Uh, Coach? Would it be okay if I sat down?"

At that, he lowered his newspaper a good six inches and gave me a once-over. "You got something on your mind?"

I took that as the best invitation I was going to get and plunged right in. "I need to learn how to swim," I said. "I mean, like really learn how to swim. By the end of the summer. Could you help me?

You know, coach me? Like you coach those kids you were telling me about the other day?"

He studied me hard. But didn't say a word.

My mouth raced ahead without me. "But I need to have private lessons," I explained. "I'm going to need a lot of one-on-one time."

Nothing. He continued to stare. My eyes darted to his neck to see if there was a pulse. "I could pay you," I blurted.

He raised an eyebrow. "Yeah? How much?"

I wasn't expecting that answer. Adults were usually more polite about money. I did some quick math in my head. I had three hundred dollars to last me all summer, but I was trying to hang on to most of it just in case I needed to blow this town and go home.

I hedged. "Well, how much do you charge?"

"More than you can afford," he said, picking up his paper again.

"My stepmother is loaded," I said. Heat rushed to my face. Man. I couldn't believe how quick I was to cash in on Skyla. If I weren't so desperate, I'd be ashamed of myself.

"Yeah?" he said. "And how much will she pay me?"

I took a deep breath and scratched at a sticky spot on the table. "Nothing. I wouldn't really ask her. Look," I said. "I'm pretty much on my own out here this summer. But I've got to learn how to swim. It's really important!"

"And I suppose I'm not going to get any peace here with my newspaper until I find out why this is so 'really important,' right?"

I tried to laugh to lighten things a bit. "I kinda told this girl I'd swim on her Adventure Race team at the end of the summer. It's for charity. And, well, I might have given her the impression that I was a pretty good swimmer."

He grunted. "Should have seen that coming. It's always about a girl."

I pinned my lower lip with my teeth and waited.

"Not interested," he said. "Nothing in it for me. Maybe you get the girl. What do I get?"

"I could work for you all summer. I'd do anything. You know, mow your lawn, feed your dog, build a fence."

He swore. "You're not going to let me read my paper, are you?"

"Please, sir? Just try me out. Here's the deal. I'll work for you all week without pay, and at the end of the week, you give me one swimming lesson. Just one. And at the end of that, if you like me okay, then we'll work out a deal for some more lessons." I ran my tongue over my lips and waited. The seconds ticked by. "It really is a win-win for both of us, you know?"

He shook his newspaper and held it up between us.

My hopes began their descent.

The newspaper rattled. "Meet me at the beach tomorrow morning at six a.m. Until then, go away!"

A smile split my face wide. "Great! Thanks, Coach! I'll see you then. At the same place I met you, right?"

Grunt.

I scraped my chair back and wiped my hands on my shorts. They were soaked from nerves. I turned to leave but then stopped short at the door.

"Oh, sir? One more thing. Should I wear my bathing suit, or—"

"You can wear a tutu, kid. Just don't be late." The paper lowered and he peered over the top. "I suppose I should know your name," he said. "And I'll I need a permission slip from your parents. I'll send one home with you tomorrow."

"Stump," I said. "The name's Stump."

He waited, his eyes boring a hole in me.

I cleared my throat. "It's Alastair, sir. Alastair Hudson."

"Go away, Alastair."

My bed was apparently rigged with motion sensors because I ran right smack into Ian at 5:25 a.m. as I crept into the kitchen to grab some breakfast to go. He had what he thought was my favorite breakfast sitting out on the counter—one onion bagel split in half with mustard and crushed corn chips on one side and peanut butter and frosted flakes on the other side. And a Coke on a doily to wash it all down. I really didn't like this breakfast all that much, but it had been worth about twenty freak-out Dad and Skyla points when I first made it. It seemed worth keeping it up.

"Good morning, Stump," he said, tidying up the counter, which was already so tidy it squeaked.

I grabbed the bagel off its china plate and wrapped it in a paper towel.

"They already know," I said.

"Know what?" he asked in his pleasant voice that always seemed a little fake to me.

"You didn't catch me sneaking out, in case you think you did. I talked to Skyla and Dad last night and got permission."

"Oh, yes, I know," he said. "They mentioned you were starting a job today and leaving early. Skyla wanted to make sure you got something to eat before you left."

"Well, thanks, then. But you didn't have to get up just for me. I'm not like them," I said, jerking a thumb in the direction of Skyla and Dad's bedroom.

"Like them?" he asked politely.

"Yeah, I mean, back home, I'm just a regular kid and stuff. I make my own meals when my mom has to work. So, this fancy servant stuff kinda freaks me out."

"Yes, well, I'm not actually a 'fancy servant.' I'm a personal assistant," he reminded me. "Can I pack you a lunch before you go?" he asked. "Perhaps a tuna-jelly sandwich?"

He kept his snooty face all prim, but I think he was having a spot of humor at my expense. I suspected he'd let loose a whole titter after I left.

I took a quick look at my watch and put it into overdrive. "No time!" I said. "Catch you later!"

I hurried out of the kitchen and then bolted out the double doors in the dining room onto the back deck. I clomped down the access stairs to the beach, taking them about four at time. I definitely did not want to be late and knew I'd probably cut my travel time by about a third if I took the beach route.

Dad offered to drive me to my new job, but I turned him down. Skyla was probably bugging him about not spending more time with me. But, he was not going to get any points off me for giving me a five-minute car ride every day. Plus I didn't want him trying to act like Mr. Cool Guy with Coach. Probably try to sell him some dumb workout equipment. I figured I could run to my new job every day and add some fitness points to my training. My version of running, though, didn't look like anyone else's. It was more like run-drag-run. But it got the job done.

I started slow, just to get myself warmed up. I wore a small backpack and it bounced up and down on my back. It was stuffed with my bathing suit, sneakers, a towel, and some snacks. I wore clean shorts, a new T-shirt for my first day on the job. I was shooting for a look somewhere left of Boy Scout and right of grunge.

My slow jog did more than warm me up. Within minutes, it felt like someone had lit a match to my lungs. Any minute now, smoke would be coming out of my nose. I stopped running and tried walking very, very fast. Checked my watch.

Five fifty-two. Uh-oh. I had eight minutes left to get there. The beach stretched on for what looked like miles. The pier looked a long ways down.

I ran like hell all the rest of the way.

CHAPTER TWELVE

COACH WITSAK WAS STANDING ANKLE deep in the water when I came tearing up the beach like a car trying to race with one flat tire.

He gave me a glance and then spit into his goggles. "You live up that way?" he asked, jerking his head in the direction I'd just come.

I sucked in a big mouthful of air so I could talk. "Yeah—just for—just for the summer," I panted.

"How'd you get down to the beach?" he asked.

"Took—the stairs—down—" I turned my head and spit. Tried to clear the sweat out of my eyes.

He grunted. "Surprised you made it. The jerk that lives next to them must have still been in bed or he would have come after you. What an imbecile. Those stairs are public property. You go ahead and use them as often as you like. If he gives you a hard time, you just let me know."

Brother, here we go with the stairs again. This is great. Turns out my dad is public enemy number one with all the locals.

Coach snapped the goggles over his head, wriggled them around, then took them off again. Spit into the lenses and spread it all around with his finger. Even though I'm a guy, that kinda grossed me out. But I'd have to remember how to do that.

He pulled his cap over his head and then snapped the goggles back on.

"Should I put my suit on now?" I asked.

"Nope," he said. "I'm swimming, you're not."

"Oh! I get it. You just want me to watch awhile. Pick up some pointers about technique and stuff. Cool."

"Nope. You're not swimming and you're not watching. You're working today, remember? And four more days after that, as I recall."

My face grew hot. "Sure! I just thought since we were down by the water and all—"

He pointed up at the parking lot. "That's my green Volvo station wagon over there. I've got a big box of garbage bags in the back. The beach needs to be cleaned up."

Garbage pickup. Oh, great. Every kid's dream for their summer vacation.

"No problem!" I said, reeking of positive can-do attitude. "Then maybe after that—"

"There's no 'after that.' You're on beach cleanup all day today."

"What if I run out of trash?"

He chuckled, his laugh rusty. Like it didn't get out much. "You won't run out. Just keep walking. It's a big long state. Miles and miles of coastline. You bring sunscreen?"

I shook my head.

"Water?"

I shook my head again.

"You thinking I was going to give you some kind of desk job?" he asked. He leaned over and grabbed his ankles, folding nearly in half. He straightened back up after a minute, his face flushed and the veins in his neck sticking out like worms—big greeny-red gummy worms. He got right next to my face. "You want to work with me, you show up prepared. You got that?"

"Yes, sir," I said.

He turned and headed out into the water. "God knows why I bother," he grumbled to the waves. Then yelled back at me. "There's a big blue duffel bag in the back of the car with sunscreen in it. Put some on, kid. You'll fry out here. Tomorrow you bring your own. This isn't summer camp, you know."

I showed up every day at 6:00 a.m. sharp in time to watch Coach spit in his goggles, adjust his Speedos, and pretty much ignore me. After he finished his swim, he'd take off for a while, probably down to the Grass Shack. Around eleven, he'd come back and bring me a sack lunch, which I thought was pretty decent of him until I saw what was in it.

Same thing every day. Three hard-boiled eggs, an overripe banana, a handful of raw almonds, and water in an old recycled mayonnaise jar. I would have pitched the whole sorry thing into one of my trash bags, except Coach sat down at the picnic table with me until I finished eating. Not that he'd talk to me. He'd bring a newspaper and read until I was done. Then he'd take the mayonnaise jar back from me and leave with a grunt.

He had a hello grunt and a goodbye grunt and not much else in between.

We did have one exciting conversation in the middle of the week. He looked up from the classifieds and asked me if I was remembering to put sunscreen on my ears. It sounded so much like something Mom would say that I had to choke down a big, dry wad of egg yolk that got stuck in my throat. Missing her nearly took the wind out of me sometimes. Like getting hit in the chest with a basketball. I blinked real quick and tried to think about something else. I was pretty sure bawling at lunch would not win me any points with Coach Witsak.

Around two he'd come back in his Volvo to pick up my recyclables but left me with the trash, which I lugged over to the Dumpster behind the Surf Burger. He said none of the shop owners minded taking beach garbage. But I'd always wait until he saw how many bags I'd collected that day. I lined them up, side by side, like commandos. It was a pretty impressive army of green.

Not that he seemed to notice. But that wasn't the point. I wasn't there to impress him with my garbage collecting. I think he was pretty sure I'd give up sooner or later and just stop showing up. Then he wouldn't have to be bothered with me the rest of the summer.

Fat chance of that. I'd *eat* garbage before I'd give up the race. For one, Jesse was counting on me to do it, and second, I was definitely picking up a strong vibe from Dad that this whole race thing was getting in his craw. That was a bonus. He didn't seem very happy with all the attention I was getting from Skyla and Jesse about it. What a loser.

I heaved the last trash bag of the day into a Dumpster. Kiki came out the back dragging a large box.

"Hey, Stump! How's the Witsak Boot Camp going?"

"Okay," I said. I held the Dumpster lid up for him while he tossed the box over.

"Had enough yet?" he asked with a big grin.

"Nope!" I said. "I'm gonna get my swim lessons. He's not getting rid of me."

He slapped me on the back. "I'm rooting for you, kid. If anyone can turn you into a dolphin by the end of the summer, it's him. But he's tough. He kicked me off swim team when I was a junior. I mean, I was born with gills. I'm a regular fish. But that was never good enough for him."

"You got kicked off the team"—Coach interrupted, coming up behind us both—"because you didn't take it seriously."

"I know! I know! I've heard it a million times." He looked over at me and rolled his eyes. "I've been out of high school for twenty-five years and he's still hassling me. See what I mean, kid?"

"I can't stand seeing someone waste themselves being mediocre." He turned toward me and gestured to Kiki. "Take a lesson, kid. This is what 'settling for less' looks like. Kiki could have gotten a scholarship and competed nationally. Who knows what that could have led to? Might have ended up doing something more than flipping grease pucks. But I guess we'll never know, huh?"

"Yeah, well, it's been a real treat reminiscing, *Coach*," he said. "But I've got to get my lazy self back to work." He walked toward the back of the Surf Burger. "Good luck, Stump!"

I wiped my hands on my shorts. "Well, I'm done here for the day. I guess I'll see you tomorrow, Coach. It'll be my last day on trash duty, right?"

"Nope. Today was your last day. I've got another job in mind for you tomorrow."

What? Digging graves?

"What is it?" I asked. "I mean, what do I wear?" Please say swimsuit, I prayed.

"What you have on is fine," he said. "I've got some flyers I want you to deliver in town and up the road. I've got a couple hundred of them. As soon as you've handed them all out, come on back here. I'll give you a lift home so I can talk to your folks."

"My folks?" I squeaked.

"Yeah, your folks. You know, the older two-legged creatures in your home that make sure you get fed and watered everyday?" He cocked his head at me. "You got a problem with me meeting your parents or something?"

"Oh, no! It's just that I didn't know we needed to get them involved. They already signed the permission slip and everything. I'm almost fourteen. And they are totally in support of this. They're like fitness freaks themselves, always working out, drinking tons of water. So, really, you don't need to meet them. You could call them, or I can just have them sign some more forms for you. Man, I hate for everyone to have to go to all the trouble of having a meeting and everything."

"Well, fine by me. But if I don't meet your parents, there's no way I'm taking you on this summer. I need to make sure they understand the kind of commitment I need from you. And I need to get a medical clearance on you."

"What if only one of my parents can come? Is that good enough?" I hurried on. "I'd hate to have to postpone this, say because my dad was tied up or something."

"Look, I need at least one adult that is responsible for you. Got it?" he growled.

"Absolutely! I totally understand. Hey, I've got a great idea!" I said. "I'll have Skyla, I mean my stepmom, meet us in town after I finish tomorrow. She loves the Grass Shack. We can knock off a cold one together, go over everything, and we'll be good to go." I waited nervously while he stared at me.

He slammed the lid to the Dumpster down, making me jump.

"You can sleep in tomorrow," he said. "We'll get a later start."

"Really?" I asked. Man, these early morning wake-ups were getting old.

'Didn't I just say so?" he asked.

"Yeah, I mean, yes, sir!"

"Meet me here at six thirty a.m. Don't be late."

"Six thirty? I thought you just said I could sleep in!"

"You want to sleep? You want to pick up trash another week? Or do you want to swim, Alastair?"

"Swim!" I said.

He turned and headed back toward his Volvo. Stopped in his tracks and came back around at me. "You try and waste my time this summer, Alastair, you're going to live to regret it. I've only got so many of them left. I'm not giving this one up for a smart-ass kid that isn't dead serious."

"I want to work, sir. Count on it. I want this so bad that I will stand right here in this very spot until six thirty a.m. tomorrow."

He studied me hard to see if I was being a wiseass. After a moment, he seemed satisfied and grunted. "Get out of here, kid."

CHAPTER THIRTEEN

THERE WERE ABOUT A MILLION stars in the sky, and my eyes were filled to the brim with them. Lumina Beach on a warm summer night was at its finest. I was stretched out on the sand on a big old towel next to Jesse while we watched the moon shine like a giant headlight on the dark water.

This was such a bad idea. No mere mortal of a boy should be subjected to such temptation.

Jesse was lying on her back with her hair all fanned out around her head. I was propped up next to her trying to make sure I didn't drool or do anything stupid. Part of me wanted to run back to the house. Part of me wanted this night to go on forever.

"I ate way too much," she said, and then popped the top button of her jeans. "Oh, better," she said with a long sexy sigh.

I rolled onto my stomach and thought about algebra. It was times like this when the two years between our ages felt more like ten. It didn't help that everything I knew about the facts of life came from my mother and lesbo aunt. I knew more about how girls worked than how boys worked. All these feelings I had were so new. I wasn't entirely convinced that at some point I might not burst into song or start speaking in a French accent like that cartoon skunk.

Jesse reached over and tugged the leg of my shorts. I almost jumped right out of them.

"Sorry!" She giggled. "Why are you so jumpy?"

"I, uh, I just drank too much Coke today. I'm wired from it." Lame, very lame, I thought. She'll be real impressed by a guy who can't handle his Coke.

"So, tell me! How's your training going, Stump?" she asked. "You didn't say much about it tonight."

As if I could get in a word edgewise. Dad wouldn't stop ranting about the bright yellow flyers that had been distributed all over town today that read:

TAKE A STEP!

TAKE FORTY-SIX OF THEM.

THE STAIRS NEXT TO 11919 BLUE COAST WAY ARE YOURS.

WE WON'T BE CHASED OFF. WE CAN'T BE BOUGHT OFF.

THEY *BELONG* TO YOU AND YOUR FAMILY.

DON'T LET GREEDY MANSION OWNERS CUT OFF OUR BEACH ACCESS!

LUMINA BEACH BELONGS TO THE PEOPLE.

Yep, you guessed it. The flyers had been made up by Coach and handed out by yours truly. I had done the flyer blitz in town, but somebody had come by before dawn that morning and stapled one to each step. Dad had gone completely mental about it. Ian had tried to clean it up before he'd seen it, but it had been too late.

Man, there was no way I was going to let Coach and my dad meet about my training. It had taken some fancy footwork, but I managed to get Coach to agree to postpone the meeting with my folks until

Saturday afternoon. Now all I had to do was to figure out how to get just Skyla to come with me.

"It's going great," I said to Jess. I was very relieved that she worked downtown in the studio all week and hadn't seen me on trash duty. "Coach is working me like a dog." That was completely true. "I'll be ready. Don't worry."

"I'm not worried. Just wondered how it was going. You're so quiet sometimes. I can't quite figure you out. Do you like it here?"

I stole a glance at her. "Well, some parts I really like," I said. My face grew hot.

She smiled at me. "Yeah? Like what?"

She was flirting with me, no doubt about it. And had been all night.

I licked my lips and wondered what would happen if I leaned over and tried to kiss her. Then I remembered I'd had two pieces of garlic bread at dinner. Saved by the bell. No way I was going to try to kiss her. It might blind her. I rolled back over and sat up, tucked my knees under my chin.

She sat up next to me, bumping shoulders with me. "Hellooo, are you still there?"

"Yeah, I was just thinking. Uh, let's see, what do I like about California? Well, I like the mocha blast frozen yogurt down at the Beachside."

"Uh-huh, what else?"

"With cookie crumbles and marshmallow sauce."

"No, silly!" she said, slapping my arm. "What *else* do you like about being here?"

"I do like being able to see the ocean from my bedroom."

"And?"

"I like not having to do any chores."

She sighed. "Isn't there anything else?"

"Well, I like to hide Ian's clipboard. It drives him nuts."

Jesse laughed and I drew a big breath. What would she do if I said what I was thinking? *I like being here with you.*

"You haven't said anything about being with your dad."

I sighed. Oh, him.

"I mean, how's that going for you? It must be kind of weird. You haven't seen him for all these years, and you really don't know Skyla at all."

I could feel her eyes on me, checking me for a reaction. "Yeah, it's weird. I totally did not want to come. My mom made me."

"That's what your dad said. But he really wanted you to be here. I know there's stuff between the two of you. I wish you guys could work it out."

I shook my head.

"Well, for what it's worth, I think your dad is a pretty cool guy, you know. He's been really good to Aunt Skyla. She adores him. And he's always been super-nice to me."

"Too bad we can't add my mom to that list of people he's been 'super–nice' to."

"Do you wanna talk about it? I'm a really good listener. After growing up on *Splendor Town*, there isn't anything you could tell me that would shock me. And besides, we're practically family!"

Family? That was so not what I wanted to hear.

"You really shouldn't keep all that stuff packed up inside. Here," she said, jumping up and reaching out for me. "I have an idea."

I gave her a hand and she pulled me to my feet before I could even think about it. Jeez, she was stronger than she looked.

Jesse hung on to my hand and pulled me half running, half skipping, down to the water's edge. I staggered behind, woozy with the crazy feelings she gave me.

"Now," she said, leaning over to roll up the legs of her sweats. "We need a couple of sticks." She raced over to a large pile of seaweed and rocks and grabbed a couple.

"This is what I do when I'm really pissed about something and I can't talk about it but I don't want to keep it inside. Watch."

She looked out at the waves and then moved forward a few feet. She took the stick and started writing in large letters across the wet sand, spelling out loud as she went—

S E R G I O I S A B I G L I A R A N D A L O S E R ! ! !

Then she ran back to the beginning and dug a big fat line under it, saying it over and over. "Sergio is a big liar and a loser!"

I stepped back out of her way. I liked this new development a lot.

"What did he do?" I asked.

"Doesn't matter," she said. But something in her voice told me it mattered a lot.

"Now, watch," she said. "Stand back."

In a few seconds, a wave crashed over just feet from us and came rushing in. It ran right over her words, then dragged them back out to sea.

"*Hasta la vista!*" she yelled. She turned toward me. "Look! All gone! It's like a giant water eraser. Takes all the crap you're carrying around and washes it away."

Jesse handed me her stick. "Now you try it."

I lifted my shoulders, embarrassed.

"C'mon, give it a go," she said, bumping against me. "It will make you feel better, I promise."

Having her bump against me again would make me feel better, but no way could I say that.

"Okay," I said. I took the stick and started writing while Jesse followed next to me.

She whispered each of the letters in a soft voice.

S E R G I—

"Nooo!" she cried, laughing. She grabbed the stick and whacked me on the butt with it. "You're supposed to write something that *you're* mad about."

"Well, you didn't say that!" I said, relishing the thrill of making her laugh. It was such a rush. "And I do think that Sergio is a big, fat—"

"You don't even know him, silly. It doesn't count."

Well, I felt like I knew him. Especially after I'd watched episode 974 about eighteen times. Not the whole thing. Just the kissing part. Man, I hated that sucker. Hated the way he chewed on Jesse's mouth like it was some kind of sandwich.

She thrust the stick back in my hand. "Write! I shared my private thoughts; now you have to."

I studied the stick. Tried to balance it on the end of my nose, hoping to make her laugh again and hoping to change the subject.

"STUMP," she said, her voice getting stern. "This will be good for you. Just write one thing that you're mad about. Let it out into the universe. If you don't want me to look, I won't."

"Okay, okay! Gimme a minute, I gotta think," I said. I walked down closer to the water's edge. Picked up a rock and threw it hard as I could. It got swallowed up and I never heard it land. I threw another. And then another.

I thought about my dad. Speaking of losers. But the sonofabitch was so much more than just a loser.

I stared hard at the moon, and its light beamed right into my brain. I took my stick and dug the letters into the sand.

EJ

Before the tide even had a chance, I slashed a line right through the middle of it.

CHAPTER FOURTEEN

GETTING SKYLA OUT WITHOUT DAD wasn't as hard as I thought it was going to be. At lunch, I asked her casually if she could ride a bike with her prosthetic feet. Told her I might need to get some new pedals to work with my prosthetic. At home, I just used a bungee cord to attach my fake foot to the pedal, but I didn't want to do that for the Adventure Race. Skyla brightened right up and said she'd take me down to the bike shop. They'd customized special clip-on pedals for her, and she was sure they could do the same for me.

Dad offered to drive us, but I cut him off.

"I need to talk to Skyla alone," I said, searching my mind for a topic that he needed to be excluded from.

He raised an eyebrow and looked suspicious. Like maybe I was planning to take her out so I could give her another shiner.

"It's very private," I said, hoping he'd just let it go at that.

Dad still looked at me questioningly. "Anything I can help with?"

Jeez, what a snoop. I pulled out the big guns. "It's about my sexual preference," I said, drawing a long sigh. Oh, this could be fun.

"Well!" Dad said, his face turning red. "If you need to talk to me about that, Alastair, I want you to know that I'm here for you. I hope we can have the kind of relationship where we talk to each other about important things."

Yeah, right. "Fine. I'm into guys. Girls don't do it for me." And until I'd met Jesse, that last part had been pretty true. But the guy part? Please. The farting alone would drive me nuts.

Dad took a deep swig of iced tea and looked at Skyla. She gave him an encouraging look and he continued. "Alastair, I think thirteen is a little too young for you to be worrying you're gay. Not that there's anything wrong with it. Your hormones are just playing tricks on you."

"I'm not *worried* I'm gay," I said. "It'd be cool with me."

"It would be fine with us—" Skyla started.

Dad gave her a sharp look. She held his gaze.

"See! You're all freaked about it. I knew you wouldn't be able to handle it. That's why I wanted to speak to Skyla. *Alone.*"

Dad got even redder.

Skyla started collecting plates. "Let's go take a look at some bike pedals, shall we, Stump?"

*

I checked my watch as Skyla and I came out of the bike shop. Right on target. Twenty minutes until it was time to meet Coach.

"Are you sure I can't buy you a bike?" she asked. "We can ship it home at the end of the summer if that's what you're worried about. You need something decent to train on."

"Naw, that's okay. Coach says he's got one I can use. I can just switch out the pedals."

I shook the box with my new ones. "These are great." The pedals had taken a chunk out of my summer money, but I didn't want Skyla doing anything else nice for me. It made me feel like a chump or some kind of freeloader.

"Oh!" I said, clapping my hand against my forehead. "I forgot! I'm supposed to meet with Coach over at the Grass Shack at three o'clock. Would you mind if we stopped there before we go?"

"Not at all. I'd like to meet him."

"Cool!" I said. "He mentioned he'd like to meet you and Dad sometime, so this works out great."

We were just a couple of blocks away, so we walked. I noticed people couldn't help staring at us. Wondering what kind of bad luck we'd had that we both lost our legs. It was kind of funny really, in a dark sort of way.

Skyla and I settled in a booth near the back. She looked so pleased about our afternoon together that it was hard not to feel bad. I'd totally scammed her. I let her order for me to try to make up for it and swore to myself I'd drink whatever she put in front of me.

She propped her chin on her hand and gave me a long, level look. "So did you really want to talk to me alone? Or was that just to keep your dad from coming with us?"

It was my turn to turn very red.

"For the record, I'm not sure I'm buying the I-may-be-gay bit anymore."

I grabbed a menu and studied it hard.

"Is there any chance you're going to give your dad a break this summer?" she asked.

"He's not who you think he is. You don't really know him." I shook my head. "But I'm sure you think you do. It's understandable. He's very handsome and very convincing."

She smiled. "And I wasn't born yesterday, Stump. When you don't have legs and you have a lot of money, you learn pretty quick who you can trust. You have to in order to survive. And I don't think your dad is who *you* think he is."

The door swung open and I was saved just in the nick of time. "Coach!" I waved, awash with relief. "Over here!"

He came to the table and stuck out a hand. Skyla slid out of the booth and stood up.

"I'm Skyla Keyes," she said with a big smile. "So nice to meet you, Coach."

"Peter Witsak," he said, not smiling, but not unfriendly either. He checked out her legs. "I like your rides. Can you run on those?"

"Run, ride, line-dance, you name it." She folded her legs back under the booth. I climbed in next to her.

He nodded with approval, then turned toward the counter. "The usual, Bridget." When he faced us again, he gave us both a long look. "I don't waste my time with people who don't mean business. I can turn this kid into a good swimmer in eight weeks, but only if I can get his undivided attention and the family's full cooperation."

"You've got it, Peter. My husband and I are both committed to fitness, and we think this race will be great for Stump."

Coach continued. "This won't work unless I have him all summer. He gets one day off a week. That means you and your husband can't decide on a whim that you all need a week in Carmel."

"I understand," she said. "I know the kind of discipline this will take."

"Okay, then. Other than the obvious, are there any medical conditions I should know about?" He opened a folder he'd brought with him. "I've got the original consent that your husband signed last week. I just need one of you to sign this medical release now."

"He's a healthy kid—just eats too much junk food," she said, taking a pen from him. She scribbled her name at the bottom. "I had a long talk with his mother before he came out. He had a full physical in the spring and he's good to go."

Coach grunted as he studied the consent form Dad had filled out and signed, then looked up at both of us. "I can't read the address here. The ink bled. Can't really read the signature very well, either."

Well, I might have dabbed a little spit on it to smear it.

"It's 11919 Blue Coast Way," Skyla said, before I could scare up a diversion like an unscheduled fire drill or something.

"And the name on this consent would be *Richard* Hudson, then, I'm guessing." He sat back against the booth and gave me a narrow look. "You all live next to the public stairway."

Skyla sighed. "Yes, we do. Though I'm not thrilled to be famous for that in town."

"Funny you didn't mention that before, Alastair," Coach said, grilling me with his eyes.

"I didn't?" I said, my voice doing one of its hormonal jumps up the scale.

"Peter, I hope that you won't let your feelings about that, whatever they are, interfere with Stump getting his training from you. This has nothing to do with him."

"It's not a problem," Coach said. He shoved my scary green drink toward me. "Down the hatch, Alastair. As of now, you're in training."

CHAPTER FIFTEEN

AT 6:45 A.M. ON MONDAY MORNING, Coach pulled into the deserted parking lot of Lumina Beach High. I'd learned over the last week that he wasn't a big talker in the morning, so I'd kept my trap shut when he'd first told me to get in the car. He set the parking brake with more muscle than most men dream of. I expected it might come away with his hand.

My trap flew open now. "What are we doing here? Do you need to pick up some swimming equipment or something?" I asked.

"Nope," he said in his grisly morning voice. "You're here to swim."

"At the pool?" I asked, and then asked again. "I mean, I thought you were going to give me ocean swimming lessons."

"Well, what you think doesn't count so much where swimming is concerned. Unless you'd like to teach yourself to swim."

"No! I just figured we'd start in the ocean, that's all. We can start at the bowling alley for all I care. Just as long as I can swim a half mile on August 28."

"We'll swim in the ocean when you can swim in the pool for thirty minutes without stopping. And when you finish the bleachers."

"The what-chers?" I asked.

"The bleachers. They need paint."

"Paint? You want me to paint the bleachers? I thought I was done working. I worked a whole week for free."

"That was to convince me you were worth my time. I'm somewhat convinced. But now you need to pay the school back to let you train in their pool all summer. And you can do that by sanding and painting the bleachers."

I opened my mouth and then shut it. This was beginning to look like a remake of the

Karate Kid. Next I'd be doing his Volvo. Wax on. Wax off.

"So, after I pay the school back, then I'll owe you too, for the lessons?"

"Yep. But I don't want your money. I'll take your labor."

I blew out a sharp, frustrated breath.

"You got a problem with that?"

"Well, I guess I didn't realize how expensive these swimming lessons were going to be."

"You want swimming lessons, Alastair?" He turned and bored a look at me. "Miss Carla at the YMCA can help you. I can lend you some water wings."

"No, sir! I want you to teach me."

"Well, if you expect me to take a kid like you through a competitive ocean swim by the end of the summer, then, yeah, it's gonna cost you."

He reached into the backseat and grabbed a big jar of water. He took a long guzzle, then wiped his mouth with the back of his hand.

"Did you hear what I told your stepmother the other day? I'm the coach, but you do all the heavy lifting. I need you thinking about swimming all day, every day. When you're painting the bleachers—and you will paint them—I want your mind on nothing but swimming. Get the girl out of your head. Focus. I want you growing a blowhole by the end of the summer. Got it?"

"I'm on board, Coach, really, whatever it takes."

He turned in his seat to face me. "Your stepmother seems to think you're already quite the hotshot swimmer."

I looked out the window while my ears heated up.

He reached over and squeezed my bicep. I tried not to cry out.

"These aren't the arms of a swimmer. The only action these arms have seen in the last couple of years are behind a PlayStation."

He started to open the door but then turned back. "When I asked you to pass out all those flyers last week, why didn't you tell me you lived in that house next to the stairs?"

"I really wanted you to teach me to swim."

He grunted and threw open the car door. Then looked back over at me. "Grab the paint."

Two hours later, I was at the pool's edge in my bathing suit. I'd taken my leg off and stood perfectly balanced. I puffed out my chest as best I could and tried not to shiver. Coach Witsak got right in my face and blew his whistle. "Hear that?" he asked.

I massaged my eardrum. Probably every monk in Tibet heard it.

"One long blow means STOP. Whatever you're doing, stop and look at me."

He raised his whistle to his lips again and I braced myself. Coach blew two short blasts. "That means GO. Got it?"

"Got it," I said. "What does 'Man, you're fantastic, kid!' sound like?" I asked, trying to lighten the mood a bit.

"Get in the water," he said.

I hopped off the edge into the pool, as manly as I could muster. The cold was a shock.

I came to the surface with a big blast of breath, grabbed the ledge, and looked up. He looked down at me, daring me to say something about it. I waited, quiet as an altar boy.

"No sense in heating the pool in the summer while school is out. Costs the school district too much money."

"Feels great," I lied.

He plugged his whistle in his mouth and blew hard. Two blasts.

"Go?" I asked, confused, looking behind me. "Where?"

He sighed. "One lap. Let's see what you've got."

Please don't let me make a fool of myself, I prayed to the pool gods. "Well, aren't you going to teach me and stuff first?"

"WRRRRRRRR—WRRRRRRRRRR!" he blew again.

I let go of the side and plunged ahead as fast as I could go, slamming the water with my arms and kicking the water into froth. I kept my head down and held my breath as long as I could. Since I was kicking with a leg and a half, I had a tendency to veer toward one side. I nearly strangled myself on the lane ropes a couple of times. When I thought I might explode, I turned my head and sucked in a big breath.

I crashed into the wall on the other side finally, grabbed the ledge, and reared up for some air.

Coach's face was right above the ledge. WRRRRRRRR—WRRRRRRRRRR!"

I turned and slammed back into the water again, pounding it with all my might, ignoring the cramp in my foot that chased me across the pool. When I got to the other side, I prayed he'd seen enough because I'd given him all I had. I pulled up on the ledge, blew a half gallon of water out of my nose, and wiped my eyes.

He looked down at me and grunted. Then shook his head. "No wonder your PT was anxious to get you back on skis."

"What-do-you-mean?" I panted.

"The sight of you swimming was probably way too painful."

I was prepared for his big tough drill sergeant routine. This was what I was paying him for. "So teach me!"

He shook his head like the prospect was just too awful. He took a long swig from a water bottle, stepped out of his sweatpants, and then pulled his shirt over his head. He dropped into the water next to me.

"We'll start with blowing bubbles," he said. "And I hope to god nobody finds out I'm out here teaching remedial swimming. This is going to cost you extra."

He put his hand on the back of my head and pushed my face underwater.

CHAPTER SIXTEEN

¡ **WOKE UP FROM A** dead sleep with someone shaking me. "Alastair, quick! Wake up!"

My eyes flew open and I saw Dad leaning over me, way closer than I liked.

He pulled off my covers. I drew them back up. "Hurry! Come on, you gotta see this!"

"What is it?" I said, still trying to shake myself from sleep.

"Come on! Come on! You'll see."

He went to my balcony and opened the doors. I obviously wasn't going to get another second of shut-eye until I followed him. I dragged myself up and tried not to yowl. I'd just finished my second week of training, and it felt like rigor mortis had kicked in everywhere. My chest hurt just from the effort of breathing.

Not that it was entirely Coach's fault. Oh, he worked me down to the bone. Had me swimming double sessions each day, not to mention sanding and painting the bleachers plus deck workouts. Push-ups, pull-ups, running stairs, and the grueling bear walk. I couldn't believe he was making me do all those things one-legged. He didn't cut me any breaks as far as that went. He said I'd be thanking him during the obstacle course at the Adventure Race. I needed more strength and more coordination.

As if that weren't all enough, I'd added my own secret training sessions in Skyla's pool before I went to bed. Swam at least another half hour. I was a train wreck, but I was getting stronger by the day.

"Hurry up, they're not going to wait for you!" Dad urged from the doorway.

I hitched up my pajama bottoms and hopped out onto the deck, where he was gesturing wildly. I dug my fists into my eye sockets to rub the sleep out and then shaded them in the morning sun.

"Look!" he cried like a kid.

I followed his gaze out to the water. It was your basic blue ocean still. Nice, but what was the big deal?

"There!" he said, coming behind me and turning my shoulders in the direction he was pointing.

Water spouts—at least a half dozen of them. And then a giant tail slammed down hard on the water. A long gray back skimmed along the top nearby, looking like a submarine. And man, they were close to the beach!

Dad stayed behind me, his hands on my shoulders. I stiffened.

A mammoth dark body nosed itself out of the water and them BLAM—threw itself over on its side, nearly making a tsunami.

"*Wow!* Did you see that?" we both cried. "Oh, man!"

There must have been ten or twelve whales that had decided to stop in our front yard and put on a morning show. I'd never seen anything like it.

"Look," Dad said, his head close to mine. "A baby—see?"

"Where?"

"There! Watch right over there. Next time that one comes up, you'll see a smaller dark shape next to it, with a tiny waterspout."

I strained my eyes on the spot, not wanting to miss it. We waited and waited, both holding our breaths, and then, the mom or maybe it was the dad, came back up with a blast of mist, and next to it, I saw a tiny puff of a spout.

"There! Oh, cool! It's really small."

I relaxed under his hands, then leaned back into him a fraction for just a second as we watched them skim the top side by side. "Do you think that's the mom or the dad with the baby?"

"Oh, it's the mom for sure," he said. "The mother whales keep the babies close to shore like this when they're that young. And they've got to keep them away from the adult males. It's too dangerous."

"Dangerous how?" I asked, looking over at him.

"Well, the males have got their minds on courting and breeding, not looking out for little ones. They could hurt them without meaning to."

I shook my head. Figures. Men were all alike. Even whale men. I was not going to be like that when I grew up.

I moved out from under Dad's hands, hopped down the railing a ways, and kept watching. I shivered in the damp morning air.

Dad came next to me, pulling off his sweatshirt. "Here you go," he said, draping it around me.

I shrugged it off. "I'm okay," I said. It fell to the ground and lay there. Dad looked at me, then picked it up and threw it across a deck chair.

He sighed and ran fingers through his hair. "Skyla thinks maybe you and I need to have a talk."

"*Skyla* thinks we should talk?" I asked, shaking my head.

"Yeah, she suggested we might go see a counselor together."

I just let that lie there a minute, like the sweatshirt, waiting to see who would pick it up.

"I dunno," he said, looking at me. "We don't know each other very well anymore. I thought maybe this summer we'd catch up, buddy around a bit."

I stared out at the water. It had gotten very still. Like the whales could feel the anger growing in me and had taken cover.

He went on. "Seems like whenever I ask you to do something with me and Skyla, you're always busy."

Yeah, well, get a clue, I thought. Maybe you should try asking me to do something with just you. Oh, right, I corrected myself. That would never work. As if Dad would do anything without at least one female in attendance. Didn't matter how young or how old. As long as she had the good sense to find him attractive, he was happy.

"Well, I'm kinda busy these days, with my training and all," I said with a shrug.

"Maybe I could help you with it. Or just work out with you. I've seen you out at the pool late at night."

"No!" I said. "I mean, Coach doesn't want me to swim with anyone else during training. Said it might throw off my game, you know?"

Dad didn't answer, and it was quiet a long time between us. I stole a glance over at him. He had his back half turned toward me. My eyes fell on a small tattoo on his lower back. It was a pair of running shoes with a bolt of lightning over them.

My scalp broke out in an icy sweat. I felt dizzy. I'd forgotten about his tattoo. Me, who in all the years since I'd seen him remembered every detail about him—the scar on his leg from a snorkeling trip and the way that his hair flipped up in the back when he needed a haircut. How could I forget his tattoo? My eyes were glued to it, and I couldn't seem to look away, even though it was making me feel sick. I gripped the railing in front of me. A swirl of pictures filled my head so fast

I couldn't sort them out. Pictures from Lake Rochester. The condo we'd stayed at. The purple–and-green ski suit EJ had bought me with all the pockets. And the jacket with the zipper that got stuck.

My mouth filled with battery acid and I felt like I might puke. I turned and left.

CHAPTER SEVENTEEN

THE WATER FELT LIKE WET concrete, and I plowed through lap four, then five, then six, barely. Coach Witsak's whistle shrieked in my ear, and I stopped at the side of the pool and ripped off my goggles.

He leaned over the edge and peered at me. "Not having a good day?" he asked.

I slicked my hair away from my face. Shrugged.

"Wanna take a break, son?" He held out an arm to me.

"Yeah, I guess," I said, reaching for him. "I'm not really into it today."

He grabbed my arm firmly and pulled me up. Then let go at the last minute. I fell back into the pool with a big splash.

"This isn't SPA DAY at the Ladies' Club!" he yelled as I fought my way back to the surface. He leaned down close to the water. "You going to swim today or not?"

"*Swim*, Coach," I said, fighting the desire to grab his ankles and pull him down into the pool.

"Well, I sure can't tell by looking at you. You're moving like a ninety-year-old woman. You got something on your mind that's bugging you, leave it outside. When you come in that door there," he said, pointing behind him, "what's the one thing I want you thinking about and the ONLY thing?"

"Swimming!" I recited, like I'd learned last Friday, and last Thursday, and every other day that I'd been out here. I blew some snot out of my nose.

"All right, then, let's see some *swimming*! Five more laps and then that's it. Go!" He put the whistle up to his lips. I pushed off the wall before he blew out any remaining eardrum I had left.

S-W-I-M, breathe, S-W-I-M, breathe, I spelled out as I moved through the water. I clicked through my mental checklist of things Coach had me working on.

Head down. Check.

Fingers relaxed. Not. C'mon. Re-laaaxxx.

Arms reaching, reaching, reaching. Check.

Pulling, pulling, pulling. Check.

Stroke-stroke-stroke—breathe.

Stroke-stroke-stroke—breathe.

I had to fight to keep my mind in the pool. But it had dug up this old video from Lake Rochester and it kept wanting to run it. Seeing Dad's tattoo had set the video on nonstop play. I didn't want to watch it. But I couldn't seem to find the damn stop button.

J-E-R-K, I spelled with each stroke. Breathe. S-W-I-M. Breathe.

His tattoo was printed on the inside of my eyelids. It was like a red flag to a bull. It made me want to kill someone. It made me want to scream.

H-A-T-E. Breathe. H-A-T-E. Breathe. I began to swim like I was riding on top of a torpedo. Faster and faster and faster. Cutting through the water.

I was pissed. Mammothly pissed. *T. Rex*–sized pissed. I wanted to rear up, roar, and tear the white right off my Dad's teeth.

My shoulders were on fire and I couldn't get enough breath. But I couldn't stop.

I finished all five of the laps and threw three more in. Ignored the whistle blast to stop. I came up gasping at the end of lap eight and looked for Coach.

He wasn't standing in his usual place at the end of the lane ready to give me feedback. I looked around the pool deck, and he wasn't anywhere. What the heck? All that work and he wasn't even watching?

I hauled myself out of the water and grabbed my towel. Even after all those extra laps, I was still cold. I mopped up my face and looked around. Coach was sitting on the bleachers. Cutting his toenails, for pete's sake.

I hopped over to him. "So, was that better?" I asked, shaking out my goggles.

"Better than what?" he asked, not taking his eyes off his big toe.

"I dunno, better than earlier or better than yesterday?"

He clipped a long nasty nail off his big toe, sending it flying off somewhere. Then leaned back and studied his work. "See these toes of mine, Alastair?"

"Yeah?" I said.

"How many you see?" he asked.

I sighed. I could smell a life lesson headed my way.

"Ten, sir."

"And how do you know that?"

"Everyone knows that."

"Ahhh," he said. "But do you know that from memory, or do you know that from counting?" He peered up at me from under his ball cap.

"Both, I guess."

"Really? Because I'm starting to wonder if you know how to count. Did your mommy forget to show you how?"

"Leave my mother out of this, please," I said, gritting my teeth.

"Well, then, maybe you could show me you know how. You know, just to put my mind at ease."

My face burned. "Look, I get it. I'm sorry! You wanted me to do five laps and I did eight. But I was really on a roll, sir."

"Show me," he said.

"Show you what?" I asked, my voice brittle.

"Show me you know how to count. Because if you don't know how, I could send you over to the YMCA day camp. They study colors, baby animals, *and* numbers."

"I know how to count," I said. "I promise I won't ever swim more—"

"Prove it," he said, snapping his nail clippers at me, which really ticked me off.

"So, whaa-a-t? You actually want me to stand here like an idiot and count for you?"

"Yep. You can count my toes if that will make it easier for you."

"No," I said.

"Pardon me?" he asked, cupping his hand around his ear.

"I said *no!*" I yelled.

He stood up and looked down at me. "I'm not quite sure I heard you," he said.

"*No!*" I screamed. "No, I will not stand here and count your toes for you, you asshole!"

"I'm an ASS-hole?" he asked.

I felt crushed by the weight of my anger, which was quickly spinning out of control. "*Yes!*" My voice broke at the end and my hands balled into fists.

He moved closer and grabbed one puny fist in his big weathered hand. "You gonna hit me, Alastair?"

I stared hard at him and tried not to blink. Because if I did, the tears would roll.

"Is Mommy's little fella gonna throw a punch?"

"Don't you dare talk about my mom!" I screamed. I tried to pull away and nearly lost my balance. He grabbed me by the shoulders and held me.

"*Let me go!*" I yelled.

"Not a chance. Not until you tell me what is biting your butt today."

I pulled and pulled and tried to get away from him. He held me tighter. "*You* are! You're what's biting my butt today, you big stupid *jerk*."

"Who do you think you're talking to, kid?" he said, getting way too close.

"I'm talking to *you*!" I twisted and yanked but he had me in a steel vise.

"Are you *sure* it's me you're talking to?"

"Yes, I'm sure it's you! Bastard!" I spit.

"*What?*"

"You heard me. Bastard!"

"So, tell me *five* times I'm a bastard and I'll let you go."

I tried to pull away and my foot slipped out from under me. He held me up like I weighed nothing. "Let *go* of me!"

He just pinned me tighter. "You heard me—let me have it five times."

I screamed right into his face. 'BASTARD! BASTARD! BASTARD! BASTARD! BASTARD!"

"Okay, then," he said after a long second, his voice quiet. He let go of my shoulders and I righted myself with a hop.

"Get back in the pool and I want to see three cooldown laps. Not four, not two, but three. Then hit the showers. Meet me back here at four o'clock sharp."

I sat down in a pool of tears and snot and rage.

"Wasn't a bad workout, Alastair," he called as he walked toward the locker room. "Those last three laps were the best ones I've seen."

CHAPTER EIGHTEEN

I EASED OPEN THE GIANT stainless steel door like a burglar breaking open a safe. I'd been back at Skyla's house for about fifteen minutes, and so far none of the staff had spotted me. Ian must be out getting his doilies dry-cleaned. I was hungry for a good old-fashioned fridge raid, without any interference.

These days, I couldn't get enough to eat. Even though Coach had told me to lay off the junk food, I'd discovered for myself that it had a pretty short life span. I burned it up faster than I could get it down my gullet.

The inside of Skyla's garage-sized refrigerator was pretty disappointing. No teenager food, really. Back home, I could always count on some fresh cold cuts, chocolate milk, leftover homemade dessert, and, if I was lucky, pizza from our last takeout night. There was no edible meat here—just a big foot-long uncooked salmon, vegetarian bacon, and leftover sushi. There were a dozen different kinds of sports drinks and deli salads that looked okay, but they'd fool you. I'd fallen for them a couple of times thinking they'd be good, but it was just tofu trying to pass for regular food and catch a kid off guard.

I grabbed a sports drink and rooted around in the pantry for the peanut butter. Figures, it was "all natural and no sugar." I grabbed the biggest spoon I could find and dropped onto a barstool. I was so hungry I was ready to keel over. Coach called it "bonking." Time to eat or die.

I dug the spoon into the peanut butter and lobbed a mammoth bite into my mouth.

My brain buzzed with joy and passed the message onto my stomach. I closed my eyes and tried to get it down as fast as I could so I could fit more into my mouth. I spooned in another shovel full, humming.

"Oh! Hi!" Skyla said, looking surprised as she came around the corner. "I didn't hear you come in."

I nodded and looked away, trying to get some spit in my mouth so I could swallow.

"Can I make you a sandwich?" she asked. "I was just going to get a snack myself."

I put down her peanut butter, feeling like a thief. I wiped my mouth with the back of my arm. "Sorry. Mom hates it when I eat it right out of the jar."

"No! You go right ahead. I used to love to do that too. When I was a kid, I'd get the mayonnaise out too and then switch bites between the mayo and the peanut butter. Helps it slide down easier."

She opened the fridge and pulled out a tub of something that looked like bird poop. She grabbed a fork and plunged right in.

"How'd your training go today?" she asked. She pulled herself up a stool next to mine and swung her mechanical legs. I studied her knee joints with interest.

"Think you might be interested in trading up?" she asked.

I shrugged like it didn't matter too much to me one way or another. But since I'd met Jesse, things like walking without a limp started to matter more. I was used to my limp, but teenage girls were real sensitive about stuff like that. When Skyla had long pants on, you could hardly tell she didn't have legs. "Yeah, maybe," I said. "Were yours real expensive?" I asked, thinking about Mom and her being off work all summer. Money was going to be kinda tight in the fall.

"Not too bad," she said. "And you only need one, so there's that."

"I wouldn't mind having a more bendable foot," I said. "Can you get different attachments, you know, like fancy vacuum cleaners have?"

"You sure can! These days, you can get one with a cappuccino machine on the end if you want. But if you're looking for a sports prosthetic, I know where you can get one for free."

"Free?" I said suspiciously.

"Yep, through the Challenged Athletes Foundation."

"Is it like charity? Because me and my mom don't need that," I said.

Skyla shook her head. "It's more like sponsorship. You know, like in the Olympics? The athletes get tons of free stuff." She licked her spoon clean. "Want me to call them for you?"

I dipped my spoon back into the jar, shrugged. "I'll think about it."

"Okay," she said.

"Thanks," I said, then spun my stool away from her, embarrassed.

"Seems like you're training pretty hard," she said. "Three sessions a day. You're not overdoing it, are you?"

"Naw, doesn't bother me."

She laughed. "Like father, like son, I guess. Your dad thinks *moderation* is a dirty word as far as exercise goes."

"I'm not really like him at all," I said, tearing pieces of the label off my drink.

"No?" she asked.

"Nope. I'm only doing the race as a favor to Jesse. I could really take it or leave it. No big deal."

"Well, that certainly is very generous of you," she said, patting her mouth with a napkin. "But I thought you liked swimming."

"I like swimming back home with my friends. Here it just helps pass the time until the summer is over and I can go home."

She stirred her snack a sec, then looked up and studied me. "Wow. I hate to think of you having to do something just to 'help pass the time.' Your dad and I'd hoped you'd have some fun with us, relax—take a break from things. We know it can be tough for you at home."

I got up and went over to the sink, dropped my spoon with a big clatter. "You two don't know anything about my life. It's tough for me *here*. Back home is easy."

I grabbed my drink from the counter and screwed the cap on tight, feeling that white-hot feeling start to surface again.

"I know I'm an outsider, and you probably think I should mind my own business."

Which was just what I was hoping she'd do, so I turned to leave.

"Hold up a sec, will you?"

I paused in my tracks, but I didn't turn around.

"Look," she said. "It's obvious that what we wanted for your summer isn't going to happen like magic. I know you're very angry with your father. Sometimes he just pisses the hell out of me too."

Yeah, right, I thought. Like when he leaves the cap off the anti-wrinkle cream.

"But I really wish you two would try to work this out. Don't you think that's part of what your mother had in mind when she sent you here?"

I whirled around and glared at her. "How would you know what my mother has on her mind?"

"Well, I know a little. I asked her, for one thing."

"You asked her?" I said, stunned.

"Sure, because in the past, she was never very open to you coming. I know about her trip this summer, but I had a feeling there was more to it. I asked her about a lot of things. We started talking before you came. I wanted to know about you—who your best friend was, what cereal you liked, what type of stuff bugged you. You know, those kind of things."

"Didn't you ask my dad about me?" I asked, my breath tight in my chest.

"Well, sure, but some of that stuff only your mom would know."

I crossed my arms. "So what did she tell you? Who's my best friend and what bugs me?"

Skyla ticked off her fingers. "She said that you didn't have a best friend, that girls seemed to bug you, that you were the best kid in the world and your dad was really lucky to have another chance with you. And that she hoped to God he didn't blow it."

My eyeballs burned. "Did you ask her about the accident?"

Her eyes held mine. "Yes."

"Well?" I said, feeling brave and sick all at the same time.

"She told me what happened. I knew a lot of it from your dad already. And he showed me the articles from the papers."

"What did my mom say?"

"She said your dad had put you in a juniors ski class that you seemed to like at first. But on the last day, you said you didn't want to go with them. Your dad thought you were just a little scared about it because they were going to do a more advanced slope. He thought you needed a little push."

I shredded a hangnail on my thumb as she talked. I could picture him crouched down in front of me. Telling me how much fun it was going to be. The smell of cologne steamed off him. His mouth kept moving, but I stopped listening. His old lady boss stood behind us, staring at me. She was wearing this bright purple ski suit with matching lipstick. She had tried to fill in all the wrinkles in her face with makeup, but when she'd smile, her face would split into a bunch of cracks. Probably why she didn't smile much.

Skyla's voice stopped.

"What else did he say?" I sucked some blood from my thumb where I'd pulled the skin down way too far.

"She said he put you on the lift with a little girl from the class that you seemed to like, and off you went."

Her name was Brianna and she had a very bad runny nose.

"Yeah?"

"Well, according to the little girl, you didn't say a word most of the way, but halfway to the top, you told her you were going to lift up the safety bar and she should hold on real tight. You allegedly gave her a hundred-dollar bill that no one seems to know where you got. And then you jumped."

My heart dropped and then pounded with the memory of the jump. It had been so much farther down than I thought.

"Is that all she told you?"

She hesitated. "No. I wanted to understand what your jumping had to do with your dad. I told her I needed to know that if you were going to stay here this summer."

I bit hard into the underside of my cheek and waited.

Skyla leaned back against the counter. "Are you okay talking about this with me?" she asked.

I didn't speak. But I sat down next to her.

"Your mom thinks your dad pushed too hard. That he was trying to impress his boss. It wasn't enough that he was perfect; Rick wanted you to be perfect too. She thinks you felt that pressure and that rather than risk disappointing your dad on the slope, you jumped."

My head bent down toward my drink, and I scratched to peel off more of the label.

"Is she right?" Skyla asked, her voice soft.

I didn't say anything but kept peeling the label. Finally I looked up. "I dunno," I said. "I don't remember much about it."

Which had always been pretty true. I didn't have amnesia or anything, but when I thought about it, it was kinda like a movie I'd seen so long ago that I'd forgotten certain parts. I knew how it ended and all but couldn't remember a lot of the stuff in the middle.

"Do you ever wonder why you might have done that?" she asked.

"Yeah, I guess," I said, surprising myself that I was talking to Skyla about this. "I went and saw this shrink guy about it for a while. We all did, me, Mom, and Dad. He probably had some ideas about it, but he never would really say in front of me. He always says that it was what *I* thought that mattered."

But even though he'd never say and acted like the reason why I jumped was no big deal, he wrote a long report about it that went to the family court judge. I wasn't supposed to read it, but I snuck it out of my mom's files a couple of years ago. It still never made much sense to me, but I could remember most of it. "*. . . eight-year-old male with acute anxiety reaction . . . projected performance expectations from father . . . confusing role reversal . . . history of maternal depression and binge drinking . . . possibility of repressed traumatic precipitator cannot be dismissed.*"

What the hell was a repressed traumatic precipitator? Sounded like something terrible you might hear about on the weather channel.

Skyla sat still, waiting for me.

Dad's tattoo started flashing in front of my face again—even now—like the most annoying neon sign. Or like a song that got stuck in your head and wouldn't stop.

"This is really hard to talk about, isn't it?" she said finally.

I shrugged. Good thing I have shoulders. Without them, I wouldn't be able to communicate with anyone.

"Nah, just boring," I said, sliding off the stool. As my foot hit the ground, I saw a whole pile of tiny white scraps of paper under me from the label of my drink where I'd pretty much obliterated the whole thing.

Looked like snow.

CHAPTER NINETEEN

DAD BACKED ONE OF SKYLA'S cars out of their massive garage and paused a minute in the driveway. He pushed a button on the dash and then said, "Top up." Like magic, the folded canvas rooftop behind us came creeping up, over, and then lay down in place.

"Close garage," he added, and the garage door slid back down.

"Why'd you put the top up?" I asked as he torpedoed out onto the road.

"Oh! Do you want it down?" he asked, looking over at me.

"Doesn't matter to me one way or another. I was just curious." Though I had my suspicions that it had something to do with his picture-perfect hair and the fact that we were on our way to the set of *Splendor Town*. He was probably hoping to land a starring role while we were there.

"It's just easier to talk with the top up."

"Oh," I said.

He turned and looked sideways at me. "You look great, Alastair. I like the new way you're wearing your hair. It's good to be able to see your face."

I turned away from him then. That was Jesse's doing. Every time I saw her, she came over and parted my hair off my face and tucked it behind my ears. "Why are you hiding this incredibly gorgeous face?" she'd say to me.

"And it looks like you've lost a few pounds, too," he said, reaching over and patting me on the stomach. I flinched, pulling away from his touch.

"Just four more weeks until the big day," he said. "You gonna be ready?"

"Sure, I guess."

"Have you seen any of the competition out in the water yet?"

I shifted in my seat and looked out the window. You kidding? Coach hadn't let me in the ocean yet. The only competition I'd seen in the water was the Blind Rehab program that came to the pool after Coach and I finished our session. I'd tried to make a joke about them having to paint the bleachers too, but Coach didn't think it was funny.

The man had no sense of humor whatsoever.

"No, I don't pay much attention to anybody else while I'm swimming. I just do my thing."

"So have you two set a goal time for your swim yet?"

"Uh-uh, Coach says it's too early."

"How's the biking going? Can you manage that with your leg?" he asked.

"It's working. Hey," I said, swerving hard off the topic. "Doesn't it bug you to have Ian hanging around Skyla all the time?" I reached over and turned on the AC. "You mind?"

"No, go ahead." He downshifted as we took a deep turn. I braced myself on the seat so I didn't lean in toward him.

When we straightened out, he rubbed his cheek. "Does Ian bug me?"

"Yeah, you know. I know he works for her and all, and she says she couldn't live without him. But you know, all the other stuff."

Dad looked over at me. "What other stuff?"

"Well, come on. You know."

"Know what?"

"The way he looks at her, for one thing. Like how a guy looks at a girl, not how an assistant looks at his boss."

"Well, Skyla is a great-looking woman. There's nothing wrong with him appreciating that. I trust him to keep things purely professional."

"Okay by me. It just surprises me that you'd let such a *young*, good-looking guy be all over your wife nearly twenty-four hours a day. And with you over at the main office so much, I just wondered if it worried you. But it sounds like it doesn't, so that's cool."

Dad looked up into the rearview mirror a minute. "Well, he's not all that young."

"Right," I said. "He's twenty-seven. And you're only what—forty-one? I personally don't think he's that good-looking. I only said that because I heard Jesse and Skyla talking about him one day out by the pool."

"They think he's good-looking?" Dad said, and I could tell he was trying to sound casual about it.

"Oh, you know how chicks talk when they get together. Mom and her friends are always doing that too. Skyla and Jesse were probably just playing around. Ian was getting out of the pool and they were saying something about him looking 'good enough to eat.'"

Actually, what they'd said was, "Oh, good, let's eat." But I liked my version better. And judging by the tight jaw on Dad, I was having just the effect I'd hoped.

The set of *Splendor Town* was nothing like I pictured. It was inside what looked like a giant airplane hangar, except without all the planes.

Instead, it was filled with hundreds of people racing around with cell phones, walkie-talkies, earphones, and giant cups of gourmet coffee. It looked like NASA. The ones that weren't walking were in little golf carts or riding up and down cranes with cameras loaded on them.

The people that worked on the show looked about as interesting as the checkers at the local grocery store. They wore old jeans, baseball hats, and scruffy shoes.

The actors looked pretty weird. They wore a lot of makeup. Tons of it. Even the men. Yeah, my dad would fit right in here.

The production assistant from *Splendor Town*, Hans, had met us at the front of the studio and gave us special badges to wear when he brought us back. He also gave me a T-shirt, a water bottle, and some big autographed pictures of the stars from the show. I was saving them all for Mom. He showed us to some special chairs we could sit in to watch. He said Jesse would come join us after she finished her next scene, and she could tell us more about the day's shoot.

I was trying to act pretty cool, like I visited Hollywood sets all the time, but I was really jazzed. Jesse had been bugging me to come watch her work for weeks, but every time she asked me, Dad had wanted to come. I kept trying to find a day that he was out of town or something, but I finally gave up. These days, I'd do anything to see her.

And I was hoping to get a good look at Sergio, too, and find out that maybe he was really thirty years old and beginning to go bald. Or maybe had problematic nose hairs that you couldn't really see on television. Even though Jesse vowed she didn't like him, the guy got to kiss her pretty regularly. For money, too. Man, what a sweet gig.

The first scene they were filming today was inside Tye's convertible, which on TV looked like a very cool silver Porsche but turned out to be a fake one without even real wheels, a motor, or anything. Hans explained to us that they'd project the scenery on the big blue screen behind the car.

Jess's and Sergio's characters, Savannah and Tye, were escorted onto the set wearing tennis outfits. I started to breathe faster like I did whenever I saw her. They climbed over the fake doors and sat down. A small swarm of people attacked the car, fussing over their hair and dabbing at their faces with little sponges and brushes.

"QUIET ON THE SET!" a woman boomed through a megaphone near my ear.

The swarm scattered, leaving Jess and Sergio alone in the car. Sergio put his hand over his mouth, leaned over, and whispered something to Jesse that made her laugh.

"*QUIET* ON THE SET!" Megaphone Woman boomed again.

A bald guy with raggedy jeans leapt in front of the car with one of those black-and-white scene markers like you see in the movies. "*Splendor Town*, scene eighteen," he said, snapping the marker shut with a clack.

Someone turned on a wind machine because all of a sudden, Jesse's hair started blowing back. Sergio's hair didn't move a bit.

The camera guys zoomed in and Dad and I had to lean over in our seats to see around them.

"Boy, I'd love to get a job on a show like this," Dad whispered, folding a piece of breath-freshening gum into his mouth. "Want some?"

"Why?" I asked. "Jesse hates it. Says that she has no real life and that most of the people on the show are shallow and only care about what they look like." Oh, I forgot. That would be just his kind of crowd.

"She's just a kid. She doesn't appreciate what a great opportunity this is for her."

On the set, Tye put his arm around Savannah and moved her closer. She pushed him away. Excellent.

"Don't you like working for Skyla?" I asked.

Dad cracked his gum. "I don't actually work *for* her, Alastair. I run all of our health and fitness facilities."

Uh-oh, Sergio was leaning over for a kiss. A cameraman cut off my view. Crap. I tried to lean across Dad.

"Here, change seats with me," Dad whispered.

"CUT!" the director yelled. He marched over to the car. Stuck his palm under Jesse's chin. She pulled something out of her mouth and gave to him. He gave it to a guy behind him and then stalked away. "Let's take five!"

The wind machine stopped and the lights over the car dimmed. Savannah and Tye climbed out. Turned back into their real selves. Sergio swatted Jess on her butt with his tennis racket.

She ignored him and rushed over to where we sat. "Hi, guys! Welcome to *Blender Town*." She gave us a two-in-one hug, engulfing me in her scent.

"*Blender Town?*" Dad asked.

She laughed, smoothing down her hair. "Yeah, that's what we call it. You know, because sooner or later, everybody ends up with everybody else."

She gave me a dazzling smile. "I'm so glad you came! What'd you think?" she asked, motioning to the set behind her. "Pretty amazing, isn't it?"

"It's great! And, you were—"

"Busted!" she said, rolling her eyes. "Hugo has a fit when I chew gum on the set. That was my third warning; now I'm going to get a memo about it. They'll dock my pay if it happens one more time. Mother is going to hang me by my fingernails. Hey, Sergio!" she called over her shoulder. "Come here! I want you to meet somebody."

I ran my hand through my hair quickly and stood up straighter. Then tried to strike a casual pose while keeping my biceps flexed. I prayed I was as handsome as Mom kept telling me I was.

Sergio jogged over and struck out a friendly hand. "Hi!"

I took his hand and pumped it hard. Jesse put her arm around me and gave me a squeeze. "This is Stump, our teammate! Rick's son— you know the one I told you about?"

"Like I could forget?" he asked, laughing, nearly blinding me with his pearly whites. "She's been talking about you all summer."

Sergio had no problem nose hairs and no chance of baldness. He was perfect in just about every sense of the word. TV didn't even do him justice.

He turned and clapped Dad on the back. "Very good, old man. What a nice-looking boy you have."

Boy? Who you calling "boy"? Jesse said he had just turned seventeen. Big deal.

Dad put his hand behind my neck. "Thank you. He has a very beautiful mother."

I turned toward Dad, stunned.

"So, Stump, you gonna help us do some serious butt kicking next month? I'm dying to break *Miami Loves* winning streak."

"Huh?" I said, still trying to process what Dad had just said about Mom.

"You're going to help us win, right?"

"Oh! You bet!" I said, drawing myself taller. "Looking forward to it, man," I said, my voice cracking.

"He's like a shark!" Jesse said.

"Well, good! We can use one. The *Miami Loves* team has two water animals—Bryce and Toby. And their girl, Kristen. They'll try to whoop ass on us from the gate."

"He's been working his guts out for weeks," Dad bragged. "He's pulling double and triple training sessions."

I shrugged, fighting off the panic that came the moment I heard about the "water animals" that wanted to play ocean whoop ass.

"Excellent!" Sergio looked down all casual-like at my legs. "So do you swim with or without your prosthetic?"

"I have a special swimming one with a secret four-horsepower propeller attached. It's retractable so the officials won't be able to see it," I deadpanned.

Sergio laughed and slapped me on the back. "My man!"

Jesse linked an arm through mine and snuggled up to me.

Sergio gave her a look that lasted a second longer than it should have and then tweaked her nose. "Let's go, Jesse. Nice meeting you, kid! Good luck with the training. We'll all get together soon and discuss strategies." He put his fist out for a knuckle rap with me, which I totally blew with bad aim. Our pinky knuckles barely grazed.

"Later, Rick!" he said, then jogged back onto the set. Didn't he walk anywhere like a normal guy? I wondered.

The director hurried over. "Jess, you about ready?" He gave Dad a quick smile and hello and then glanced at me. He put his hand out. "Hi! Do I know you?"

"Oh! Sorry! Hugo, this is Rick's son—"

"Alastair," Dad interrupted before she could say "Stump." I know he didn't like people calling me that.

"Hi," I mumbled.

"I've—seen—you—on—" Hugo said, pumping my hand with each word.

"No! He's not in the biz," Jesse interrupted.

"Well, God, he should be," Hugh said. He put his hand toward my face. "May I?" he asked, and then proceeded without waiting. He turned my head gently side to side and then stepped back and gave me a long look.

"You've got The Look. The little girls would just eat you up. Isn't he just perfect, Jess?"

"*I* think so," she said with a laugh. "But I bet you're just embarrassing him to death."

Hugo turned to Rick. "Nice work, Rick."

"Can't claim much credit. He came this way," Dad said. "Say, do you have a sec?" He pulled him over to the side, though Hugo kept staring at me. I could hear Dad whispering something about a package he'd sent over. Hugo patted Dad on the back, nodding.

Jesse leaned over to me and whispered, "Your dad's been trying to get a shot on the show."

"*Why?*" I asked. "It's not like he needs the money."

"Who knows? But they just keep putting him off. I'm not sure why. He's probably too old for *Splendor Town.*"

We both looked over at them. Dad was handing him his business card, and Hugo was all polite smiles.

"You, on the other hand, my little junior hunk," she said. "You he'd take on in a heartbeat, I bet. Did you see the way he was checking you out? Wouldn't it be fun if you could do a guest bit on the show while you're here this summer? Let's see," she said, tapping a finger against her lips. "Where could we fit you in right now?"

What about as your new boyfriend? I thought. Maybe I could

come into town, beat the snot out of Sergio, and make you my woman.

"I know!" she said. "You could be one of the extras swimming in the pool at the country club when Sergio and I go there next week. We're scheduled to have a knockdown, drag-out fight. Maybe I can throw him in the pool and you can help him out or something."

"Or try to drown him," I said to myself, but accidentally out loud.

"Drown him!" Jesse giggled. "Oh, my hero! I love it."

An earsplitting bell rang, making me jump.

"Oh, darn. I gotta get back to work. *Don't leave*," she said. "When I'm all done, we'll go over to the commissary. I'll introduce you to everyone, okay? And you and I are going to gorge on burgers and fries. Sergio will never eat junk food with me, and I know your dad won't, but you will, won't you, Stump? And malts, big fat creamy ones, okay?" she said backing onto the set.

"Absolutely!" I said.

"Promise?"

"Burgers and fries with the hottest-looking girl in LA? I think I can fit you in," I teased boldly, the near scent of her making whatever trace amounts of testosterone I had nearly boil over.

"Jess!" Sergio called from the set. "C'mon! We're burning daylight here."

She turned and gave him an annoyed look. "Yes, Father!" she said. The two of them held each other's look for another moment, and then Jesse turned toward me. She grabbed a piece of T-shirt from my chest and pulled me close. "Kiss me," she whispered.

My mouth dropped open and my heart went wild. She covered my mouth with hers and the whole world disappeared in my first kiss.

CHAPTER TWENTY

¡ GAVE THE BENCH A final swipe of paint and then threw the brush down into the bucket. "Done, Coach!" I yelled. I took a big swig of water and pulled off my shirt. And then carefully laid it down on top of my swim bag. It was my favorite T-shirt, the one I was wearing last week back when Jesse had grabbed the front of it and laid a long, sweet one on me. That had to be the world's hottest first kiss ever. She was a pro. I would never forget it.

The *Splendor Town* crew hooted and hollered, but Sergio just stared. Even my dad nearly laid a brick. He tried to talk to me about it in the car on the way home, but I pretended I'd fallen asleep. I didn't want to talk about it with anyone. Dad was probably all fired up to give me a lecture about how Jesse was too old for me or how we were almost family, but I didn't want to hear it. Least of all from him.

There'd only been one quick hurried kiss after that—more like a mother peck at the airport when Jesse took off with the *Splendor Town* gang to film on location in Mexico. I couldn't wait until she got back.

I sat down on the bench and pulled off my leg, gave my stump a good scratching.

"Can I swim now, Coach?" I yelled over at him. He was busy repainting some lines around the pool. I had to hand it to him. Sure,

I'd repainted the bleachers all by myself, but he'd done a lot of work too. Probably more than he should have, being elderly and all. But I wasn't about to point that out to him.

He sat back on his haunches and looked down toward me. He got up with a grimace and shook out his arm. Then walked down toward me. "Okay, same as yesterday. Thirty minutes, nice, even tempo—no hotdogging." He picked up my goggles and tossed them to me. "Give me a four-lap warm-up first."

"Then can we start ocean training tomorrow? For real, I mean, without the boards?"

"If you do a good clean thirty minutes today, we'll talk about it."

I dropped in the water, goggles in hand. I spit into each lens, rubbed it around, and stretched the band over my head. Pressing the goggles into my eye sockets, I squeezed out all the air.

I shook out my shoulders, turned, and looked back at Coach.

He peered at his stopwatch. "I've got you on three! Two, one—go!"

I lowered my body into the water, took a deep breath, and pushed off. I cruised through the water with the momentum and then surfaced like a dolphin to skim the top, turning my head easily to take in a long deep breath. After logging nearly a hundred hours in the pool, moving through the water had begun to feel more natural. Like I could almost breathe through some invisible gills. It was so quiet, almost church-like underwater, and everything looked so clean and clear. And nothing was confusing.

I wanted to swim well for Coach today. He had to cut me loose out in the ocean. We'd gone out a few times, but just on a couple of old boogie boards he brought. It was kind of like Ocean School. He wanted me to get a feel for the swell, the cold, the tow, and we'd even practiced what to do in a riptide. We'd see some of his swimming buddies when we'd go out, and he'd point out the mistakes some of them were making with their stroke. One day there was a real hotshot swimmer out there, and we'd cruised behind him for a long time. Coach called it "neuromuscular training." He said we had to train my mind, not just my muscles. Sometimes Coach would swim awhile and I'd tow his board. And watch. He was amazing. A total sea creature. The water loved him, and he loved the water.

I wanted to be just like him.

Coach and I talked more out in the ocean. Just seemed easier. *He* was easier out there. I told him about my accident. He didn't act like I was a total job for jumping. Just listened, nodded a bit now and then. Asked me how Dad felt about me jumping, which if the truth be told, I couldn't really tell you. I mean, everyone just kind of assumed Dad felt really bad about it. Maybe he didn't. Maybe he was sorry he had such a freak for a kid.

Jesse's face leapt across my mind, and I had to blink to change channels. She was not a good focus for me when I was swimming. I'd get all loose and frisky and I'd lose my edge.

Thinking about Mom wasn't any good either. I knew how hard everything was for her when she wasn't drinking. Even though Aunt Clem was taking good care of her, I worried anyway. When we talked last Sunday, she was having a hard day. She tried to act like everything was okay, told me a funny story about trying to ride this donkey that only wanted to go backward. Even still, I could hear the shadows in her voice.

Dad was my best bet. I could think about him—obsess about him, really, and the minutes in the pool would just slip away. My body would follow my mind down that path, chasing it, trying to keep up with the anger that didn't let up stroke after stroke after stroke.

At Skyla's house these days, I felt like a caged animal. I wanted to growl, bite, rip up the carpet—something. And it just got worse every day. Even the smell of Dad ticked me off. When I slept, I dreamed about EJ, his old lady boss. The night before last she'd been chasing me naked and she was wearing the running shoes that looked just like Dad's tattoo, with a little lightning bolt over them. I'd caught Dad on the phone yesterday with Jesse when she'd called for me. He was almost flirting with her. I could have torn his arm off. And then I would have stuffed it down his throat till he choked. He handed over the phone before I got a chance.

I turned away from him and took the phone into the living room. I told her I missed her like crazy, then would have given all the money in my wallet to take that back. Idiot! She laughed and asked me about my training.

Then she said that shooting had gone way past schedule, and she was so ticked about it. But Hugo had promised her and Sergio they would be back in plenty of time for the race. She said the ocean was so much warmer down in Mexico and the two of them were swimming a lot. She said they'd be ready.

I reached the wall at the end of the pool and flipped underwater, pushing off my leg. I got stronger every day. Sore, but stronger. Bone-crushing sore. I liked it. I liked feeling this ripped up. It matched how I felt inside.

I told Aunt Clem on the phone Sunday that their big plan had backfired. Instead of me warming up to Dad, being here this summer had just made it worse. I told her how he was living off Skyla, and Mom's idea about him finally having a decent job was just a joke. That he was just living with his boss, and as far as I was concerned, he was worthless. He played with Skyla's fancy gym toys for a living and used his good looks to con people into buying things they didn't need. And I told her that no matter how many high colonics Dad had, he was and always would be full of it.

Aunt Clem was quiet a minute and then asked if Skyla had talked to me about me and Dad getting some family therapy while I was there.

I snorted into the phone.

"You mind translating that for me?" she said.

"That means that I'm not going to counseling with him! He'll just con his way out of it. I know how he works."

"Con his way out of what?"

The "what" flared up like lava in my chest. And thinking about it now was making it hard to breathe. C'mon, two more laps. Smooth it down. Focus. I turned my head on the stroke to take a deep breath and sucked in a big mouthful of water.

Even that didn't put out the fire.

With Jesse out of town and my whole life devoted to training, I decided I needed a diversion. Something to help pass the time when I wasn't working out. I called it Operation You're Losing It, Buddy! I mapped out a plan.

Object: Drive Dad crazy
Subjects: Ian, Skyla, Dad, and the entire community of Lumina
           Beach
PLAN A: Try to convince Dad he is losing his hair.
PLAN B: Try to convince Dad that Ian is moving in on Skyla.
PLAN C: Help give the stairs back to the public.

Plan A was pretty simple. Dad was going to do most of the work for me. All I needed to do was to plant the idea and let him run with it. But I needed to gather up some hair. I pulled some off my brush, but they were too long, so I had to cut them into smaller, Dad-sized pieces. It was pretty tedious work but well worth the effort. I snuck into his bathroom when he and Skyla were out running on the beach.

I hadn't ever been in it before, but after living with richies all summer, it didn't really surprise me all that much. Their bathtub was the size of a school bus and had a killer view of the ocean. It was all done in this black marble stuff, and there were enough bath gels and fancy soaps to bathe everyone in Lumina Beach.

It was kind of like being in a maze, and it was even more confusing because of the floor–to-ceiling mirrors all around me. If you hung a left at the tub, there was a room with a wooden floor and some yoga mats. That room smelled really good, like incense and other stuff. If you went to the right of the tub, you ended up in Skyla's closet, which really looked like a whole women's clothing store. Minus the high heels section. It was big and roomy with built-in dresser drawers and different racks, and it even had a couple of chairs where you could sit down. Man, she had tons of clothes. But she mostly wore sweats and shorts around, which I kind of liked.

I took a turn at her fancy dress section and ran smack into Dad's shoe store and the entrance to his closet. It had to be twice as big as Skyla's. And his mirror had those side panels on it and lights like in real dressing rooms. I was betting this part of the closet was supposed to be for a lady, but he took it. Figures.

I walked around a bit looking at his stuff, checking myself out in his mirror.

I looked different. I patted the place where my belly used to jiggle and it was rock hard. I got real close up to the mirror and studied my armpits in the light. Finally! Some little hairs were growing there. Excellent.

I eased open some of Dad's drawers and pawed through them, careful not to mess anything. I don't really know what I was looking for. Clues? Maybe his journal that would explain everything?

Dear Journal,

Today I got a facial, a back waxing, and a eucalyptus body wrap. And I thought a lot about my son and my ex-wife. I was a complete fool to leave Nan. She was the best thing that ever happened to me. I wonder if she'll take me back. Alastair is such an amazing kid. How could I have ever left him? He turned out better than I ever hoped. Jesse is a lucky girl.

I'll talk to Skyla later and tell her this was all a big mistake. And that Ian really loves her. I'll get her to see that she is really better off without me.

Gotta run for now. I'm going to take my Jag down to the dealer and trade it in for a couple of road hogs for me and my boy. We'll drive those back to Taombi Springs. Won't Nan be surprised?

Yeah, right. I shoved his sock drawer closed, hard.

I spied his hairbrush on a dresser top near the mirror and pulled the plastic bag out of my shorts pocket. I grabbed a big gob of hair and stuck it on his brush and worked it down through the bristles. There! That ought to get his attention. Before I knew it, he'd be like one of those middle-aged old guys who are always patting down the back of their hair with that nervous look.

I set the brush down on the dresser, angled it so it would catch the light just right and he wouldn't miss it. Oh, man, I wish I could be here to see the look on his face. Chances are he'll be making a 911 call to his hair stylist and doctor by the end of the afternoon.

Dad had three bottles of man perfume sitting on his dresser top, two more than even my mom had. Make that three more than Aunt Clem had. I pulled the top off one and sniffed. They ought to call this one Fruit Gone Very Bad. Gross. He had that one on when we went to *Splendor Town*. Probably why that director guy didn't want to hire him. Didn't want him stinking up the set all day. I put the cap back on and set it back next to the big leather box that nearly screamed "open me."

It was his jewelry box, complete with everything except the dancing ballerina. Full of necklace chains, single-earring studs, hoops, and rings. I fingered through his things, a bitter taste growing in the back of my throat. The contents of this box alone could probably pay my and Mom's rent for the next five years. I flipped open a compartment in back and drew in my breath.

It was a stack of hundred-dollar bills as thick as a deck of cards. All nearly mint condition. What was this? His nest egg? His allowance? I pulled one off the top and studied it. I hadn't seen one of these babies since—I turned it over and stared into the face of Benjamin Franklin. A burst of images and sounds came at me all at once. And fury— throat-ripping fury. I ground the hundred-dollar bill in my fist and tried to find my breath. I hurled it across the room. Grabbed another one, balled it up, and threw it. Damn him! I picked up the whole wad. It felt like someone was standing on my chest.

"Stump!" A voice stopped me and I whirled around. Ian stood in the doorway, staring. Like he couldn't believe what he was seeing.

Couldn't believe that he'd found me standing in Dad's closet, next to his open jewelry box, one hand wrapped around a stack of cash.

CHAPTER TWENTY-ONE

AUNT CLEM TOOK A DEEP swig of Skyla's green iced tea with wheat grass and looked like it was work not to spit it out.

"I'm not here to take him home," she said, "if that is what you're all thinking."

She gave me a pointed look.

Dad and Skyla looked at each other and then at me. "We don't want him to go," Skyla assured her. She picked up Dad's hand and folded his stiff fingers into hers.

"But we can't go on like this," she added.

Aunt Clem nodded.

"So, if he stays, we are going to have to address this—this incident. And not just this, but the issues that are behind it."

"Agreed," Aunt Clem said.

"I wasn't stealing!" I blurted.

"Well, well," Aunt Clem said. "It talks!"

It had been hours since I'd spoken to anybody. I sure as hell wasn't going to talk to the crazy therapist guy that Dad and Skyla had come to the house after Ian found me in the closet freaking out. They tried to take me to go see him at his office, but I refused. So, they brought him to the house, and the guy actually came into my bedroom. I threatened to beat him with my leg if he didn't get the hell out of my room.

That's when Dad decided to call in the heavy artillery—Aunt Clem. He called her on her cell and arranged for her to get picked up in the middle of the Wild Women in Recovery camp and put on a direct flight out of Denver. She'd gotten in after dinner.

She looked tired and mad, but I was so glad to see her. I wanted to talk to her but nobody else. From the looks of things, they'd already made up their minds about what I was doing. Well, Dad at least. He looked like he wanted to throttle me. The jury was still out on Skyla.

"Okay, Alastair, let's take it from the top," she said. "We're all ears."

"What's the point?" I muttered. "*They* already think I'm guilty."

"Can we lose the attitude, please?" she said. She squeezed the back of my neck. "*They* are your family, and *they* are sitting right in front of you. We're all in this together, and we can solve it."

"Did you tell Mom?" I asked, digging my teeth into my bottom lip.

"Not yet, but I will. For now, I just told her I was making a quick business trip out to UCLA and would stop in and check on you."

Dad cleared his throat. "She's lucky to have you, Clem."

"Yeah, yeah, I'm a regular saint." She looked over at me. "Your mom is going to be fine, Alastair. She is made from some tough stuff. And she can't wait to get home and get the new place set up before you come back. So I'd hate like hell to tell her you won't be coming because you're in juvenile detention for robbery."

"I wasn't *stealing*!" I yelled.

Three faces stared back at me.

I stuck out my chin a bit more and stared back.

"You know, Alastair," Dad said, his voice hard, "I've put up with you being mad at me all summer—figured I probably had it coming.

But this goes way beyond. If you needed money, all you had to do is ask. I would think you would know that by now. Haven't we given you everything you needed this summer?"

"I'll say it one more time and then that's it for me—I wasn't taking your money!"

"Okay, then what were you doing in your dad's jewelry box with cash in your hand?" Aunt Clem asked.

I turned to look at her. "I'll talk to you but not them. HE won't listen anyway."

Aunt Clem shook her head. "No deal, Alastair. This is a family issue. It comes out here."

Skyla cleared her throat. "I can leave if you think that would help."

"Nope," she said. "You're family. This is about you too."

I looked around at them all and knew I'd never make them understand. I wasn't even sure if I understood. I just knew that I was mad enough to chew glass.

I glared at them all. Threw up my hands. "All right, then. I needed some cash. Figured in a place like this, there would be some lying around. I took it. It's not the first time. Just the first time you caught me."

That shut everybody up. For a minute at least.

Then they all started talking at once while I dug at a hangnail and tried to look like a real jerk. Dad was royally mad, and that suited me just fine. Skyla was stunned and willing to let me work off the money. Aunt Clem was ready to turn me over on her knee and give me a good wallop. But nobody was saying the thing I wanted to hear. Time for me to go home.

"Are you done with me here?" I butted in.

"Oh, boy, not by a long shot," Aunt Clem said. "Look at me, Alastair."

I turned my head a smidgeon toward her.

"Why would you do something so completely stupid and beneath you?"

"I dunno. Just to have it to buy stuff if I wanted. I mostly just blew it all," I said, covering for myself in case they wanted to see some actual merchandise.

"How much?" Dad asked.

"Not barely enough," I said, glaring at him.

Aunt Clem sighed and laced her fingers together. "I think we're done here for now. Alastair, in your room *now*."

"Suits me," I said, unfolding myself from the couch and sauntering off like a real cool guy.

"No phone, no computer, no DVDs," she added. "I want you thinking about what you're doing to this family."

That stopped me dead in my tracks. I whirled around. "What I'm doing to this family? Are you kidding? What have I ever done to this messed-up family?" I looked at Dad. "What about *you*? What about what you did to Mom and to me? If I stole a hundred dollars a day for the rest of my life, I'd never even come close to the damage you've done. You make me sick!"

And with that last word, in the uncoolest way possible, I started crying and ran from the room.

My neck was stiff and my face was crusty from salt when I woke up later that night. Somebody was knocking on my door. They turned the knob, but I'd locked it when I first came in.

"Who is it?" I snapped.

"Your aunt. Open the door, Alastair."

I rolled out of bed and went and unlocked it. Then threw myself back onto the bed, facing the other way.

"I'm leaving," she said. "Thought I'd come say goodbye."

I rolled back around and looked at her. "You can't leave me here with them."

"Yeah, I can."

"I'll run away, then."

"That would be really stupid. And I won't come back for that show."

"I want to talk to Mom *now*."

"No, you don't. You can't even imagine how much this would upset her. I won't let you do that to her. Not this month, kid."

"Please take me home," I said, almost in a whisper. "I hate it here. I hate them. And now they hate me."

"Surprisingly, they don't. Skyla is a very nice woman, and she just wants to make this work. Your dad is mad at you, but you're mad at him, so you two will just have to work it out. If you don't want to see a counselor, fine—do it the hard way. I can't force you."

"I'll keep stealing," I threatened.

Aunt Clem opened her hand. A balled-up hundred-dollar bill was in her hand. "Ian just brought this to us. A housekeeper found it in the bathtub. This is not stealing. This is pitching a fit." She ironed the bill between her fingers. "You can stick to your crime story if you like, but I'm not buying it. I'll never believe in a million years that you are stealing from them. Snooping where you have no business, I buy. You got that gene from your mother. I could never keep her out of my stuff."

I rolled over on my back and the tears fell into my ears. I scrubbed my face with the heels of my hands. "When you're old and in a nursing home and beg me to come home, I'm going to say no."

She laughed. "Please just make sure there are some cute chicks in the nursing home. I'll be fine."

She planted a kiss on my forehead. "I miss you like the dickens, Alastair. You'll be home soon enough."

And with that, she was gone. Leaving me to fight my own demons.

Damn her.

CHAPTER TWENTY-TWO

"OKAY, OFF YOU GO," COACH said, tipping my boogie board. "Let's take it nice and easy." He peered down at his watch. "I want a ten-minute warm-up."

I'd been doing my workouts in the ocean all week now and was still shocked by the icy cold. Even with a wet suit. The sun was just coming up, and we'd already paddled out toward the buoys. Coach said this was the best time, when the water was still smooth. This morning it was smooth like glass—but felt like a glacier.

It was hard. Harder than I thought it would be. It wasn't just the cold. The water was dark, and you couldn't really see where you were going. There weren't any lane lines painted under you that you could look at or colorful flags hung overhead to let you know you were getting close to the turnaround. All your markers had to be different. Coach was teaching me how to track my progress and keep myself going in a straight line without stopping to look around. The horizon and the buoys were my new guides.

Even though the water was smooth, there was a good swell this morning. I could feel it lifting me up and bringing me down. It could make you sick after a while. I'd thrown up from it after my first ocean swim last week. Coach acted like it was no big deal and just kicked some sand over it.

Mom would have had a quilt over me and a cup of soup ready if she'd been there. But I'd gotten used to how Coach treated me. Made me feel sorta manly.

My arm hit something very un-water like at my next stroke. I gasped and jerked my head up. I was surrounded by what felt like dozens of dismembered body parts. And things crawling between my legs.

"Coach!" I shouted.

"It's just kelp. Keep your head now," he yelled back, watching me from his boogie board.

It was like Spider-Man had just thrown a giant web over me. I tried to kick my way out of it, but there was too much of it.

I spun back around to face Coach. He wasn't coming any closer. He was just watching me from his board. Bastard.

I tried to dig a space around me. My heart was pounding. I couldn't get out of it! I started to pick the biggest pieces of it up and hurl them away from me.

Coach paddled closer to me. He propped himself up on his elbows to watch. "Now, that is going to make you very tired."

I cursed him under my breath. A giant whip of a piece was wrapped around my waist, and I tried to pull it out of the water.

"Use your head, Alastair."

"I'm getting out of here! No way I can swim through this." I shifted to reverse and looked for the back door. I kicked as hard as I could to motor out. But it felt like someone had tied my legs together.

He paddled closer and grabbed me by the scruff of the wet suit. "Okay, time out. Stop!" He whirred his whistle next to my head. After weeks of training, my body had become his slave. I stopped.

"You're getting your heart rate all jacked up and you're wasting energy."

I tried to not let him see my teeth chattering. "What am I s-s-supposed to do?"

"Problem-solve. This is not the pool, and there is no cute girl in a red suit to save your bacon."

"I can't g-get through—"

"Sure, you can. How'd you get in it?"

"I swam into it."

"Then swim out of it."

"I was trying to, for pete's sake!"

"Forward, not ass backward."

"How? Look!" I said pointing. "There's tons of it ahead. I'll just back up, and then we can go around the whole thing."

"Is that your plan for race day? Do you think that is what the other swimmers are going to do? Everyone is going to stop, put it in reverse, and swim around it?"

I blew my nose out and coughed. "Well, if they were smart—"

"They are smart. And they'll be going through it. And I can pretty much guarantee you that you won't be winning the girl if she sees you swimming backward."

"All right, all right! So, s-s-how me!" I was really starting to get cold.

"What is the correct position for swimming?"

"Head d-d-own," I recited.

"Right, and if your head is down, your body is horizontal. If your head is up," he said, grabbing my chin, "the rest of you is vertical. That's all the more surface area to get caught up in the kelp. So what's the best position to get through a kelp bed?"

I sighed. "Horizontal, sir."

"Yep," he said. "Swim on top of it. Keep your arms and legs above it."

I nodded. "G-g-got it."

He let go of my wet suit and backed away from me. "Now, easy does it. Don't fight it. Go with it."

I put my face down and began to tread water—nice and slow. Arms on top for now. I did a small frog kick to push forward.

Raised my head for a breath and then back down again. Tried to get into the whole Zen of just being with it. Mom was always trying to teach me about that. It was kinda pretty, actually—yellowish gold in some parts.

I eased over a small forest of it, inch by inch, and then hit a clear patch. I kept treading water, though, for a bit longer, past some long whip-like stragglers.

Coach's whistle shrilled and I came up.

"Okay! Now get your bearings."

"Yes, sir!"

"You've got to use your head out here. This isn't just about swimming. It's about being prepared and solving problems."

Figures he'd known I was going to swim right into it and he let me.

"I'm r-ready."

Coach rechecked his watch. "Gotcha. Go!"

I slipped into the back of the meeting, my hoodie over my head. Not that I could actually get by going incognito anywhere, but I hoped for some invisibility. I'd been working on that particular act for a few days around the house, moving ghost-like best I could—not talking to anyone. The minute I'd see Ian leave the house, I'd duck into Dad's bathroom to plug his hairbrush full of more of my hair.

Ian had left a pair of his flip-flops out by the pool one day, and I'd scooped those up and put them at the foot of Dad and Skyla's bed.

Tried to imagine Dad's face when he saw them—what he might think had been going on while he was at work. It made me feel a little sick inside to think about getting Skyla in hot water. None of this was her fault. In the end I moved Ian's sandals. I just didn't have the stomach to do that to her.

And now here I was, working on plan C of Operation: You're Losing It, Buddy!

Helping the public get back their beach stairs. I wanted to rattle Dad's cage hard. He had left right after dinner to go to a city council meeting. I'd been eavesdropping on Ian and Skyla and found out. Dad wanted Skyla to go with him, but she told him it was his battle and he could leave her out of it. He'd left the house steaming. Skyla said she wished he'd just give it up.

I took a seat near the back of the room. The mayor and all the council members sat at a big table in front facing the audience. Some lady was standing at a podium pleading with them to spend fifty thousand dollars to install several more doggy poop bag dispensers at the beach. And she wanted a personal attendant for the stations to make sure people were using the bags.

I could see Dad up near the front clutching a folder, looking impatient. After the doggy poop lady, we had to sit through a man ranting about the number of homeless people that were

panhandling in front of his yoga studio, and the police weren't doing anything about it. One guy had even grabbed a latte right from one of his students' hands! Mr. Yoga said it was very distressing to his clients to encounter them. There was a long debate, then, about the lack of jobs and affordable housing in Lumina Beach. I felt like raising my hand and suggesting they be offered jobs manning the bag dispenser stations, and could we move on with it, please.

The tension in the room nearly blew sparks when Dad stepped up to the mike. He cleared his throat and launched into a brief history of the beach access issue. The mayor interrupted him, told him he only had five minutes and everyone knew the history of the issue. Some people laughed at that, a few booed, and there was hissing from behind me.

"I'll get right to the point, then," he said. "I am prepared to finance a free trolley service for all locals and tourists on Blue Coast Way. This would ensure immediate beach access for anyone. The trolley would stop at eight different locations for pickups and drop-offs all day long." He pulled a stack of papers from his folder and said he'd drawn up a full business proposal.

One of the council members interrupted him. "Mr. Hudson, this just moves everyone away from your house and doesn't address the real issue at all—"

"Yeah!" a surfer chick behind me yelled. "What if I want to surf right in front of your house?" Her pals cheered.

"Quiet!" the mayor said. "She has a point, Mr. Hudson. There is no reason that anyone should *have* to take a trolley away from your house all the way down to the pier. If they wanted to surf near your house, they'd have to walk all the way back up the beach."

"Mayor, I have to think about the safety of my family! We have not been afforded protection from thugs who have continued to come on my personal property, on my deck, in my pool! A few weeks back some surfers threw property signs at the windows of my dining room while my family was eating. Someone could have been hurt! I get firecrackers thrown on my property regularly and threats in my mailbox. If the police can't protect me, what do you expect me to do?"

The back rows erupted in jeers, taunts, and yelling. "Yeah, we threw your bogus Private Property signs, all right!" someone shouted. "And we'll keep doing it!"

Dad threw up his hands. "See what I mean, Mayor? They're impossible."

I yanked down my hood and jumped up. "That's all bull! You just don't want anyone or anything to mess up your perfect little kingdom!"

The mayor shouted, "I'll have QUIET here!"

Dad stared at me, dazed.

"Free our stairs! Free our stairs! Free our stairs!" The back rows got to their feet and started stomping.

"Officers!" she said. "Escort these young people out!"

"Free our stairs! Free our stairs!" I yelled loud as I could.

Dad's eyes locked onto mine. I held them.

"Loser," I said, not really caring one way or another whether he heard me.

CHAPTER TWENTY-THREE

i **WOKE UP THE NEXT** morning with a gut-grinding, bone-crushing hunger that wouldn't let up. After the city council meeting last night, I'd done a long, "illegal" workout session in the pool at home. Coach would have killed me. But it was the only way that I could get rid of the tsunami inside me.

Now I felt wasted. Hung over. I needed to eat or die.

I dialed the kitchen's extension and waited for someone to pick up. Hoped it wasn't Ian. I knew he didn't like me eating in my room. Crumbs were the stuff of his nightmares, I was guessing.

"Felipe! Oh, good!" I said. He was a cool guy. "Hey, can you make me a big ham-and-cheese omelet? And some of those home fries—"

"Sorry, kiddo," he interrupted. "Your dad said no room delivery for you today. He wants you to come out when you get up."

I slammed the phone down, yanked my blanket off, and sat up.

Fine! You want to mess with me today? Here I come.

I jammed my leg on and hiked up my pajama bottoms. But I didn't put my shirt on. Didn't comb my hair. Didn't bother to brush my teeth.

Dad was sitting alone at the breakfast bar, reading the paper. Every one else was either done or had taken cover somewhere.

I walked right past him without a word. Went to the pantry and pulled out some cereal. I started eating it by the fistfuls. I needed an appetizer until I could get my brains back from starvation mode.

Dad watched me, but I ignored him.

Eggs. Now I needed eggs. I pulled a carton out of the fridge and started cracking them. Didn't care that an awful lot of shell was ending up in the bowl.

"Do you have a shirt you could put on, please?" Dad asked, his voice level.

I whipped around. "Why? No one's here."

"I'd prefer you wear a shirt while you're cooking."

"You want me to go all the way back to my room and get a shirt?" I asked, incredulous.

"Yes," he said, looking down at his paper.

I slammed the bowl down on the counter and stared at him.

He looked up. "It's for your safety, Alastair. You could get burned."

"Fine, I won't cook." I picked up the bowl and brought it to my mouth. Sucked down four raw eggs and some shell. And willed myself not to gag.

We stared each other down.

I wiped my mouth off on the back of my arm. I wasn't completely sure those eggs weren't going to come right back up. I prayed they wouldn't.

"Thanks for breakfast." I dropped the bowl into the sink and turned to leave the kitchen.

"Stop right there," he said.

"*What?*"

"If you're not going to eat with the family, then you'll clean up your own mess. Wash your bowl and put the cereal away."

"Well, will that make you feel better?" I asked. "'Cos I can tell that you just aren't going to be happy until you can make my life completely miserable today." I grabbed the bowl, egg carton, and cereal box, opened the trash compacter, and dumped it all in. Rammed the door closed. Put my hands on my hips. "Done."

Dad stood up and I felt a moment of fear. He came toward me, but I held my ground.

He yanked open the door to the trash and pulled the bowl out. "Wash it."

"No!"

"NO?" he shouted.

"No." A mere whisper.

Dad glared at me, and I didn't know what he would do. He dropped the bowl into the sink and filled it with water. And then soap. Scrubbed it so hard I thought he might break it. I wet my lips, now not sure what to do.

He set the bowl into the dish drainer and turned to me. "You and I are going to talk. Go put your shirt on and meet me in my office in five minutes."

"I have nothing to say to you," I said, folding my arms across my chest, chilled.

"You apparently had quite a bit to say last night."

"It's a free country. I have rights."

"Not the right to interfere with something that has nothing to do with you!"

"So send me back to my mom."

He shook his head. "Don't think I wouldn't *love* to, Alastair."

And even though I was so angry I could have blown flames, hearing that hurt.

Hurt bad.

Beebe swung me around in her chair and leveled a long gaze at me with eyes that were honest-to-God purple. I guess you could pretty much get anything you wanted in LA, even purple eyeballs. She probably had a different set of colored contact lenses for every outfit she owned.

"You do know that you are going to be an absolutely lethal lady-killer, don't you?" she asked, and then pumped my chair up higher with her foot. She raked her fingers through my hair. "You hair feels like straw, though." She turned toward Skyla. "Well, the old apple doesn't fall far from the tree, does it? I bet this is exactly what Rick looked like at his age."

Skyla's face came up in the mirror behind me. "Oh, he's okay to look at, I suppose."

"*Excuse* me. My hair, please?" But I flashed Skyla a grateful look. She smiled back at me.

I'm not sure what had happened, but things were changing between us. Seemed like the madder I got at my dad, the less pissed I felt toward Skyla. I felt kind of bad for her. Bad that she had to be stuck with such a gold-sucking scumbag like my dad.

"So, what are we doing for you today—besides a deep conditioning, Mr. Salty Hair?" she asked.

"I want you to dye it," I said.

She raised an eyebrow. "Really?" She looked over at Skyla.

She shrugged. "Don't look at me. It's his hair. Whatever he wants."

"Black," I said. "Real, real black."

"Hmm," Beebe said, swinging me around toward her. "Not more blond, huh? I could give you some nice highlights. It would really bring out your eyes." Beebe tilted her head to look at me as she continued to stir up my hair with her fingers.

"Nope. Black," I said. "And matching eyebrows, too."

Ian did a double take when he saw me and then got very busy shuffling the mail in his hand. "Oh, hi! Great, you're back. Sky, you've got a ton of calls you need to return."

Sky? I wonder if he called her that in front of my dad. Ian couldn't return my look. I think it was my eyebrows. Made me look kinda scary.

Cool.

"So what do you think of my hair?" I asked.

He handed the mail over to Skyla and gave me a once-over. "Well, turn around. Let me get a look at the whole new you."

I did a slow spin.

"It's quite an exciting color. It's very—hmm, very Sergio-esque. Don't you think, Skyla?"

"Not at all!" she said. "Sergio's hair is more purple-black. This is *black*, black."

"Well, but the cut—don't you think—?" he went on.

"Nope—Stump is an original. A real head turner."

Ian paused and studied a magazine cover. "Speaking of the devil." He turned to flash the cover to Skyla. "Have you seen this?"

She took and quick look then tossed it facedown onto the table. "What else have we got?"

"Mail aplenty. C'mon," he said, leading her away. "You've got to spend some time in your office this afternoon. I cannot fend off one more hungry nonprofit."

Skyla turned back toward me as she walked away. "Don't forget what Beebe said. Stay out of the pool for at least twenty-four hours, okay? You look great! And thanks for letting me go with you. That was fun."

"Yeah, sure," I said, waiting until they were out of sight before diving for the magazine that was "speaking of the devil." It hadn't escaped me that Skyla had put it facedown.

It was one of those soap star magazines. Half of the cover was a glamour shot of Sergio and Jesse in their show clothes and makeup on sailing on a yacht. Mexico, probably. The other half was a slightly blurry shot of them sitting way too close together at an outdoor café. And this was no shot from the show. This was real life. No glamour— just one teenage girl in cutoffs and big sunglasses with one black-haired guy without a shirt. Jesse had her legs curled around his under the table. And her mouth stuck on his.

My head felt like a missile that had ignited and was ready for launch. It was going to explode off the top of my head. Then it was going to find, lock on, and blast Sergio to smithereens.

What kind of girl was Jesse anyway? Just two weeks ago she had given me my first hot grown-up kiss. And now she was off with *Puke-io*, laying those lips on him?

I should have never let her kiss me. She was no better than Dad. Hopped from one person to the next. I couldn't stop staring at the picture even though it was nearly giving me a brain hemorrhage.

I said a very, very bad word and ripped the cover off.

The front door slammed shut and I looked up, startled. Dad pulled off his sunglasses and looked at me. And kept staring at me like he couldn't believe his eyes.

"Alastair! What in God's name did you do to your hair? Your mother is going to kill me. Has Skyla seen you?"

I leveled him a long, mean gaze. "She took me. She likes it."

"Did you actually dye your eyebrows, or is that just—" He stepped toward me and put a hand behind my neck. With his other hand, he rubbed his thumb across my eyebrow.

I knocked his arm away and jumped back. "Keep your hands off me!" I yelled.

He planted his hands on his hips and sighed with disgust.

Skyla came rushing into the room. "Rick! I was just trying to call you—"

"I can see why! What were you thinking, letting him do this?" he said, his voice loud. "He is too young to be dying his hair. You should have asked me or his mother about this first."

Skyla's cheeks turned bright red. "Let's go outside and talk about it."

"No, we're staying right here. If he's old enough to dye his hair, then he's old enough to hear how I feel about it. You had no right to help him with this, Skyla. You aren't his parent."

"Honey, it's hair color. It's not a big deal. Relax, would you?" She put her hand on his arm, but he pulled it away.

"It's more than hair color and you know it," he growled.

"Yeah?" I asked, my voice getting all squeaky. "What is it, Rick? You think maybe I don't want to look like a 'chip off the old block'?"

"Watch your mouth, young man. You will not call me Rick in this house. I am your father."

"This is freaking unbelievable!" I screamed. "I have been here for weeks and this is the first time you're playing the father card.

And because of *hair*? You've let Skyla do pretty much everything but breast-feed me and NOW you're pissed that she's crossed the line? You're pathetic."

"Alastair, that is enough! Go to your room."

I continued like I didn't hear him. "All that has ever mattered is that I make you look good. Just like with—with EJ! The only reason you took me to Lake Rochester with the two of you was to show me off. 'Woo-hoo, EJ. Check out my boy. Aren't we a pretty pair?'"

"That's not true—" he started.

"Yes, it *is*. And you know it. You were pimping me off."

"That's enough!" he roared.

"Yeah, it is! I've had enough and I'm out of here, you sonofabitch!"

Back in my room—correction—the guest room at Villa Skyla, I was burning up the phone keypad dialing Aunt Clem, Jesse, and Coach.

Not a single one of them picked up. I hung up on Coach and Jesse but left Aunt Clem a very pissed-off message.

I yanked open the balcony door and hurled the phone as far as I could. And fired off a string of dirty words behind it.

My eyes burned like someone had just stabbed them with a hot poker. There was a loud rap at the bedroom door, so I hurried over and locked it.

"Just leave me alone!" I yelled through the door.

"Alastair, we need to talk *now*," Dad said.

Man, he was really mad. If I'd known dyeing my hair was going to make him this angry, I would have done it the first day.

"I'm giving you ten minutes to calm yourself down, and then I want you back out here. We are going to talk this through."

I balled my fist and considered flinging the door open and giving him a good sucker punch. Be just my luck, though, that Skyla would be there and I'd accidentally give her another shiner.

Instead I socked the door with my fist. "Go away!" Pain tore through my fist up to my elbow, but it felt good.

Dad started mumbling to someone, and I moved closer to the door to hear.

" . . . get this door open . . . if you . . . hinges off . . . he better . . ."

Oh God. He was getting ready to pull a Mr. Tool Man on me and take the door off.

I scanned the room like a magic portal might suddenly appear. Nothing but the balcony.

I wiped my runny nose with my shoulder. "Twenty minutes!" I said, banging the door with my other fist. "I'll come out in twenty minutes, not ten."

"Fine!" he yelled back. "But I'm not leaving this door, in case you think you're going to slip out. IAN! Get me a chair and a drink, will you?" he bellowed.

What was up with him? Was the man *mental* all of a sudden?

A softer rap sounded on the door. "Stump?"

"Don't *call* him that," Dad yelled.

It was Skyla. I bit my lip but ignored her.

"Let me come in, will you? Just for a couple of minutes— please?"

I grabbed my backpack from the closet and started pulling things out of the drawers that I would need . . . bathing suit, goggles, sunglasses, some triangles of clean underwear, shorts, a couple of T-shirts. I was out of here. There was nothing he could say to make me stay. I'd sleep on the beach if I had to—if Mom wouldn't let me come be with her. She would—if she knew. I know she would.

I sat down on the edge of the bed. I pulled up the front of my shirt and mopped off my face. Checked my watch. I had eight minutes left until he got the power tools out.

No way was I putting up with this. I tucked my fist under my armpit and squeezed it. It was really throbbing now. I was regretting throwing the phone out the window. I wanted to try calling Aunt Clem again. Maybe she'd answer this time.

I went out to the balcony and paced its length. Looked to see if there was a place I could climb over and down onto something. The outdoor patio was below me. Ian was out there with a cell phone stuck to his head. Probably calling someone who might actually know how to operate power tools to get a door off a hinge. To the left of the balcony, I had a clear drop, all the way down to some boulders and the beach. About twenty feet or so down. My mouth grew dry. I drew a deep breath.

I raced back to the room, grabbed my backpack, and pulled it on. Checked over the balcony again to see where Ian was and then climbed up onto the railing and balanced there a minute. I was going to have to do more than drop. I'd have to jump wide to clear the rocks.

Hasta la vista, jerk.

I do remember I thought sand would be softer.

CHAPTER TWENTY-FOUR

I HIT THE SAND LIKE a sack of rocks.

Knocked the wind clean right out of me.

Tried to find one single breath of air.

Maybe I would suffocate.

B R E A T H E!

They'd find me laid out here one day. Eyes pecked out by seagulls.

B R E A T H E!

I caught a thin wave of air and rode it in hard.

Sucked for another.

Another.

I rolled over to one side.

I could still roll. That had to be a good sign.

Sat up slowly. Looked up to make sure nobody could see me.

My head was heavy and swimmy and felt way too big for my body.

I tried to hoist myself up on my foot. It all seemed to still work, but in slow motion.

I had to get away. Had to get out of here. Away from all these crazy people. I staggered and tripped over a piece of driftwood. Shook my head and got back up again.

I headed for the shoreline. I'd follow it until I got to town. Then I'd call EJ.

No, not EJ—I'd call Mom. That's what I meant.

But EJ's face kept swimming in toward me. Closer. I blinked to change pictures, but it wouldn't work.

Tried to see Jesse instead, but EJ was playing on all channels.

Doesn't matter. Just keep moving forward. Faster.

EJ had kissed him with her old woman wrinkly lips.

And he'd been kissing her back.

In the bedroom. That morning.

And they'd been so wrapped up in what they were doing, they didn't see or hear me come in. The zipper on my new jacket was stuck and I needed help.

EJ had her own room. She shouldn't be in Dad's bed. So I stood frozen and stared at the tattoo on his back.

Until EJ saw me over Dad's shoulder, but she didn't say a word.

Not until later.

CHAPTER TWENTY-FIVE

I RAN.

But I couldn't outrun it. It came faster than my legs could take me.

The video of Lake Rochester came in high resolution, high definition, and with surround sound—like it had just happened yesterday.

My lungs gave out. I slowed to a stop and leaned over at the waist, trying to catch my breath.

When EJ had seen me standing in the doorway holding my jacket, she sent me away with her eyes. With a look that said, "He's mine." Dad never even turned around. Didn't know what I'd seen.

And she came back at me with the same look a couple of hours later, when she leaned down and whispered in my ear as she zipped my parka so close to my throat that I could hardly breathe.

And she put a brand-new hundred-dollar bill in my hand. Told me to be a good boy and keep our secret.

If you tell your mother, she'll be very upset, and I won't be able to keep your dad on at the firm. You don't want your dad to lose his job, do you, Alastair?

Dad had come back after signing me up for the last day of the juniors' class. EJ leaned over me like she was kissing me and breathed hot stinky coffee breath on me. I turned my head. She snapped the money from my hand and stuffed it deep in my pocket.

They'd meet me on top, they'd said, with big smiles.

But I'd never made it to the top. I couldn't.

Couldn't bear to think of them waiting for me.

Couldn't bear to think of what they were doing right that second. Probably kissing and rubbing up against each other like in the movies. Like Dad should only do with Mom.

I didn't want to be with them. It was wrong, and I wanted to go home.

I wanted to go home so bad and make the nightmare stop.

I thought I might start bawling or slugging somebody.

I had to get off.

Now.

Had to get off the lift now. So I could run. Far, far away. Maybe I could get a ride home somehow. Tell some nice family that I'd been kidnapped and they had to take me home to Taombi Springs.

Down was really far away.

I pulled the money out of my pocket and gave it to Brittany, who was next to me in the lift. And then I told her to hold on to the sides real tight for a minute. I lifted up the safety bar. She looked at me like I was crazy.

I jumped and sailed downward like a bird set free, until I hit the ground.

And the pain took me home.

CHAPTER TWENTY-SIX

IT WAS LATE WHEN I finally ended up at Coach's house. It was cold and wet out from a thick fog. My hair was wet and my nose was runny. I could have called him, but he would have never let me come over. I'd found Kiki and he told me where Coach lived. Warned me about going over there, though. Said Coach did not like visitors. Probably turn the hose on me.

Coach didn't look too surprised to see me, but he didn't look happy about it either. He just shook his head. "Well, that was stupid," he said.

"What?"

"Dying your hair. Is that what your dad is so pissed off about?"

"Did you talk to him?" I asked.

"Yep—he called a couple of hours ago."

I shifted my backpack. "I just came to say goodbye—and, well, to thank you and all for coaching me this summer." I wiped my nose on my sleeve.

"No, you didn't," he said. "You came here to get me to talk some sense into that fool black-haired head of yours."

"No, I didn't. I'm going back to Colorado."

He looked me over hard.

"But I didn't want you to think I was just bailing out on the race and all."

"I see," he said, leaning up against the doorjamb. "And do you think saying you're not 'bailing on the race and all' when that is exactly what you're doing makes it all right?"

"I'm not bailing. I just can't stay here, Coach."

"Did you jump?"

"What?" I asked, startled.

"Did you *jump* from your balcony to the beach?" he said.

I looked down at my shoes. They were wet and crusty with sand. "Yeah," I said quietly.

"I'd call that bailing. Did you hurt yourself?"

I lifted one shoulder. "Not really. Well, maybe twisted my ankle a bit."

"You know what, kid? That hair dye has gone right to your brain."

He yanked the door open all the way. "Get in here. Now. Let me see your ankle. Take both your shoes off."

I tried to walk with just my regular limp as I moved past him and not with my new limp. Truth was, walking was killing me. I dropped my backpack and sat down on the edge of the closest chair. I pulled my shoe off. Which hurt a lot. My ankle was swollen, but not too bad. But now that I had my shoe off, it hurt like a mother.

Coach held it in his hand and gave it a good once-over, pressing different places, trying to make me scream, I think. "Let's get some ice on this," was all he said finally.

He headed off to the kitchen, and I collapsed against the back of the chair.

He came back with a giant package of frozen lima beans and another one of frozen peas. He laid one over the front of my ankle and one behind the back. "Now hold that there!" he said.

He ducked into the hallway and then was back in a second. He had a small red bag with him that had 1984 US Olympic Team written on it. It looked like it had been through a war or two. He dug through and pulled out a small box with dials on it. Looked like maybe the first radio that was ever invented.

"What's that?" I said nervously, sensing that we weren't about to listen to some old-time music together.

He unclipped a cell phone from his waistband and tossed it on my lap.

"Call your parents," he said.

I licked my lips. "I can't call my dad."

He pulled a sticky Band-Aid looking thing from a small envelope and attached it to one side of my ankle and then put another one of the other side. Then he hooked some wires to it that he plugged into the box.

"Call your parents, or I'll call the police and tell them I've got a runaway sitting in my living room."

"I'll call my mom but *not* my dad."

He put the vegetables back around my ankle and foot, then wrapped it all together—tight—with the ace bandage. Man, it hurt.

"You sprain your finger, too?" he asked.

"No—I just . . . I just—well—"

Coach dragged some pillows from his couch and put them under my ankle, propping it up. Then he started fiddling with the dials on the old radio-looking thing.

"Are you going to shock my ankle?" I asked, getting worried.

"Yeah," he said.

I drew a deep breath.

"Tell me when you can feel this," he said, turning one knob slowly. He watched my face.

I braced myself, not sure what to expect. "Oh! It's like pins and needles. Is that what you mean?"

"Could you stand it if we go higher?" He turned it up.

I nodded. "It's okay. What is it?"

"It's electrical stimulation. It will help the swelling come down. Won't hurt you. Now call your dad." He stood up, stretched his back.

I called Jesse's number because I knew she wasn't home.

"Hi, Dad?" I said. "It's me, Alastair."

I paused as if he was saying hi back to me.

"I just wanted to let you know that I'm fine—"

I paused again.

"No, don't keep dinner for me. I'll eat out and be home later."

Coach snatched the phone from my hand. He listened a second to Jesse's recording, then hung up.

"Don't mess with me, Alastair," he said.

"Look, I'll leave. I'm not talking to that bastard." I tried to pull the wrap off my foot so I could get up.

Coach knocked my hand away. "Leave it! You're not going anywhere on that ankle." He put his hands on his hips and shook his head at me. "I knew you'd be trouble that first day we talked in the Grass Shack. Should have sent you and your sorry story packing then."

"I didn't mean to get you into this mess."

"Sure, you did. If you really just wanted to thank me today, you could have sent me a card and a fruitcake. You want me to fix this—I know you, kid. But I am not Father Flanagan and this sure as hell isn't Boys Town."

"Sorry," I mumbled.

"Did he beat you or something?"

I shook my head. "No. I just don't want to see him."

Coach's phone rang. He rubbed his palm over his whiskers. "Well, that's probably them again." He pointed a finger at me. "Don't you move!" he barked. He went into his kitchen and I strained an ear to listen, which was hard on account of my foot being shocked and all. I took a deep breath and laid my head back on the chair.

Coach was doing a lot of listening and grunting. Hard to tell what was going on.

I looked around his living room, which was very tidy. Against one whole wall was a big wooden display case. With rows and rows of watches—tons of them. The stopwatch kind and some that looked like the old kind that men used to carry in their pockets on a chain. The case was very fancy, like something you might see in a store with little lights in it and velvet on the shelves. I wanted to get up and go look closer, but I was trapped having my foot shocked.

I heard Coach slam the phone down. He came back and stared at me.

I stared back.

He checked the meter on the shock box. "Can I take this up higher?"

"Sure," I said with a gulp, knowing that was the right answer but bracing myself. The vibration on my ankle went from pins and needles to an intense buzz. Weird, but it didn't really hurt.

"That was your stepmom," he said.

"Figures," I said. "Dad is probably busy getting his nose hairs highlighted."

"Don't be a smart-ass, Alastair. You've got two choices."

I raised an eyebrow and felt heat rush to my face.

"She said she'll come get you and everyone will leave you alone for the rest of the day. You can talk in the morning."

"I *don't* want to see him!"

I waited, but he didn't continue.

"What's the second choice?" I asked.

He rubbed a hand over his chest like he'd just eaten something bad and it was giving him heartburn. "I told her you could bunk up with me—but just for tonight. You give me any grief, so much as fart in your sleep, I'm tossing you and your gimpy ankle right out the front door. You got that?"

I nodded. "Yes, sir."

"Will that crap wash out of your eyebrows?" he asked.

"No, sir, it comes with the hair. It's permanent."

He guffawed. "Nothing's permanent, kid."

CHAPTER TWENTY-SEVEN

AFTER LIVING IN THE FAT lap of luxury at Skyla's, being at Coach's was—well, different. Real manly, that's for sure. I liked his house. It was older but had a good feel to it. I added it to my sketchbook right away. That night, after he fed me some liver, onions, and kale, Coach went out back for a while. I thought I smelled cigar smoke coming in from the window, but I didn't mention it. At 8:30 p.m. he called "lights-out" and sent me to my "bunk."

"Breakfast at five thirty and then suit up. The cold water will be good for your ankle."

I wasn't in any position to argue. With all I had ripping through me, a sore ankle was minor stuff.

I lay down on top of the bed, too beat to even get under the covers. I stuck a couple of pillows under my ankle like Coach had told me.

I felt like the scarecrow from the *Wizard of Oz* after he'd been beaten up and had his straw pulled out of him. Lying there on the road, with his guts all over.

Man, you can't just do that to a boy and expect to be able to stuff him back up. You'd never get him put back the way he was before. And most of the straw I didn't want back. I just wanted my house in Colorado, my mom, and Aunt Clem. All the stuff that was my feelings for Jesse and Dad—just leave it out there in the road. I was through with it anyway.

I threw my arm over my eyes and tried to block out all the pictures—EJ kissing Dad, Jesse kissing Sergio. I tried counting zebras like I used to when I couldn't sleep. Sheep had always freaked me when I was as a kid with their big woolly heads. One zebra, two zebras, three zebras—Dad riding a zebra—EJ chasing a zebra. I gave up until sleep finally came and clobbered me a good one.

Coach and I sat at the same picnic table where I'd first met him back at the beginning of the summer. Now the worst summer of my life was almost over. And instead of pigging out on candy bars, I was eating an endurance bar that tasted like a stale iron-flavored brownie. After our swim, though, it tasted pretty damn good. I twisted the cap off the mayonnaise jar and took a big swig of the tap water from Coach's kitchen. I wondered how long it had been since tap water had even passed my Dad's lips.

"How's your ankle doing?" he asked.

"What ankle?" I said with a shrug.

"Don't be a smart. How's your ankle?"

"It's fine, really. I can do some more—let's go."

"Nope. Not today. Go on back to the house and get it up on ice. I'm going to finish my swim. When I get back, I'll put some more stim on it for a while."

"C'mon, Coach! Please?"

"What's it to you, anyway? You're not racing next week. Take it easy, kid."

I tried to shake some water out of my ear. "Maybe I want to race next week."

He turned to give me a long look. "You decided to go back to your dad's?"

"No."

"You planning on renting yourself a bachelor pad, maybe, and paying for it with your good looks?"

I shook my head and swallowed down the rest of my bar. Tried to think of the most convincing way to say it. "I'll just go ahead and stay with you," I said, nodding, like I'd finally made up my mind.

He turned to face me. "No, you won't."

I stared back. "Yes, I will."

He gave me one of those rusty grins of his that would scare most kids. "You're a piece of work, Alastair." He stood up and dropped over in a forward bend to stretch.

"You've got to agree with me. It would be very bad for my character to drop out of this race."

"Cut the crap, kid. You don't give a gnat's ass about your character."

"I do care about the race, Coach, I'm serious." And the funny thing was, it was true. After flipping and flopping all night long in bed like a beached fish, I realized that swimming had become very important to me. And as much as I wanted to leave Lumina Beach, I really wanted to do the race. My body was geared for it. I *needed* to do the race. I felt like it was the only thing that would release me from all of this.

"I didn't jump off the ski lift because I was scared," I confessed to his backside.

"Yeah?" was all he said, still bent.

"I jumped because I'd just seen my dad's boss in his bed. She was kissing him." The truth slithered right out of me like a snake. I put my head down.

Coach grunted, and that was the only sound except for the waves crashing in.

"She knew I saw them. He didn't. She gave me a hundred bucks to keep my mouth shut. And somehow that made me guilty too. So I jumped—it was all I knew how to do to get away from them both. Somehow if I'd gone all the way to the top, where they were waiting, it would be like the deal was sealed."

Coach straightened up but still didn't turn around to look at me. I took a big, deep shaky breath.

He turned finally and eased himself back down on the table next to me. We both just stared straight ahead.

"Parents really screw up sometimes, kid. I've done my share."

"You have kids?" I asked. For some reason, I couldn't imagine him married or changing diapers or anything.

He snorted. "Not exactly kids anymore. I got a daughter, a son. Heck, they're practically elderly now."

"Where are they?"

He lifted his shoulders and then dropped them. "My ex-wife left with my daughter a long time ago."

"Why'd they leave?"

He shook his head. "Beats the hell out of me. I tried to do what I thought I was supposed to do. I guess I just don't understand little girls or grown women. I was raised by my dad and only had a brother."

"Did you ever think about trying to find your daughter?" I asked.

"No point. She could find me if she wanted. I've been here the whole time."

"Where's your son? Did he go with them or stay with you?"

"He stayed with me. For a while. I finally let him go when he was sixteen. His mother had ruined him and I couldn't fix it."

"Did you ever see him again?" I asked.

"Yeah. But I don't claim him and he doesn't claim me. End of story."

Coach spit into his goggles. "I'll tell you what. You can stay with me until the race, but there are two conditions."

Relief rushed through me. "Really? I mean, sure! What are they?"

"Get rid of the black hair. Buzz your head or dye it back to the regular color. You look like a punk."

I nodded. "No problem, Coach. I can do that."

"Second, you've got to get your dad to stop harassing the locals about using the stairs. Get him to agree to share access the way it's supposed to be."

"Did you hear what I just told you? The man is a maggot. I don't want to see him or talk to him."

"Have it your way, then. Now get on back to the house and get the ice on. When you're done, call Skyla and make your arrangements with her to pick you up."

He stood up and pulled his cap back on. Shook out his legs and started back toward the water.

"Wait! How about if I get Skyla to agree to talk to him about the stairs? Can I stay then?"

"Is that how you want to go through life solving things? Sending Mommy to fix things for you?"

"She's not my MOMMY!" I said, my voice getting shrill.

"Then don't act like you need one. If you really wanted to race, wanted it bad enough, we wouldn't be having this conversation. Per usual, you're still looking for easy street. Kids," he said, muttering as he moved down the sand.

"Bastard," I muttered back.

CHAPTER TWENTY-EIGHT

MY CELL PHONE RANG, AND I pulled one hand out of soapy water and fished into my shorts pocket for it. Ian had found it where I hurled it off the balcony. Being on a cell was one of Aunt Clem and Skyla's conditions for letting me stay at Coach's. They wanted to be able to have complete access to me around the clock. Whatever.

"H'lo," I mumbled. A warm trickle of water ran down the underside of my arm.

"Hey, gorgeous!" Jesse cooed into my ear. "How *are* you? God! We haven't talked in ages."

Blood pounded in my head and I took a deep breath. "I'm great!" I said, trying to sound like I was having the time of my life washing up Coach's dishes.

"I'm just back. I didn't think we'd ever finish filming. It was such a drag! It kept raining, so we couldn't shoot the final sequence. I thought I might die of boredom."

Apparently, her version of boredom included snuggling over lattes.

"I kept trying to call you," I said. "I started worrying you weren't going to get back in time for the race."

"I know! Wasn't that gruesome? No cell service for days. Anyway, I called Aunt Skyla's to get you and she said you weren't staying there.

You're at your coach's? What is going on, Stump? She said I'd have to ask you that."

"Nothing, really. I just wanted to spend my last week focusing on swimming completely. Coach is working me day and night." Well, chores, mostly. Dishes, mopping floors, mowing his lawn.

"Wow!" she said. "You must be in fabulous shape. I'm so jealous."

I looked down at my gut, which wasn't really there anymore. It was brown, flat, and taut.

"I want to see you!" she said. "Are you busy right now?"

"Um, not really—" I lied. I promised Coach I'd help him stain his back deck today.

"I really need to work out. Come with me, will you? We can go use the gym at your Dad's office. I've got a key, in case he isn't there yet. Can you meet me at ten?"

My guts started churning. Man, I did not want to see him. But I wanted to see her bad. Even still. Maybe she and Sergio had broken up. Maybe it was a fake picture that someone had rigged up. Maybe she'd been missing me. Maybe I wasn't mad at her anymore.

"Sure—" I said. "How will I recognize you? It's been so long."

She giggled and my knees nearly gave out. "Meanie."

My luck was running like gold today. Jesse was back, she was dying to see me, and Dad's car wasn't out front. I'd be able to get in at least without having to see him. I did need to talk to him soon, though. I had to get him to agree about the stairs. I wasn't sure how I was going to pull that off. Well, I had an idea, but it wasn't pretty.

The front door was open and I eased myself in, quiet as a cat in case Dad was lurking here somewhere. I wheeled Coach's bike inside so no one would take it. I'd put some serious miles on it getting ready for the race.

I turned, then jumped at the site of Dad's giant pearly whites smiling down from his portrait on the wall. I wished I had the nerve to grab a marker from the desk and black out a few of his teeth, maybe add a really hairy mole on his face. But since I wasn't actually in junior high anymore, I just cursed him as I walked by the picture.

I made my way up to the gym on the third floor. Tried to calm myself and did a quick breath check into my hand. Nearly knocked myself over with the fumes of an entire pack of breath mints I'd inhaled on the way over.

Jesse was already there on the treadmill, running at full clip. She didn't see me, so I had a minute to just soak up the sight of her. She had her hair up in a ponytail, and I could see the sweat running down into her sports bra—which was drenched already. I loved a girl who could really sweat.

I walked around to the front of the treadmill and waved. She pulled out her earphone and gave me one of her giant real-girl smiles that I loved. Not a fake Savannah smile. Her whole face got into it. She shouted over the noise of the machine. "Oh-my-God! Love your HAIR! They told me you dyed it, but they didn't tell me you shaved your head."

I ran a quick hand over it. I didn't have the cash to have it dyed back—and I wasn't about to ask Dad to pay for it. Coach shaved my head for free. Can't remember when I saw him look so happy about anything.

She nodded over at the treadmill next to her. "Hop on! I've got fifteen more minutes. Then you owe me a big hug."

I looked over the treadmill and at the massive control panel.

Jesse's was all lit up like it was about ready to launch. I wondered for a second if I could fake it. I saw a dog on TV once that could do it. It couldn't be that hard. I stepped on it and grabbed the handles. Tried to find the go button.

"Hey, Jesse!" I yelled over. "Where's the puree button?"

She laughed with delight and toweled off her face. "Try program three! That's what I'm doing. It's great!"

I stepped up onto it, pretended to be stretching my calf and then my neck while I read the directions as fast as I could manage. *Press on . . . choose program . . . choose speed . . . choose incline . . .*

I pressed on and the belt took off under me and I nearly did a split. Jesse laughed again and said, "You clown!"

So I kept clowning around because I never wanted her to stop laughing, and by the time my goofus act had gotten old, I'd actually gotten the hang of the thing.

Jesse was singing under her breath to the tunes on her iPod. I could hear the bass

beat coming from it and before I knew it, I had adjusted my stride to it. I looked out the window at the Pacific Ocean spread out before us. It was like the view from my old room at Skyla's, only better because Jesse was next to me and we were running together, like in slow motion off into the horizon. It was very romantic. I stole a glance at her and she looked at me too. She shot me a grin. Right through my heart. Man, any hope I'd had that I was over my crush was a giant delusion.

"You wanna swim while you're here?" she yelled, nodding toward the pool below us.

"Nah," I said, trying not to sound too winded. "I'm-going-out-with-Coach-later," I huffed.

After a bit, her treadmill began slowing down and she mopped at her face with her towel. "Okay! I'm through! Keep going if you want. I'm going to do some weights."

"I'll be right there!" I said optimistically, hoping to be able to get the thing to stop sometime today.

Jesse went into the ladies' room, so I took a moment to towel myself off and get ready for our reunion hug. I hoped she could still smell the cologne I'd put on. Aunt Clem had given it to me, and I sure hoped to God like it wasn't lesbian perfume. But it smelled pretty good.

Music came on overhead and I looked around. Just in time to see Dad coming through the door. He looked very surprised to see me.

I licked my lips. "Hey," I said.

He put his hands on his hips. "Hi. You come over with Jesse?"

I nodded.

"You cut your hair," he said.

I shrugged. "Better for swimming."

Jesse came back in, twisting her hair back up in a knot. "Oh, great! You're both here! Hi, Rick!" She went over and gave him a quick kiss on the cheek and then gave me a big squeeze and the same quick kiss on the cheek. My lips nearly died of disappointment. Of course, she couldn't really lay a big one on me in front of Dad. But why did he have to show up just then?

"I need to talk to both of you, so this is perfect!" she cooed.

"What's up?" Dad asked.

"Well, it's about the race. Sergio just called me and said that his brother, Philip, who was supposed to be our alternate in the race, crashed on his mountain bike this weekend. He's broken his clavicle and a few ribs. So, we need a new alternate for our team. I mean, we probably won't use one at all, but we need to have somebody just in case. That way if one of us needs to drop out, the team still has a shot."

"You mean if one of the racers gets fatigued or in some kind of trouble, you can put in a fresh player in the middle of the race?" Dad asked.

Jesse nodded. "That's right. But if you use your alternate and win, they take off ten thousand dollars from the prize. That's to keep people from using their backup guy without a good reason."

I started getting a bad feeling about where this all might be headed.

"Would you be interested, Rick?" Jesse asked, sidling up to him. "I know it's late notice, but you're the only other person I can think of that could probably whip out an Adventure Race without training for it. You're like Mr. Fitness USA." I watched as she gave him total girl eyes.

"Aren't you racing in the teen division? Can you use an adult alternate?" he asked.

"Yeah, Philip was over twenty-one," she said. "We *have* to have an adult as our alternate. It's an insurance requirement for the race. They don't want any of us kids getting lost or mangled over on Adventure Island. It would be bad for the show."

Then she flashed a look over at me. "But it's got to be cool with you both. Stump? What do you think? Would that be okay with you if your dad was on our team?" She looked from one of us to the other.

Dad shrugged. "It's up to Alastair. His call."

Then she turned the girl eyes on me. When I didn't answer right away, she turned up the power a notch.

"Doesn't matter to me one way or another," I said. "I won't need an alternate."

She grabbed us both around the neck and whooped. "Woo-hoo! This is going to be such a blast! A real family affair."

Dad and I both pulled away at the same time. He looked as uncomfortable as I did.

"Oh! And guess what?" she said, her excitement mounting even further. "I was talking to Aunt Skyla about what might be a good charity to race for. We have to pick by Monday. Sergio thought we should race for the Screen Actors Guild retirement fund, but I don't know, that seems a little self-serving. Anyway, she suggested the Challenged Athletes Foundation. Isn't that a great idea? And here's the best part. She says if our team races for them and we win, she'll match the pot and throw in another fifty thousand dollars! Isn't that cool?"

"I'm all for that," Dad said.

"Stump? What do you think?" she asked.

I shrugged. "We can race for whoever you want—paraplegics, prairie dogs, death row inmates. Makes no difference to me. I'm just there to get the job done."

And with that, I left them in my wake.

CHAPTER TWENTY-NINE

I SLEPT, IF YOU CAN call it that, with one eye propped open, watching the clock make its trek around to 4:00 a.m. I was freaked out about oversleeping and Dad jumping in and taking my place in the race. Wouldn't have put it past him to slip me a sleeping pill in my soda last night at the Adventure Race Kickoff Dinner. It was at this fancy joint in Hollywood, and all the teams from the shows were there. And about a million celebrities. Dad looked like he'd died and gone to heaven. He was so busy trying to charm the pants off everyone that I don't know if he ever even got to eat. I got kissed and squeezed and patted on the butt by everyone. After a while, Skyla came over and stood guard over me. She didn't say that, but I knew what she was doing. I had to admit I was happy to see her. I'd missed her. Wow. Who would have thought?

It was 3:43 a.m. I could hear Coach moving around down the hall. Guess he didn't want me to oversleep either. He was driving me up to Vedanta Beach, where the race started. He wasn't saying so, I but I knew he was keyed up about the whole thing. He'd said last night he wouldn't mind having his morning workout up the coast for a change. No big deal. Wasn't doing anything else anyway. Right, no big deal. Saved me having to ride up with Sergio and Jesse or, even worse, Dad.

I threw the covers off and stretched my legs. Coach hadn't let me swim for the last three days, so I was feeling pretty good. He wanted me fresh and raring to go.

My cell phone chirped and I grabbed it off the nightstand. A text message had come in. It was from Jesse.

c u ther. dun b l8. al grlz on our sho r n luv w u. bt u luv me best, rght?

Did I love her best? I shook my head. I wondered if she sent the same message to Sergio. I hesitated a second, then tapped in a reply. *c u ther.* I needed to stay focused.

Coach rapped on the door. "You up?" he asked. He opened the door before I had a chance to get it. "Let me take a look at your ankle."

I sat back down on the bed and he squatted down in front of me. He rotated my ankle in a circle, then flexed it back and forth, watching my face. "Feel okay?"

"Fine," I lied, just a little. It still stung a bit, but it was race day. I was going to tough it out.

"Okay, he said, giving it a thwack, still watching my face. "Breakfast in twenty minutes, then we're on the road."

I held my expression until he left, then grimaced and rubbed my ankle. Took a long, deep breath. It was showtime.

It was still dark when we hit the road, and we got to watch the sun come up. The water was still and glass-like. Coach said we lucked out and had the perfect day for the race.

He shoved a jar of water toward me. "I want you to finish this before we get there. You need to be good and hydrated."

I took a big swig, though I thought I might spew it back up. My stomach was getting nervous.

"Did you talk to your dad last night at the dinner?" he asked.

"Nope, not much," I said. "He was pretty busy schmoozing all the producers."

"You don't give him much of a break, do you?"

"Why should I?" I said, watching a pelican drop into a high dive.

"There are always two sides to everything, Alastair. The sooner you figure that out, the better off in life you'll be."

"I see both sides. That's the problem."

"No, you don't. You just think you do."

"Do you understand why your wife left you?" I asked.

He looked over at me sharply. "Yeah. She thought I was too hard on the kids."

"Were you?"

"Probably. Thought I was doing the right thing at the time."

"So, who *was* right?"

He just shook his head. "That doesn't matter anymore." He turned to look at me.

"That much I learned."

"Did you ever cheat on your wife?" I blurted.

"Excuse me?"

"Sorry," I muttered.

Coach's face looked gray in the early light. "Look, there's all kinds of ways that husbands and wives cheat on each other. Having an affair is just one. I never did that, but I put my work and sports before everything. That's kind of cheating on your family too."

I chewed on that awhile. Took some more long drinks of water. "Do you ever think about trying to fix things up with your kids?" I asked.

"Yeah, I think about that every day," he said. He turned to look at me. "How about you?"

"What about me? "

"You think about trying to fix things up with your dad?"

"There's no 'Dad' to fix. Just a pretty face."

"Can't see past that, can you?"

"Nothing to see, Coach. Believe me. I know."

"Yeah, I forgot. The world according to Alastair."

We stopped talking then and just let the miles fill the air between us.

I finally broke the silence. Figured anything was fair game at this point. "Did you really throw a social worker lady in the pool in front of all the kids?"

He barked a dry brittle laugh. Put his hand over his heart like the effort hurt him. "That old story still going around?"

"Well, did you?"

"Of course not. Do I look stupid? But when people start seeing you in a certain way, they have a way of making everything else fit with their picture. Whether it goes there or not. She fell in the pool, Alastair. Came out to talk to me in these fool high heels and with her mind already made up about me. She tripped right over her own feet. I tried to grab her, and the rest is Lumina Beach folktale. Nobody considered that maybe there was another side to it. All they saw was a fully dressed lady in the pool and me standing there watching it all. Small minds jump to the nearest-possible conclusion. You ought to watch out for that, kid. A mistake like that can change a whole life."

CHAPTER THIRTY

EVEN THOUGH IT WAS BARELY 7:00 a.m., there was a crowd of die-hard soap fans mobbed up behind barriers when we pulled in. Big speakers blared music, and workers were hurriedly putting up tents and banners.

"Over there." I pointed to a tent with a large *Splendor Town* sign over it. "Jesse said to just pull up front and someone would take our car and park it."

"I don't need anybody parking my car," Coach said. "I'll drop you off, though." He looked over at the water jar and said, "Bottoms up."

I took a last swig and wiped my mouth on my arm. I grabbed my race bag from the floor and hoped I'd remembered everything I needed. I took a quick swipe through it.

Wet suit, goggles, cap, bike shoes, socks, shorts. Some gel packets. I looked over at Coach as he pulled up in front of the tent. All of a sudden I felt like a five-year-old arriving for the first day of kindergarten. I licked my lips. "Are you going swimming now?" I asked.

He shrugged. "Why?"

"I just thought maybe you could hang out until I take off. You know, if you want to. No big deal," I said, ducking my head to hide my embarrassment.

"Sure, I'll stick around a bit. Make sure you get a good stretch before you get in the water."

Relief rushed through me and I jerked the door handle open. "Okay! See you in a minute."

I walked past the fans on the way to the tent, and teenage girls and middle-aged women started squealing and whispering about me. Well, barely whispering.

"Oh, he's cute!"

"I think he's from *Now and Ever*—you know, that kid that was on the sailboat with Bella?"

"Hey, there! Can we have your autograph?"

Just for the heck of it, I went over to one large woman waving a small book. I took her pen and scribbled my name, then dad's cell phone number. I gave her the flirtiest look I could muster at this hour and then hurried away.

"Alastair! Over here," Dad called. He waved me past security into the tent.

Jesse and Sergio were bent over forms, and Dad motioned me over. "We need to get you signed in and legal."

Jesse came over and gave me a big squeeze. Sergio gave me a hug too and then clapped me on my back. "You ready to rock and roll?"

"Been ready all my life," I said, trying for the coolest voice I could dig up. He gave me a blinding white smile. He smelled really good. Even better than Jesse. And his abs made mine look like a kitten's belly.

I leaned over the form and hurriedly filled out my full name, birth date, age on race day, and address at Coach's. I also put him down as the person to contact in case of emergency. Signed my name with a big flourish and then paused at the part that had to be filled out by my legal guardian.

I looked up to see where Dad was and predictably, he was in the corner of the tent trying to charm someone. I took it over and thrust it at him. "You need to sign this."

He gave me a nod and read it quickly. He hesitated just a moment, then signed on the bottom line.

"Thanks," I mumbled.

I took the form back to Jesse and Sergio. Their production assistant from the show, Hans, was there. "Great, thanks," he said. "Now, let's see." He consulted his clipboard. "I've got yours, Jesse's, Sergio's, and Rick's. I'll go turn these in to the officials. They're briefing the teams in twenty minutes down by the kayaks. Don't be late!"

Jesse put a hand on my shoulder for balance, then folded her calf behind her to stretch. "I've tried bribing everyone I know to find out what the obstacle course is going to be like," she complained. "But the course info has been seriously hush-hush."

"I don't want to know beforehand," Sergio said. "It's more exiting this way. I'm ready for whatever they've got for us. How about you, Stump?"

"I got the full scoop last night," I said, making it up on the fly. "I was talking to one of the guys on the setup team. He'd been out on the island all yesterday afternoon. He'd had a few drinks, and I got it out of him. But I swore I wouldn't tell anyone."

Jesse pounced on me and threw me into a headlock. "Tell me now or die."

I peeled her off me. "No way."

She put her hands on her hips and gave me one of her famous

sex kitten Savannah looks. "I could make it worth your while," she purred.

I took a look at Sergio, but he just laughed. Didn't seem the least bit jealous, which really ticked me off. Like he didn't consider me any competition.

"Okay, make it worth my while," I said boldly. I closed my eyes and pointed to my lips. "Right here."

A pair of soft lips landed on mine, and my heart thumped.

"Serg-i-o!" Jesse screamed. "He meant me, not YOU!"

My eyes flew open and Sergio grinned at me from about two inches from my face.

He laughed as Jesse swatted him. "Oh-h-h! You wanted Jesse to kiss you, Stump? My mistake!"

My face blazed and it was all I could do not to wipe my mouth off, but I wouldn't give him the satisfaction.

"Might want to give that some work," I said, my voice flip. "Have to tell you that I've had better." I spied Coach in the tent opening. "I'll catch up with you two outside."

"Wait!" Jesse called after me. "You didn't tell us what you found out."

I turned back. "I was only kidding. I don't really know anything."

"You big tease!" She laughed.

I hitched my bag over my shoulder and caught up with Coach. "We're meeting down at the kayaks in a few minutes. Let's go."

"Who was that guy in there that just planted one on you?" he asked when we got a ways down from the tent.

"My teammate, Sergio. He's such a jerk."

"Doesn't sound like a promising start. You two better get over whatever it is between you. And quick. You're going to be out in the ocean together. There's no room for hotheads. Is this about *the girl?*"

"Doesn't matter what it's about. I'm out of here in just a few more days," I said, though I couldn't imagine not seeing Jesse again except on television.

"Don't forget about our deal, kid. You promised me to get your dad to back off about the stairs."

"I will! I already told you I would."

"I've got your plane ticket, you know," he said. "You're not getting it until I see a welcome mat out next to your dad's. And if you don't talk to him, I'm afraid it's going to get ugly."

"Why? What do you mean?" I asked.

"The entire swimming and surfing community for a fifty-mile radius is planning a demonstration."

"A demonstration of what?"

"A demonstration of our rights as citizens to peacefully assemble and march—on the public stairs daily until he backs off. If he thinks having an occasional person walking up and down them is a loss of privacy, just wait until he gets a load of us marching up and down them for hours. A lot of us, too, are retired coaches and teachers. We have really loud whistles. We'll keep it up as long as it takes. Be good exercise for us."

"He's going to go out of his mind," I said, and for some reason that didn't make me as happy as it should. And it made me feel bad for Skyla. She didn't want any trouble with the locals, I knew.

"OKAY, TEAMS, EVERYBODY GATHER AROUND!"

The sound of the bullhorn made me jump, and Coach grabbed my shoulders and gave them a painful squeeze. "Save all that for your swim."

Wet suits of all sizes and colors gathered. Jesse, Sergio, and Dad jogged across the sand to where we stood. Hans followed in their wake with a phone plugged to his head.

"Okay, okay, everyone, settle down!" Mr. Bullhorn said. "We're going to let the

E! TV cameras join us in a minute, but I want to go over some things with everybody first. I need all the team captains to come stand up here with me."

Sergio flashed us a smile and went over to the announcer. Team captain? Figures.

"All right, listen up!" the bullhorn continued. "We've got eight teams." He consulted his list and read through it fast. "Captains, report in when I call your name!"

"*Now and Ever!*"

"Ready!" the team yelled in chorus, and whooped.

"*Chicago Central!*"

Their buffed captain snorted and pawed at the sand.

"*Lost in Love!*"

Their captain was a girl, and she beat on her chest and gave a Tarzan yell.

Jesse elbowed me and said, "Stay away from Sasha. She'd eat you as an appetizer."

"*Splendor Town!*" he called next.

Sergio curled his biceps, struck a dumb pose, and said, "Come and get us!"

"*Sunset Cove!*"

Their captain threw his head back and howled.

"*Miami Loves!*"

"All present and accounted for and ready to kick some celebrity booty!"

"Rodeo Drive!"

"HERE!"

"And our newest soap on the block that is running away with the ratings," he blared, *"Reality Soap!"* The whole team threw themselves on their knees and mimed like they were ready for a firing squad. The crowd booed and hissed.

Jesse shouted into my ear, "People hate them because the show makes fun of soaps. I think they're hilarious!"

"All right, settle down now, folks!" the announcer boomed. "Let's remember this is for fun and charity. We don't want anyone getting hurt. There are no losers today. You're all winners by volunteering to participate. Remember, the winning team gets fifty thousand dollars donated to the charity of their choice. Second-place team gets twenty-five thousand dollars. He lowered his voice an octave and whispered deeply into the horn. "And the last team in, folks—he paused for dramatic effect—"last team to finish donates one week's salary to the winning team's favorite charity." Everyone howled and booed at that.

"Listen up! In just a minute, I'll meet with all the captains and give them the course maps and a list of the official rules. But I want to go over a couple of things together. While on the course, your alternates carry the show's flag. This is to help keep you all in sight of one another. Remember, all three members of the team must stay within one hundred yards of one another at all times. It serves no purpose to get ahead of your own teammates. Does everyone understand that? We want you working together, helping each other. If an official sees your team all spread out, you'll be d'qued."

"What's 'd'qued'?" I whispered.

Coach leaned over. "Disqualified."

Bullhorn continued. "Only the team captain can bench a racer and call the alternate in. If your captain benches you, you are OUT. Get off the course and flag down an official for transport back in. They're the ones in the bright orange vests. Everyone got that?"

"YE-E-S-S!" the group shouted.

"Okay! The *Orca* leaves in thirty minutes from the dock," he said, pointing behind him. "Last chance to use the facilities and call your mommies, your agents, your attorneys. I'll meet with the captains now and they can brief you on the ride out. It will take about an hour to get to the starting buoy for the ocean swim." He paused, pressed his lips around the bullhorn, and gave a maniacal chuckle. "Oh, have we—got—some—wicked—fun—in store for you folks. You people ready to PARTYYYY??"

As the racers screamed and kicked up sand, and me right there in the midst of them, I decided that I was in way, way over my head.

CHAPTER THIRTY-ONE

WE WERE ALL HERDED TO the harbor, where we would board the
Orca. The team from *Miami Loves* got there first, and their captain
had them drop down and do push-ups. They looked dead serious, and
when they finished their push-ups, they pulled on their wet suits like
they were suiting up for surgery. I pulled on my wet suit like I was
dressing for my own funeral. Dad put his on, "just in case" he needed
to be called in.

Not on my account, I vowed.

Coach stood talking to Hans and a couple of the race officials who
were on walkie-talkies. He had his hands on his hips, and he looked
unhappy. He shook his head and spit off the dock.

I watched Jesse pull on her wet suit and tie up her hair in a tight knot on
top of her head. She yanked on her cap and grinned at me. Our team had
yellow caps. *Miami* would be in orange. That was who I had to watch for,
Sergio told me. He was bent over in half, his tiny celebrity butt sticking up
in the air, stretching. I had a brief fantasy of giving him just a gentle little
push over off the side. But he was holding our race instructions in one
hand, and I didn't want those getting wet. They were sealed, and none of
the captains could read them to the team until we hit the open water.

Now Coach was yelling and waving his hands at the officials. Uh-
oh. This couldn't be good.

"What do you think is going on over there?" Jesse asked, looking at me and Dad.

I shrugged. Dad capped his Chapstick and headed over that way with his shiny lips.

"Do you think he gets his chest hairs waxed?" I asked, watching Jesse bend over to one side like a ballerina.

"Of course!" Sergio butted in. "Chest hair is so out." He rubbed a hand over his own.

"Clean as a baby's bottom," he said with a grin toward Jesse. "Want to feel?"

"Get over yourself, Soap Boy," she said.

I darted a glance at the two of them. There was some bad mojo flowing between them, but I wasn't sure what it was about. He'd been everywhere but Jesse's side last night at the banquet, and I'd caught her giving him some heated looks. A very skinny blonde with stick-straight hair was never far from his side. I just hoped it meant that Jesse had come to her senses. Since they'd been back from location, I'd dropped a bunch of hints to try to get her to talk about them—I even tried to make a joke about the picture I'd seen of them. She'd just gotten all tight-faced about it and changed the subject.

Whatever it was, I wanted to believe it meant that it was over between them. If it had ever even started. Hard to tell with these Hollywood people. Nothing was ever as it seemed. About the only person in the whole town that seemed to be straight up was Skyla. She was who she was. Didn't try to be anything else. Didn't try to hide anything. Too bad she married my dad. He was going to break her heart one of these days. I just knew it.

Coach came storming back, muttering under his breath.

"Hey!" I said when he passed me right by. "What's going on?"

"Those damn fools don't know anything about swimming." He waved his arm at the ocean. "This is not the lap pool at the Bel-Air County Club. Anything could happen out there. You've got twenty-four people ready to race, some just kids, and they've got two—just *two*—support people out in the water. It's not safe." He turned on his heel and took off, muttering to himself.

"So, are you leaving?" I said, hurrying after him.

"No! I'm going to get my stuff! I told that fool race official that he needed two more people out in the water. He said he didn't have anybody else. One guy called in sick, and it was too late to replace him. So, I'm going out. If this isn't the damndest thing I ever heard of. I just hope to god everybody can swim."

"RACERS! IN THE BOATS!" came the call from the bullhorn.

"*Splendor Town!*" Sergio hooted. "Let's shove off!"

The *Orca* was a big, fast boat that ate up the channel waters between Vedanta Beach and Santa Therese Island, where the course was. I would have been happy to have a nice, slow boat. Man, I was not in a big hurry to get into the water. Coach still looked mad as hell about everything, except when he discovered one of the other two lifeguard guys was Kiki. He gave a short grunt that meant he was pleased, but he didn't necessarily want that to get around.

The teams all huddled together in small groups the minute the boat launched, and the captains pulled out the instruction sheets.

I read over Sergio's shoulder while he read aloud.

"Okay, here we go," he said, clearing his throat. "First off is the half-mile swim, which we already know about. Piece of cake, right, team?" he asked with a cheerful grin.

"Would you please just keep reading, Sergio!" Jesse said.

"All right—during the swim, the alternates will be given a boogie board and will follow us in the water with the team flag. Rick, you have to make sure we all stay together and don't get off course. Got that?" he asked. "Oh, and it says if any of the swimmers get into any kind of trouble, you need to raise the flag over your head and wave it big and wide."

"Got it!" Dad said.

"Let's see. Once we hit the shore, we'll see a transition area with a big sign with each of our team's names. And there will be mountain bikes for all of us. Cool! All our stuff will be there already, so we can change out of our wet suits, but we've got to be fast. No time to stop and blow-dry your hair, Jesse," he teased. "You either, Rick."

Dad ignored the joke. "Once I see you're all almost near the shore, I'll ride in real quick and get your stuff organized."

"Right," Sergio said. "Great, Rick. Okay, next is the bike ride— just a short one—thirteen miles. Some hills, but easy squeezy. And there will be race officials all along the way. Looks like we've got a couple of water crossings to do, and it says something about a cargo net crossing."

"What's a cargo net?" Jesse asked.

I jumped in. "One of those big old scratchy nets you see on old ships that they used to use to lift and unload stuff. Now they have forklifts, so they don't really use them much."

"What else does it say?" Dad asked.

"Just that riders have to get themselves and their bikes under the net," Sergio said. "How hard can that be?" he said with a shrug.

"What comes after the bike?" I asked. I was getting impatient with Sergio and trying to eavesdrop on the other teams, but everyone was whispering and being very private about their instruction sheet. Like it was a treasure map or something. Jeez.

"After we finish the bike ride, we have another obstacle, probably some kind of climbing." He flashed Dad a look. I caught it and translated it. Or in other words, "Be ready, Rick, we may need to dump Stump there."

What? You don't think a one-legged kid can climb? Just try and bench me, sucker.

Jesse grabbed the sheet from him and scanned over the rest. "Then the last thing is kayaking. We'll have two doubles. The alternates get to paddle too. Unless"—she continued—"unless the alternate is already in as a racer, then we only get three people to spread over both double kayaks."

"That's no problem," Sergio said.

She continued. "Kayaks leave from the rear of the island and then paddle back out to the *Orca*." She looked up from the sheet. "And that's it! First team to reboard is the winner!"

"We need to figure out the kayaks," Sergio said. "I'll take Jesse. Rick, you take Stump. Okay with you guys?" he asked, like an afterthought.

"I say that whoever gets to the kayaks *first* picks their partner," Jesse said.

Sergio looked from me to Jesse and back again. "Well, okay, but I really think we need to have the stronger paddlers with the—"

"With the what?" I asked, thinking I'd like to deck him now and get it over with.

"I mean, well, no offense to anyone here, but clearly Rick and I are going to be the stronger paddlers," he said.

"Well, then, the stronger paddlers better get their butts to the kayaks first, right?" I said.

Things quieted down on the *Orca* after all the teams had a chance to review the instructions. It was a major psych-out to be sitting in the boat with all these buffed-out celebrities and their jock-a-lot teammates. I looked like about the youngest one, though there were two other girls about Jesse's age that kept staring at me. They were both from the *Lost in Love* team. Man, as soon as I got back to Colorado, I was going to grow my hair out over my face again. But I didn't think I wanted to grow my old potbelly back. I liked having a hard center. Made me feel like I could handle just about anything. I'd never felt so healthy and strong in my whole life.

Except for the fact that I was getting seasick. At least that was what I thought it was. Or maybe it was a bad case of nerves, but I really wanted to throw up. I caught Coach giving me a look now and then, and I gave him a thumbs-up. Last thing I needed was him coming over and making a big deal about it.

"Okay, listen, everyone!" one of the race officials yelled. "We're approaching the swim course. Lifeguards, we'll drop your kayaks off the back. Alternates, grab one of the boogie boards and get off with your team. Stay on the far side of the swimmers so you don't block anyone."

Coach, Kiki, and some lady with gnarly biceps stood up. Oh, boy, Aunt Clem would probably go for her in a big way.

The official pointed to them. "Any of you racers get into trouble, you let these people know. I want everyone watching everyone's back, you hear me? This is not the Ironman. This is a *fun* charity race.

Take it easy. I don't want to see any of you swimming over the top of anybody. Any questions? Now or never!"

It was quiet as a church.

"One last thing. We've got two kayaks out there with cameras filming this. They've got green KNBC life vests on. They've been told to keep their distance from the swimmers. Lifeguards, if you see any of those hotdogs getting too close, I want you to get over and make them move. We'll try to keep an eye on them too. You got me? And if you see anybody else out there on the course, I want them out of there. We've promised the soap mags we'll get them photos and film. But we don't need problems with paparazzi today."

"Got ya!" Kiki shouted as he pulled his lifeguard vest on.

The *Orca*'s engine quieted and we slowed down. Some knarly old guy in the back dropped anchor.

Coach motioned me over before he climbed down the ladder. "Keep your head out there. Don't worry about anyone else and how fast they're going. Follow your breath. Just keep it slow and easy. Got it?"

I nodded and pulled off my leg. I handed it to Coach. "Can you get this out to the island for me?"

"Sure, kid." He gave me a slap on the back, then, he, Kiki, and Ms. Biceps took their paddles and went over the back.

"Gather around, teams, if you can't see from where you're at," the official said from the front of the boat. "Look, we're starting here at this buoy," he said, pointing. "I want you to follow the buoys in and beach between two blue flags. It's kind of overcast, so you can't see them right now. I don't want you coming out of the water anyplace else. You got that?"

"Got it!" teams yelled.

"You get out of the water anywhere else and you're not going to have a bike to get on. Does everyone have some kind of aqua socks on? There could be some rocks on your way in." He looked at the stopwatch hanging around his neck.

"Okay, teams, let's go! Alternates, grab your boogie boards and flags. Line up as I call you. Once you are in the water, swim over to the first buoy and hold tight a sec. We are—" he said, checking his stopwatch, "T minus three minutes. Let's move it out!"

CHAPTER THIRTY-TWO

SERGiO DROPPED iN FiRST, THEN Jesse, then me. Dad came behind us on his boogie board. The water bit me hard with icy jaws, but I was damn glad to get out off that boat. We all paddled over to the first buoy, where *Miami Loves* were huddled. And not leaving us any room.

"Here, hang on to my board," Dad said, circling us. "Save your strength for the swim."

Jesse adjusted her goggles and shivered. "This water has got to be ten degrees colder than Lumina Beach!"

"Ten?" Sergio asked. "I'd say twenty! So, let's not waste any time once we get going, huh? You guys ready? Jesse? Stump?"

"Just remember you all need to stay together," Dad said, looking at Sergio. "Doesn't do any of you good to get too far ahead."

Another swell lifted me up and over. Ugh. This was almost worse than the boat.

"You okay, Alastair? You getting sick?" Dad asked.

"No!" I lied, and then turned so he couldn't watch me anymore.

Coach pulled up nearby. I give him a weak smile and another thumbs-up. He still looked gray to me. Well, I was feeling green. We were a pair.

"Hurry up, people!" Jesse called. "We're growing icicles out here!"

Within seconds, everyone had hit the water.

"OKAY, TEAMS!" the official called. "Alternates, get on the other side of the swimmers. Racers, you're off in ten—! Nine! Eight!"

"Seven! Six!" the teams chanted.

I pulled my goggle strap tight one last time and took a deep breath. Blew it out hard. My stomach churned like an old washing machine full of stomach acid.

"Three! Two! And you're OFF!"

The *Orca* blasted a horn, and Sergio struck out with Jesse on his tail. I put my face down and headed out after them.

Steady now. Find your rhythm. Coach's voice found its way into my head.

Arms and legs flapped all around me.

Chopping up the water.

Stay calm.

Follow the yellow caps. Lock your sites.

Find your breath. Follow it.

Follow the caps.

Follow Jess.

Ten-four. Anywhere.

A body too close next to me.

Let them get ahead.

A foot kicks my head hard.

I gasp and rear up.

Cough.

Head back down. Can't swim vertical, Coach says.

Steady breath.

On course.

Yellow cap.

She's close.

Back off her a bit.

"C'mon, Jesse!" I heard Dad yell. "Keep it up, son."

He called me "son."

Focus.

Yellow cap next to me.

"Stump!" Jesse's voice.

Pulled my head up.

"Get in front of me."

She's way out of breath. Too early.

Giant swell.

Up and over.

Then another.

"Climb on," I say.

Jesse following me.

Yellow cap in front.

Too fast.

Go ahead.

I'm with Jesse.

Quick look back.

Yellow cap way back.

Dad's got her covered.

Big deep swell lifts me high.

Drops me.

Stomach drops.

Seizes in hard sharp ball.

Up it comes.

Breakfast vomit.

Head up. Cough. Spit. *Gaaack.*

And again.

Little Cheerios on water like life preservers.

Coach's voice. "You're fine, kid! Happens all the time."

Long paddle spoons the barf away.

"You done?"

Nod. "Where is she?" I gasped.

"A ways back. You'll feel better now. Head back down. *Go!*"

Shake it off.

Stroke.

Follow the cap.

Follow the cap.

CHAPTER **THIRTY-THREE**

A CRASHING WAVE DROVE ME the rest of the way in, and I ended up beached on my belly in shallow water. Sergio hauled me up and then pounded me on the back.

"My MAN!" he crowed. He crooked an elbow around my neck.

I did it! I absolutely freaking did it!

"Don't-even-think-about-kissing-me," I heaved with what little breath I had left. I coughed, cleared my nose, and turned to check on Jesse. She was still about fifty yards out, but Dad was right with her. She was moving slow, but she'd make it all right.

"I gotta tell you, I wasn't sure you'd make it, kid," Sergio said, his voice approving.

"Gee, thanks," I said, and leaned over and spit. I looked to see where the orange *Miami Loves* caps were. I counted all three still offshore. Their team captain, Bryce, that Sergio had warned me about, was just now coming in. God, I'd beaten him! Unbelievable. Orange cap number two was almost in, and the third was just barely ahead of Jesse.

"C'mon, let's get you ready, Stump. Here's your stuff." He looked around. "Where's your leg?"

"Oh, man!" I said. "I left it on the boat!" I swore under my breath. "Now, that's gonna hurt us."

"You WHA-AT?" he screamed.

"Kidding! I'm kidding! Lighten up, will you?" I said, smacking him on the shoulder.

I nodded over to Coach in his kayak, who was just beaching now.

He hurried over to me, breathing hard. "Strong work! That's the way the job gets done."

I smiled at him, and then I couldn't help it. I gave him a hug, and he froze like I might explode if he moved so much as a muscle.

I let him go. "Thanks, Coach."

"JESS! JESS! JESS!" Sergio hollered as she came nearer and nearer.

I peeled off my wet suit as fast as I could. My teeth were chattering, and my gut was very glad to be on dry land. I sat down in the sand, covered myself, and pulled my bike shorts on. Put my leg back on. Sergio did his whole change without a towel, just barely turning away from me when he dropped his pants.

"Hey!" I said. "We're being filmed, you know. You want your ass on TV?"

He turned and grinned. "Okay, sure."

I shook my head. What a perv. I pulled a T-shirt over my head. Then dug for my sunglasses and raced over to the water to be there for Jesse.

She was doing the sidestroke now, and Dad was right next to her.

I cupped my hands around my mouth and yelled, "C'mon, Jesse! You're almost home!" Bryce came over, whistled, and clapped for his teammates. "Bring it home, Ashley!"

He turned to me then. "So how'd you lose the leg, kid?"

"Mountain bike race," I said. "Got in a pileup on a descent. My leg got caught in this guy's wheel. I had to cut it off. It was kind of a mess, but I won the race."

Bryce threw back his head and laughed. "Awesome!"

Sergio came up and shoved me my helmet. "Buckle up, kid. Let's be ready so we can pull her out and get her on the bike. She's slowing down, and we're losing seconds." He looked at his watch. "Bring it HOME, babe—" he hollered.

A big wave caught the back of her, Dad, and the last *Miami Loves* swimmer. It brought them in fast and hard. Dad jumped off his board and turned to catch Jesse. All three of us corralled her to the transition area.

"God!" she panted. "Sorry—so—soo——slow—"

"Too many burritos!" Sergio said. "I warned you! C'mon, let's get you on the bike."

"Give her a second, will you?" I snarled. "Are you okay to ride?" I asked her.

She pulled off her cap and nodded. "Think—so. Need—water."

I grabbed a bottle and unscrewed the top. She poured some on her head and then took some long gulps.

"Give me your foot, Jess," Sergio said. She stood flamingo style while he pulled off her aqua socks. Then he pulled the zipper down on the back of her wet suit and pulled the shoulders down.

She shrugged him off. "I can do it!"

She bent over at the waist and dug her fingers into her side. "Damn stitch in my side—won't let up!"

Dad stooped down next to her. "Cough, Jesse—and keep coughing. It'll let up."

"Great idea!" Sergio said. "Let's get you up on the bike, though, and then you can cough all you like." He glanced over at *Miami*, who were all huddled around their last swimmer in.

"Back off, will you?" I said, pissed.

Jesse put her hand out toward all of us, waving us to stop. She hacked out a few big ones and then slipped out of her wet suit. Sergio handed her bike shorts and her tank top, which she put on over her bathing suit.

"Moving out, team!" Sergio yelled, and we all wiggled our cold feet into our bike shoes.

He slapped Jesse's helmet on her head, and she tried to buckle it with frozen fingers. "Here, I'll get it," I said, leaning in close.

"Thanks," she whispered, her voice shivery. She gave me a peck on the cheek.

"Hey, no kissing! This is racing!" Sergio yelled.

Man, the guy had turned into Mr. Testosterone all of a sudden. Do or die!

"Hold up, everyone!" Dad said, stepping in front of the bikes. He was holding some bottles of water. "Quick gear check! Helmets! Sergio, buckle yours. You take off like that and you're going to get disqualified. Water! Everyone good?"

"I'll take another one—" Jesse said.

"How's the cramp?" he asked, jamming the bottle in her water cage.

"I'll be fine!"

"Okay, the course is marked. But Serg—you have the map, right?"

"Check," he said.

"You all need to eat as soon as the course straightens out up here." He handed us each a packet of sports gel and a bar, which we stuffed into the legs of our bike shorts. "I've got bananas, more gel, and the first aid kit. We're good to go!"

Sergio laughed. "I doubt we'll starve to death. The ride is only thirteen miles, Rick! Let's go! Let's go!" He whooped like a crazy man, and we headed off on the dusty path. "Stay close!" he yelled over his shoulder.

We ate up the trail for the first three miles—it was quick and flat, but we were sucking dust the whole time. Don't think the island had seen any rain in a century. I tried to eat my gel, but it was like eating raspberry dirt. I gave up.

I kept an eye on Bryce, who seemed to be riding the whole way with his head turned back to his team. Looked like they had a weak link in the rear, and Bryce was probably trying to decide if and when to dump him.

The course began to climb.

And we climbed some more.

Dad shouted encouragement from his bike. "Jesse, Alastair, get into another gear!"

I downshifted or maybe upshifted—I couldn't remember which was which. My chain caught and fell off. "Damn!" I swung my good leg over the bike before I tumped over.

Jesse turned around, panting. "You okay?"

"Yeah! Go ahead, I'll catch up."

Sergio turned back. "Hurry up, man! We've got bikes crawling up our ass."

Dad dropped down beside me. "Can you get it back on? I'm not allowed to help."

I pulled up the chain.

"If you lift it over this top gear—"

"I can do it!" I said, sounding like a two-year-old, even to me.

He backed off.

I hopped back on, quick as I could and just in time. Barely.

Bryce was on my tail. I managed to get into my small chain ring and motored as fast as I could. Which was pretty fast. I'd been training a decent amount on Coach's bike, and I was surprised how strong my legs were from swimming. He told me not to sweat the bike race or the hiking. Said that whatever the course offered me, I could take it. Plus some. He told me swimmers were the strongest athletes there were because you train your arms, legs, trunk, and lungs.

I was on Jesse's back and hung on while Sergio pulled us through over the top of Mount Everest or whatever it was we were climbing. We crested the top just about the time my chest was going to burst into flames. Jesse spit off the side of her bike.

You gotta love a girl that can spit.

"Heads up, team!" Sergio shouted over his shoulder. "We've got some single track coming up. Stay tight!"

Once we'd gotten to the top, the road disappeared right under my tires. What was left of it was a tiny shelf jutting out from the mountain with a big, long drop down into a canyon. Crap.

"Whoa!" I heard Dad say behind me. "Careful, team!"

The track took a deep dive, and Sergio hollered like a kid on a roller coaster. Jesse hunkered down and blazed after him.

I wiped some sweat out of my eyes and started to descend. It was too fast! I pumped my brakes hard. My bike skidded, lurched, and then slid. I fell over, my foot just catching the ledge. I did a face-plant into a bush. I hung on to my bike as it started to go over the side. I grabbed it and righted it fast as I could. My face burned from being scratched.

I wished to God that Dad wasn't behind me to watch all this.

"Good save!" he called. "Just ease up on the brakes."

I sat back on, trying to jump-start my nerve. I was not going to let Sergio show me up today. I took a deep breath. Up ahead, they'd both stopped to wait for me. I wrapped my fingers around the handlebars and just let the bike do its thing and tried not to fight it.

"Woo-hoooo!" Jesse and Sergio cheered my descent all the way down, and as I neared the bottom, they both got back on and took off.

I took a big slug of water and tried to get my breath back. Up ahead, I could see the trail evened out but got very rocky.

A really tall, pretty girl I'd seen on the boat came up next to me, wrestling her handlebars over some big flat rocks. "Hi! I'm Ashley!" she said.

"Stump," I said in return.

"Man, don't you hate this technical stuff?" she said.

"It's rough!" I agreed.

The next few minutes we all rode with our heads down, navigating as best we could. All of us dumped over a few times and had to carry our bikes over some big boulders.

Sergio turned and pointed at something ahead, but I couldn't hear what he said.

"What was that?" I shouted to Jesse.

"Furry octopus ahead!" she yelled.

Furry octopus? Was she kidding?

I turned to pass it on to Dad. "Watch out for a furry octopus!" I yelled.

"Furry what?" he shouted.

Ashley was still near me, and she laughed. "Furry octopus! I think she said *first obstacle*."

Jesse cursed up ahead. "Shoot! I got a *flat*!"

Sergio stopped his bike and circled back. Dad and I caught up next to them.

Ashley sailed past us. "Later, taters!"

It was a total blowout.

Jesse's hands flew to her seat pack for a new tube. "I'll be quick."

"Leave it," Sergio said. "We'll fix it after the net. Let's get through it quick! Pick up your bike and run!"

Dad and I climbed off our bikes, and we all hefted them onto our shoulders and ran.

Jesse stumbled and fumbled with her bike. She tried hiking it up on her other shoulder. But then changed back when she couldn't control it.

"Let me help you!" I said.

She shook her head. "I got it!"

"Go ahead, Alastair! You and Sergio get started on the net," Dad yelled.

Jess nodded, her face strained. "Go!"

I raced ahead and around the next corner. The road opened up again, and there was the giant net, laid out with stakes driven into each corner. A couple of race officials with clipboards and enormous drink bottles stood nearby, sweating.

The net was about a foot off the ground. We just had to get ourselves and the bike under it. How hard could that be?

Sergio was already on the ground, wriggling himself and the bike under.

I dropped my bike on its side, then slid next to it in the dirt. I lifted the net over us both and copied the shimmy-drag-wriggle that Sergio was doing.

The net pretty much caught on everything. The more I pulled, the stucker I got. Sergio shouted instructions at me as he went through. But I noticed he was getting nowhere fast. Ashley was only inches ahead of him.

"Get behind your bike! Get on your side! Try holding the net up with your foot so you can have both hands!"

"O-kay, I'm h-e-eere!" Jesse shouted. She slipped under the net, dragging her bike with her.

Dad stood at the edge and watched. The alternates weren't allowed under the nets.

"Stump!" Sergio yelled. "What are you doing? Move it!"

"I'm thinking!" I shouted. "There's got to bes a better way."

"He's right, Sergio! Come on, let's think this through, team," Dad said.

"Well, in the meantime, everyone keep *moving*!" Sergio grunted.

"Lighten *up*, Captain!" said Jesse. "We're all doing the best we can!"

"It's a Zen thing, I bet," I said. "We need to be the bike or the bike needs to be us."

"Oh, great!" Sergio said. "Buddha is here to guide us through!"

I crawled over the top of my bike crab style and hovered over it. Okay, I'm being the bike, I thought. Lowered myself a little closer. Sent Coach a mental thank-you for all the grueling bear walk drills at the pool. Gave the bike a shove a few inches forward and went with it. No catches. Tried another few inches. One small catch on the pedal, but I unsnagged it easy.

"I think you've got it, Alastair!" Dad shouted. "Sergio! Jess! Crawl over the top of the bike and drag it under you."

Bryce came tearing toward us. "We got 'em now!" he shouted. "These guys couldn't find their way out of a makeup bag."

"Eat my dirt!" Sergio shouted.

"Hey, Sa-van-nah!" Bryce called. "I brought a little something off the trail for you!"

I turned just in time to see him fling a small snake over onto Jesse. She saw it coming and screamed. Dad hollered, "Interference!"

I dragged myself back to where Jesse was squirming like she was having a seizure.

"I got it!" I yelled, picking it up behind its head. "It's harmless."

Jesse rolled around, batting the net out of her way. "I didn't hurt it, did I? Please tell me I didn't hurt it!"

"*Miami!* You just earned a five-minute course penalty. Off the course!" the official yelled, pointing to an area behind him. "Sit! All of you!"

Bryce exploded in protest. "No fair! We were just having a little fun. Show me in the rules where it says we can't have fun out here!"

"Would you like five more minutes?" the official asked, his face grim.

I reached up through the net. "Dad! Here! Take the snake!"

He stretched over and took him by the tail. "Got it!" he said.

"We're sorry, little snake!" Jesse called to it.

Ashley crawled from the side of the net and moved over to the time-out area. She socked Bryce hard on the shoulder. "Idiot!"

She and Bryce dropped to the ground just as their third teammate came up to the net.

"Toby! Over here!" Ashley shouted. "We're having a picnic," she said, sounding disgusted.

"C'mon, Jesse, let's GO!" Sergio yelled. "Stump, let's move out!"

"Like this, Jess," I said, showing her how to hold herself over her bike and pull it through.

"I'm out! Yee-haw!" Sergio yelled.

"Great job, you two!" Dad said, clapping. "Keep it going!"

"Glad—I've—been doing—push-ups all summer," Jess panted.

"C'mon! C'mon! You two! Haul ass!" Sergio whistled and hooted. "Almost got it!"

Jesse collapsed next to her bike. "I've—got to stop—just for a sec."

I turned toward her. "You're doing great, Jesse. You're an Amazon!"

"I'm a filthy, disgusting one," she said. She pulled her bottle from its cage and sucked it down. She wiped her mouth on her dusty arm and gave herself a big brown mustache.

Sergio was nearly busting his vocal cords. "LET'S GO! LET'S GO!"

I grinned at her and said, "Ignore him. Ready?"

She nodded and got back in position. "Last one out of the net has to have dinner with Sergio tonight!"

CHAPTER THIRTY-FOUR

THIRTY MINUTES LATER, THE THREE of us were ready to surrender our bikes to the course monitors. *Reality Soap*, the race underdog, had surprised everyone and finished the bike course first. We were still battling it out with *Miami Loves* despite their time-out. *Chicago Central* had caught up with us as well. We all looked like we had done a stint mud wrestling. The last hundred yards of the bike course included wading through the only standing water on the island. It was the biggest mud hole I'd ever seen. I'd gotten ahead of Sergio going through it and hit the last obstacle first.

It looked like a big wooden garage door, propped up in back by two by fours. But it was taller than a garage door.

I yelled over at the official nearby. "Can we help each other?"

He nodded. "Racers can. Alternates can't. But once you're over, you can't come back to help."

Jesse and Sergio came running up. "Here!" I said. I laced my fingers together in a stirrup. "Up, Jesse!" She put her foot in and I hefted her up.

Sergio came from behind and started pushing her butt. "Oh, I like this job!" he said, huffing.

"Jesse!" I yelled up. "Put your foot on my shoulder!"

"Mine too!" Sergio yelled.

She was still short. I grabbed her foot from my shoulder and pressed it farther up, straining.

"I'm there!" she screamed. She pulled herself up the rest of the way and swung a leg up high, tucked it over the other side. In a moment she dropped over the top and disappeared.

Sergio and I looked at each other.

"You go!" he said. "I'll give you a boost."

"No, you go!" I said.

"C'mon, man! You'll never make it by yourself!"

"GO!" I screamed at him.

"Suit yourself," he said, "But if you're not over this in sixty seconds, I'm benching you!"

Jesse came around from the back and stood at the side, watching. "Hurry, guys!"

He stuck his foot out and I gave him a boost, straining under his weight.

"Higher, I need to be higher!" he shouted.

I hugged his leg close to my chest, grunting, then took the heel of my other hand and shoved it under his butt, then pushed with both hands hard as I could. He stepped onto both my shoulders, his bike cleats digging into me. It felt like he weighed twice what Jesse weighed.

He lunged up then but didn't make it and landed back down on me hard, one wayward heel kicking me in the forehead.

"Damn!" he yelled.

Ashley from *Miami* ran up next to me. "Drop him! He's a creep."

"GO!" I yelled at him.

Sergio took a final lunge and he was over! I heard him land with a thud and a yell on the other side.

Ashley looked at me. "Now how do you get over?"

I rubbed my shoulders. "I dunno! Just didn't want him helping me." I stood back and gave it a long look.

"Come on, kid. I can get you over," she said. "You weigh what— 120? Piece of cake. I can bench more than that on a bad day."

I stared at her. "You're gonna help me over?"

"Sure! I can if I want to."

She looked down at my legs. "Which one you gonna give me?"

"I've got to give you the fake because I'll need the real one to swing over."

She bent down and made a saddle of her hands. "In you go!"

I looked over my shoulder to check to see if Bryce or Toby was near. "Your team is going to kill you."

"Probably. So hurry the heck up, will you?"

She vaulted me up and I strained, reaching as far as I could. Dad, Sergio, and Jesse screamed and yelled for me. "Almost there! Don't stop!"

I was still short, way short, and couldn't get my fingers in the grooves enough to pull myself up.

I heard Ashley growl and grunt under me. She gave me a massive butt push and I was able to get one hand over the top. I pulled with all my might to bring the rest of my body up. Got it! I swung my foot once and missed, hanging on hard.

Jesse screamed the loudest for me. I swung again and my foot caught the top edge.

"Whooo!" Ashley screamed below me.

I dropped over the back, landing on some soft cold sand. I pulled myself up and ran around to the side.

"Thanks!" I yelled.

"See you at the finish!" she said.

Sergio saw Bryce and Toby coming and hung back. "Hey, fellas! Guess who helped our boy over the wall? Do you think Ashley might be available to paddle for us too?"

Jesse and I sprinted over to the kayaks.

"Which ones are for *Splendor Town*?" I shouted at the official.

"Those two yellow ones—" he said, pointing.

I grabbed one, hauled it into the water, and turned to Jesse. "Oh, miss! Your taxi is ready!"

She hesitated a second and glanced over her shoulder.

"Hey!" Sergio jogged over, dragging the second kayak. "Jess! No way you go with him. Over here, babe."

"I got here first," I said. "I get to pick my partner. That was the deal. And I pick her."

He shook his head. "Look, no offense, guys, but you two aren't strong enough to paddle together!"

"We're wasting time, boys," Jesse said. "But Stump is right. He got here first. If he wants to paddle with me, he can paddle with me."

Sergio glared. "You two want to lose this race or *what*?"

"We had a deal—" I said.

I looked at Dad. He put his hands up and said, "Keep me out of this. Just tell me what kayak you want me in."

"C'mon, Jesse," I said. "You want front or back?"

"Don't you dare, Jess!" Sergio yelled. "You going to throw away the race so you won't hurt his feelings?"

"Stop it, both of you!" she shouted. "We don't have time for this."

"That's right!" Sergio said. "We don't have time for this pretend romance."

"Shut up, Sergio!" I said. I shoved a paddle at Jesse.

Sergio knocked it away from her. "C'mon, Jess. I've tried to be a good sport about your little rehab project here. But enough is enough!"

"Shut up, Sergio!" she said. "You are *such* an ass."

He laughed at me. "This was nothing more than her good deed for the year. But you had to fall for her, and she just couldn't resist using that to try to piss me off. As if it would."

"That's *enough*, Sergio," Dad said, moving closer, his voice low.

But it wasn't enough for me. I came at Sergio like a rocket. Grabbed him around the neck and pulled him down. Got him from behind then and shoved his face in the water. He flipped me onto my back and shook me, yelling. He was strong and wild, but so was I. I wanted to kill him with my bare hands. I shoved the heel of my hand hard up under his chin and he fell back, splashing into the water.

Jesse screamed at us both to stop, and I felt a pair of strong arms yank me up. I was dizzy with animal rage.

"ENOUGH!" Dad yelled.

Jesse ran over to Sergio and helped him up. He wiped his hair out of his eyes and looked at me. "Did you really think you had a chance with her? What a joke!"

I lunged again, but Dad had my arms pinned.

Sergio grabbed the kayak from behind and put it in the water. He looked at Jesse.

She couldn't even look at me—she just climbed into his kayak, her mouth tight. He pushed off into the surf, jumping in before a wave hit them. He shouted back at us, "Let's just finish this damn race."

Dad pulled the other kayak next to me. "Let's go!" he said.

I was stunned. Could hardly move. I couldn't believe she was riding off with him. He was such a creep and a liar. Or was she the liar?

"Alastair!" Dad called again. "Let's go! Get in! You can finish kicking his hide when we get to the boat. I'll help you. He's a punk."

"NO!" I shoved the kayak away from me. "I'm not going back with you!"

"We can't finish the race if you don't get in."

"I don't care about the race!"

"Look—" he said. "Here comes *Miami*. We can still beat them. Come in second for sure. Maybe even first if we hurry!"

"Why? So, you'll look like a big shot? So Sergio will? Think I care about what *any* of you want?"

"What about the money? We've got a real shot at it!"

"I don't give a damn about the money! That's your thing, remember? Not mine."

"Alastair, use your head. That money will go to good use. And you've trained so hard all summer. Do you really want to bail now?"

"Maybe! Maybe I want to be known as the Bail-Out Kid! The Quitter! What do you care?"

Bryce and Toby flew by, shouting taunts.

"What's wrong, *Splendor Town*? Can't find the ignition?"

"Fuck off!" I yelled, waving a finger at them.

"Knock that off right now!" Dad roared. He grabbed me by the arm.

I ripped it away from him. "What's wrong? Am I embarrassing you?"

"No! You're embarrassing yourself!"

I laughed like a crazy person. "I couldn't embarrass myself if I tried. You've done that enough for me for a lifetime. You're pathetic."

"Stop it right now, Alastair. You're upset, and you need to calm down. Take a deep breath. C'mon." He took a step toward me.

"Get away from me!" I backed up. "You're disgusting! You know that?"

He shook his head, his face full of hurt and anger.

I couldn't stop. "What kind of man cheats on his wife with a *senior citizen*? What was she, Dad? Seventy? Did she pay you? Was that it?"

Dad's face froze, and I could see that I'd just made a base hit. But I wasn't done. I was going for the whole game.

"You knew she paid me, didn't you? A hundred bucks to keep my mouth shut!"

A bark of pain escaped me and I swiped hard at my nose.

"Oh God, Alastair—!" He came toward me and I backed away.

"I saw you two in the bedroom that morning—you're pathetic!" I screamed.

"Oh God, that's why—" he started. "Son—please," he said, reaching for me.

"Stay away from me!" My voice caught and I had to hold it strong so I didn't cry.

He raked his fingers through his hair. "We've got to talk. But not here. Get in the kayak. Let's go home."

"No! It's too late for talking. I'm out of here!"

I leaned over and yanked off my leg. Then cocked my arm back ready to throw it at him. Instead, I just shook my head in disgust and hurt and hurled it as far as I could in the sea.

I threw myself into the water and began to swim. Hard, angry strokes. I'd swim back to the boat. To hell with this damn race. To hell with Jesse.

And to hell with him.

CHAPTER THIRTY-FIVE

I SLICED THROUGH THE WATER like a shark, every fiber pulsing. I imagined leaving a trail of blood in my wake. I flew, faster and faster—icy waters stinging my skin. I'd never swum in the ocean without a wet suit—not since that first time when Kiki had to bail me out—but I didn't care. Coach would kill me if he saw me. Didn't care about that either right now. Just wanted to get back to the boat, back to the shore, back to the airport, back to my mom.

My lungs burned and my arms began to ache, but I knew how to swim past the pain, past the exhaustion. But not past the cold. The truly wicked cold of it. The farther I got from the shore, the colder the water got.

I kept a close eye on my course. Before long, Sergio and Dad would probably come after me, but I had the stealth advantage. And I didn't have a big plastic tub to navigate.

My leg was getting stiff, and if I wasn't careful, I was going to get a cramp. I notched my kicking down a bit and tried pulling harder with my arms.

I swam like a fool farther and farther from the shore. I spent all the anger I had, then drummed up some more. I started shivering. I'd never make it to the boat like this. This was stupid and dangerous, but I couldn't tell yet if I cared.

Minutes ticked away, and the boat wasn't getting any nearer.

One shrill whistle startled me and I halted in my stroke, popping up in the water.

Coach was propped up on top of a surfboard with a terrible look on his face.

"What the hell are you doing out here?" he asked with a mean grimace. He reached over to pull me toward him, and as he did, he grunted and swore.

"Get . . . out . . . of . . . the water!" he said, his voice strained.

"Coach! I-m-m sorry!" I tried to keep my teeth from clattering.

Man, I'd never seen him look like this. He looked like he was to going to kill me.

"Get . . . out . . . water—can't swim—without a wet suit." He reached a hand out to me and I grabbed it. But it was weak, like someone had drained all the strength from him. It scared me.

"Get—up—here," he whispered, nearly out of breath.

"Coach, what's wrong?"

His face ripped up in pain then. He bared his teeth and squeezed his eyes shut. Then he just crumpled forward on the board.

"COACH!" I yelled, and tried to push him back up. But he was as limp as a rag.

My head spun around and I screamed. "HELP! HELP, SOMEONE!" The nearest kayak looked like it was miles from me.

I grabbed Coach by the shoulders and yelled, "*Coach*!" I felt on his neck for a pulse and thought I'd felt something, but I was shivering so bad, it was hard to tell.

Oh God, had he stopped breathing? "No!" I yelled. 'Cause if he had, I didn't know CPR or anything. Dad did. I'd watched him in that video back at the house, doing big breaths on that blond dummy.

If Coach wasn't breathing, he'd need air. I needed to get him lying on his back. I moved around to the front of the board and pushed his shoulders, then eased him back as best I could without dumping him off.

This couldn't be happening. Not here. Not Coach. I couldn't handle it. Oh God. OH GOD!

I tried to steady and center him on the board. Luckily, it was a big one. I hefted myself up onto the board and slid up, spreading his legs apart so I could find a small place to dock. The board dipped and rocked and I held us both on. Steady! I crawled over the top of him and shook him.

Nothing. Okay, okay, what was I supposed to do? Pinch his nose. My fingers were so cold I could hardly work them, but I managed to get them squeezed together around his nose. I clamped my mouth against his and gave him a big gust. Waited a second, then did it again.

I needed to push on his chest, but things were too rocky. I was barely keeping us both out of the water. I didn't think I could get up over him.

Had to.

I spread my legs over him and sat up.

Tried to remember how Dad did it. Like with two hands put together. He'd made some dumb joke about a hand sandwich with the heel on the bottom. I pulled the zipper of Coach's wet suit way down and spread it open. I shoved the heel of my hand into his chest. Where I hoped to God his heart was. I gave him several shoves there and then felt for the pulse in his neck.

Pinched his nose again. More breaths.

More chest thrusts.

Shook him a good one. "C'mon, Coach! Knock this off!"

I pulled his whistle to my lips and blew. Loud and shrill, and I hoped somebody could hear me.

And pressed my face onto his again.

Pinch. Breathe. Breathe. Breathe.

I wished I had some of those electric paddles you see on TV so I could shock him back.

Why wasn't he waking up? I was doing everything right. How could a guy be swimming one minute and dying the next? I took the deepest breath I could and blew it into him hard as I could.

"Alastair!"

I jerked up.

"*Dad!* Help! It's Coach!"

He swung the kayak up next to me.

"I think he's dead!" My voice cracked into a sob. "I've been doing CPR, but he's not coming back!"

"Trade places with me! Quick!" he said.

I was so cold it was hard to move. Dad dropped into the water next to me. "Easy, now. I got you," he said, pulling my legs around. "I've got Coach, steady—go!"

I dropped into the kayak, nearly capsizing it. Dad held it upright with one arm and grabbed the paddle.

"Now! Hold the board steady if you can," Dad shouted.

He climbed over top of Coach, turned Coach's head, and opened his mouth. Then propped Coach's neck with his hand and blasted some breaths into him. Then did chest compressions.

"How-long- has- he-been-out?" His voice heaved with the thrusts.

"I dunno! Two minutes?" I wrapped my arms tight around me to try to stop the shaking. I grabbed the team flag from the bottom of the kayak and waved it overhead, back and forth, hoping someone would spot us.

I grabbed Dad's pack. "Dad! Is your phone in here?"

Dad shot up after another round of breaths. "Won't work out here! Go get help! Quick!"

I looked down at the paddle on my lap. Then at Dad. I couldn't tell him that this was only the second time I'd sat in a kayak. And I'd never paddled before. I knew Jesse could paddle, so I hadn't worried about going with her.

"GO!" he yelled. "Tell-them-we-need-air-rescue-NOW!"

"Go *back*?" I asked, looking around me wildly.

"No! Nobody's cell on the island will work. You need to get back to the *Orca*! Hurry!"

He ducked down for a couple of breaths, and I stuck the paddle deep into the water. Dug into the water as fast as I could. One side, then the other. One side, then the other. There was a swell coming my way, and it was tough going. I was going left, then right and hardly forward.

Please, please, don't let Coach die. Now I was going in circles.

"Dad!" I shouted. "I don't know how to do this!"

He pulled his mouth off Coach's and watched me a second. He held his arms straight out in front of him. "Like this! Side to side. Not so deep! Don't dig!"

The harder I tried, the worse it got. I tried to remember how Kiki had done it. I couldn't move the blasted thing in a straight line.

"I can't do it!" I looked at Dad.

"It's okay!" he shouted. He dropped down for a couple of breaths, then came back up.

"I'll go!" he said, heaving over Coach's chest. "You can do this! Watch me, okay?"

Oh, no. No. Please don't leave me with him. But even as I said that, I knew there wasn't another choice. I dropped over the side of the kayak into the water and towed it over to Dad.

"I saw you doing the breaths—" Dad said. "It was good! Just tilt his head back a bit so you can blow right into his lungs. And here—" He showed me when I got closer. "See this spot right here? I want you to put the heel of your hand right over the center of his chest. Don't be afraid. Give him fifteen steady compressions and then two big breaths. Just keep at it."

Dad felt Coach's neck for a pulse. Then he turned his head back toward me. "There's a life jacket in the front compartment. Hurry! Put it on! It will keep you warm and make it easier for the chopper to find you."

"He's not dead, is he?" I asked, my voice raw and cracked.

Dad finished off some chest thrusts before he answered. "This old guy?" Dad said. "Not a chance—but you keep at it until he sits up and tells you to knock it off. Okay?"

I nodded and threaded my arms through the life jacket.

Dad swung his legs around and dropped down into the kayak. I kept a steady hand on him and one on Coach's leg so he didn't drift off.

"Go!" Dad said once he was in. He held the board steady, and I pulled myself over the top.

I tilted Coach's head back and started the breaths again.

Then braced myself over him and pressed into his chest. "You— can—not—die—dammit!" I panted over him.

In response, his lips began to turn blue.

CHAPTER **THIRTY-SIX**

DAD BLEW AWAY ON THE kayak, and by the time I finished round number two, he looked miles away. We definitely picked the right guy for the go for help job.

Note to self: learn how to friggin' kayak!

I put my mouth over Coach's and he groaned up into me. Scared the living bejezus right out of me. I jackknifed up and stared. Waited for another sound. Nothing. Did I imagine it?

I put my mouth back on his and blew. He blew back!

"Coach!" I yelled.

His eyes fluttered.

I rubbed his scratchy cheek. "Can you hear me?"

I put two fingers on his neck like Dad had done. I felt something! *Definitely* felt something that time!

He moaned and started moving under me.

"Hold on, Coach! Stay still!" I patted his chest gently. All the same, I did not want him rearing up like Shamu under me.

He tried to lift his head and started mumbling.

"Stay STILL," I said, using my best no-nonsense voice. "Dad went to get some help."

His eyes opened halfway and he peered at me. Like he couldn't place me. Licked his lips. "My—son," he said.

"No, I'm not your son," I said. "It's me—Stump!"

Coach turned his head from one side to the other. "Get—my—boy."

Okay, he'd apparently fallen off his rocker, but I didn't care. As long as he was breathing.

"No worries, Coach. Once we get rescued, we'll look him up. Promise!"

Coach lifted his hand like in slow motion and moved it to his chest, over his heart.

"Yeah," I said, "It's your heart. It went on the blink. But you're fine now. We'll get you out of here."

"Where's . . . my . . . boy?"

Okay, back to that. "He's coming, Coach," I lied. "Dad went to get him. Just close your eyes and relax."

A big breath escaped him and he looked satisfied. I mean, I guess as satisfied as an old guy could look this close to death's doormat.

The sky began to hum, then vibrate. Within seconds, the sound of chopper blades filled the air around us. Getting closer and closer.

Amazing! Dad had hardly been gone five minutes and he'd already gotten someone to rescue us. The man could kayak! I slipped off my life vest and waved it overhead, keeping one careful eye on Coach.

"Hang on, Coach! The cavalry is here!" As the chopper got closer, I could see the markings on its side—E! TV. Oh, crap. It was reporters!

But wait—they had radios. They could still help.

The chopper circled me and dropped lower, then tipped to one side. Somebody was leaning out with a camera or maybe binoculars—I couldn't tell. I waved the vest higher and faster and hoped they knew that meant HELP and not HOW'S IT GOING UP THERE? And I prayed they could see that I wasn't just sitting on top of a surfboard, but on top of a real sick guy.

The chopper dropped lower and the water started swirling and frothing around me and Coach. The board tipped and rocked and made a couple of full revolutions. I lay flat on the top and tried to keep us upright.

I turned my head and yelled, "Hey! Back off!"

"HANG ON THERE!" a voice from a speaker blared. "WE'VE CALLED FOR HELP!"

"Id-i-ots," Coach mumbled.

I smiled. My man! He was coming back.

CHAPTER THIIRTY-SEVEN

I TALKED NONSTOP TO COACH until the Coast Guard chopper arrived. I couldn't remember if keeping people awake was what you were supposed to do when somebody overdosed or had a heart attack. Didn't matter. I wasn't taking any chances that he might wander back to the light and try to check out again.

He didn't tell me to shut up, and anyway, I couldn't have if I wanted to. All this stuff came pouring out—like maybe a delayed shock thing. I told him all about what Sergio had said and what a jerk he'd been. What Jesse had done. And how pretty decent my dad had been during the race and how he didn't even give me a hard time when I couldn't kayak. And how he'd been such a whiz at CPR and everything. What I didn't say out loud, but what I couldn't stop thinking about, was the look on Dad's face when I was screaming about EJ. Like I'd torn his heart out with my bare hands and ground it under my heel.

Coach was quiet and still, but he was breathing. He was probably in a world of hurt. I couldn't wait to turn him over to some doctors that could fix him all up. I couldn't wait to get out of the water.

By the time I'd given him a blow-by-blow account of the whole race, the Coast Guard came charging through the sky. They hovered overhead a minute, and then the door opened and a guy in a wet suit was lowered down a rope. He had some kind of coffin-shaped cage with him that was going to be for Coach.

"ALASTAIR!" boomed a voice out of the sky. "JUST HANG ON! WE'LL HAVE YOU UP IN A MINUTE!"

I nodded and gave a thumbs-up. I had to flatten my body then over Coach to hang on. The water chopped up again. It felt like some kind of crazy ride at Raging Waters.

"Almost home, Coach!" I yelled in his ear over the noise of the chopper.

He circled his arms around me and patted my back like he was trying to burp me.

I tucked my head into his shoulder and tried not to cry.

The Coast Guard guy on the rope hit the water with his big basket. Then another guy dropped from the sky in a scuba outfit and popped up right next to me. Except he was a girl and she had eyes the same exact color as the water. "You okay?" she shouted.

"He started breathing!" I shouted.

The guy with the basket broke into a big grin. "Good! Now let's get him out of here."

I dropped over the side, my body numb to the water.

"Okay!" the man said. "Let's move him!"

And before I could even blink, they had him off the board and into the basket, snug as a bug. The girl gave the chopper a high sign and they started pulling him up.

Then the two of them swarmed around me, checking me, and she gave me something hot to drink from a thermos on her belt, which tasted like honey and burned so good all the way down.

The rope came back down with a big harness this time, which

she slipped over my head and shoulders. She grabbed onto me from behind and held on tightly as they raised us together.

And as we were hauled up into the sky, I saw Sergio and Jesse paddling toward where the chopper hovered. Really fast, like they were on their way to a fire.

Funny how small they looked. And they just kept getting smaller and smaller until I couldn't see them at all anymore.

Jill was the name of the girl with the ocean-colored eyes, and she was a paramedic. She and the other rescuer, Silas, got busy right away cutting off Coach's wet suit and trying to warm him up. The other guy who got hauled up behind us was working on getting me all settled. He gave me a big soft blanket to warm up.

Jill helped hook Coach up to a special machine so she could watch his vitals until we got to the hospital. She gave him an IV. He didn't like that and tried to pull it out.

"Is he going to be okay?" I asked her.

She nodded back at me. "You did it, Alastair."

I shook my head. "It was my dad."

An hour later, I was still wrapped in a blanket and still shivering even though I had no reason to. It wasn't like I'd been adrift at sea all week—though it felt like it.

The chopper ride was beginning to feel like a blur already. Everything happened so fast once we took off. It had been so hard watching Coach lying there all exposed—the man that seemed a giant to me all of a sudden looked like someone's grandpa, all white and frail-looking. I wanted to go over and pat his hand or something, but I didn't have my leg, and I would have had to hop over there. I'm pretty sure hopping is frowned upon in a Coast Guard air rescue chopper. It was kind of embarrassing when they pulled me out of the chopper and I tried to hop off the landing grid. Hopping and ducking at the same time is no picnic.

I was starting to regret throwing my leg into the ocean. Mom was going to kill me.

Now I had no foot and no place to stay. Coach was probably going to be in the hospital a while, and I didn't have my own key to his house. I didn't have anything at this point except my swimsuit and this borrowed blanket. Not even money for the phone to call Aunt Clem.

But compared to what Coach was facing, it all seemed pretty stupid. He might be losing his whole life and all the things he loved—his stopwatches, his swimming, his coaching, and maybe the chance to see his son again.

Man, I had my whole life ahead of me.

One of the nurses at the hospital came bustling up to me. "Here! I snitched this from the ortho unit!" She handed me a crutch. "Stand up and I'll give it a tweak for you."

I stood up and the blanket fell.

"Arm out," she said, and she did a quick measure with the crutch. "Great!" she said, satisfied, as she tightened the screw. "Give it a go now."

I took a few steps with it. "It's good, thanks," I said, turning back.

And there was Dad, standing next to her, watching me. Looking at my leg. Looking at me.

Me looking at him.

Both of us looking at each other—well, different-like.

He came over then. Put an arm around my shoulders. Cleared his throat.

I took a big breath.

"You saved his life, Alastair."

I leaned into my crutch and looked up at him. The whole thing was so incredible. Taking any credit for anything seemed—well, stupid, really.

Kiki came hurrying down the hall and spotted Dad. "They won't let me see him yet." His eyes landed on me, and he came over and put his arm around me. "I heard what you did. Thanks, kid!"

"Wasn't me," I said, surprised at how shook up he seemed. I thought he and Coach hated each other.

Kiki leaned up against the wall and massaged his forehead. "I should have known something was going on this morning when I saw him. He actually smiled at me."

"I guess it's my fault—" I started, finally putting words to what had been chewing on me. "If it hadn't been for me, Coach would have never been out there in the first place. I could have ridden to the race with Dad and Skyla, but I was being stubborn."

"Don't even go there, kid," Kiki said. "Even if he hadn't pulled through, he would have died doing what he loved—coaching and being in the water. You can't ask for more than that. I'd sure love to leave the world surfing!"

"Right," Dad said. "And really, when you think about it, he picked a great place to have a heart attack. He had you with him, Alastair—"

"Yeah," Kiki said. "And then a CPR instructor on the scene—"

"And celebrity chasers overhead," I said, my voice weak.

A nurse stepped into the hallway and looked down at us. "Mr. Witsak?"

I looked around, confused. Mr. Witsak?

"Yes?" Kiki said, hurrying toward her.

She smiled. "You can see your dad now."

My brain went dark then, like I'd blown a fuse and couldn't get any lights to come on.

"That's Coach's *son*?" I asked.

CHAPTER THIRTY-EIGHT

DAD AND i SAT iN the waiting room, not talking, even though there was tons of stuff that needed to be said. It felt like a bomb had gone off between us. You can't undo that. Kiki came back to us after a while and told me I could go in and see Coach if I wanted. I jumped up. I had to see him. Needed to see for myself that he was still breathing.

His eyes were closed, and he still looked old and frail. But more peaceful now.

"Did you get to talk to him at all?" I asked.

Kiki nodded. "He told me I needed to charge more for my burgers. Said they were too good to pass off that cheap. I almost fell over when he told me that. I figured he'd never even been inside the Surf Burger. He must have snuck in one day when I was out."

"I can't believe he's your dad," I said, my head still reeling from that. "Why did you guys keep it a secret?"

"It wasn't a secret. We just stopped claiming each other a few decades back."

I pulled the towel closer around me to fight off a shiver. "So do you ever regret that?"

Kiki looked at me, then looked back at Coach. "I'm not much for spending time on regrets. I like the present. You know, before he fell asleep, he took my hand. That makes this a good day." He came around the bed then and gave me a big squeeze around the shoulders. "Thanks again, Stump, for everything you did."

I lifted my shoulders and dropped them. "I didn't do much. I'm just glad I didn't drown him while I was trying to save him."

Coach groaned, and Kiki went back over to him. "I'm still here, Dad."

"I'll come back later," I said. "When he wakes up, will you tell him I'll be back?"

Kiki nodded as he sat down on the bed, patting Coach's hand.

My eyes were leaking as I left the room, and I realized I was dog-tired. Between the race, the fight with Sergio, the explosion with Dad, and trying to save Coach, I felt like I'd just lived about three lives.

Skyla was sitting with Dad, and she jumped up when she saw me. She came over and handed me a sweatshirt. She held my crutch while I drew it over my head. Man, it felt good. I wondered if I'd ever warm up again.

She gave me a quick once-over, rubbed her hand over the bristles on my head. Then she gave me a kiss on the cheek. "Nice work, Stump."

"Thanks," I said. I leaned across and kissed her back. She turned bright red but looked very happy.

Dad came up to the two of us then. "How about we all go—uh—" He stopped before the word "home," but it hung in the air. "You need to get in a hot shower."

I hesitated, looking back at Coach's room.

Skyla read my mind and said, "It's okay. Kiki won't leave. You know Coach would want you to eat, right? It's been a very long day."

"Okay," I said. "But can I see him later?"

The nurse that was working on her charts overheard and shook her head. "Come back in the morning. He needs his rest."

And even though Coach was sound asleep and hooked up to all those monitors, I could hear him loud and clear, like he was standing right next to me growling.

"Get outa here, kid! Go home with your dad."

Back at the house, after a very long hot shower, I made my way down to the kitchen. On the way home, Skyla had called ahead to Ian and put in a grocery order. They had put together a massive submarine sandwich with all my favorite meats and cheeses. And it had a big double row of tortilla chips right down the middle of it. They ate yogurts and watched me work my way through it. Then they brought out some killer chocolate chip cookies and I ate five of them. I could have stopped at three, but watching me dig in for the first time all summer was really making the two of them happy. I figured it was the least I could do.

Dad joined us toward the end of the food orgy. He had just gotten out of the shower and as usual smelled good enough to eat. He patted the top of his wet hair a bit nervously, I thought.

I took a deep swig of milk and tried not to burp. "Dad?" I said. "Uh, you're not losing your hair."

He looked at me and shrugged. "Happens to the best of us."

"No, I mean, really—" I did burp then. "S'cuse me! I've been putting hair in your brush. It was mine. I did it so you'd think you're going bald. You're not."

It got very quiet then, and Skyla covered her mouth with her napkin. Ian got busy taking things to the sink.

I wiped my fingers off on my napkin. "I'm sorry—it was a dumb joke. Mean, too, I guess, if you were worried about it."

Dad put his hands on his hips and just stared at me like he couldn't believe it. Then he dropped his head back and laughed.

I laughed too, nervous-like, and then everybody started laughing. In minutes, we were near hysterical.

Skyla stood up and went over and hugged him. "You poor guy. Have you been worried about that, Rick? God, I can't wait until you lose your hair. I think bald guys are very hot. Don't you, Ian?"

"So the ladies say," he agreed.

Dad wiped his eyes and looked at me, still chuckling. "Boy, you got me. Remind me to tell you someday what I once did to your grandfather."

He looked over the bare remains of my lunch. "Get enough to eat?"

I nodded.

"Let's go down to the beach," he said.

I slid off the stool and landed on one leg.

"Oh! You don't have your leg," he said. "I forgot."

"It's cool. I'm good with a crutch." Normally I didn't need one, but I was shot from the race.

"Great!" He reached into a drawer by the sink, pulled out something small and shiny.

"Heads up," he said, hurling it my way.

I plucked it out of the air. Looked down and rubbed my fingers over it. "What's this for?" I asked.

"For later," was all he said.

There was one of those gorgeous, show-off kind of California sunsets happening, like the kind we had the first night we'd all had dinner together. The night I'd first fallen for Jesse. My heart turned over on its side and choked a bit, remembering. I took a deep breath and sighed.

"You okay?" he asked.

I picked up a small pebble and hurled it. "Yeah, mostly. Just beat."

Dad and I were sitting on one of the giant rocks on the beach in front of their house. He seemed nervous, and I was too. I think we both wondered if we'd survived the explosion.

"I'm going to gather up some of this driftwood. Then we can have a fire."

Ah, the lighter he'd tossed me. I thought maybe he was going to want to do a father-son dope pipe or something. Frankly, I was relieved.

"Want some help?" I asked.

"Sure!"

Within just a few minutes, we had enough driftwood and kindling piled to light several bonfires. I think he was putting off talking to me about what was on his mind. But I could feel it hanging over us.

The fire leapt to life. He fussed with it a few more minutes, then sat back next to me.

"I need to talk to you about what happened in Lake Rochester. I can fly back with you and talk with your mom there or with a counselor—whatever will work for you. But we've got to talk."

"Why not now?" I asked, my voice small.

He turned to look at me. "Well, we can start," he said. I could tell he was surprised and not expecting that. "I guess I'm not sure where to begin."

I broke in. "Well, I obviously already know about you and EJ. I just don't get why you'd pick her for your girlfriend when you had Mom."

Dad rubbed his hand across his face. He looked even more tired than I felt. "This is so hard. I never thought I'd have to have this conversation with you." He looked into the fire, and I could tell he was seeing the whole thing play out in his head. "I feel like such an ass. She wasn't my girlfriend, though she wanted to be. Well, I'm not even sure about that. EJ got what she wanted when she wanted it. And that winter, she had her sights set on me." He broke a small stick in two and threw it into the flames.

"I've never been very good with women," he said.

I looked at him, an eyebrow raised.

"I mean, I'm not very good at saying 'no' to them. When you look like I do—and *you* do," he added, "you get a lot of attention."

"Maybe you should try a stump," I said, trying to lighten things up.

He attempted a grin, but it looked sickly.

"I had a good job with EJ, and it looked like I could really go somewhere in the company. Your mom's business was kind of slow, and we'd been worried about money. EJ was leveraging my interest in getting promoted to—uh, well, get what she wanted from me. I was stupid. At first, I was just flattered and thought all of her attention was about mentoring me. Then I realized, well—"

"That she wanted to sleep with you?" I said.

Dad paused a moment, looking down at his hands. He nodded, cleared his throat. "Yeah. I kept trying to divert her. Put her off. When she insisted I go to Lake Rochester to meet some new clients, I panicked." He stopped and dug a hole in the sand with his foot.

I tried to imagine it all. How he felt. I knew I hated it when girls at school got too friendly with me. There were a couple of them in particular that always stood too close to me or would rub against me. I'd wedge my backpack between us. Try and fend them off.

"Oh!" I breathed. "That's why you took me with you on the trip."

He nodded and hung his head. "I've never regretted anything more in my life."

We sat there quiet a second with the weight of all that. I could feel his shame and guilt like a dark ghost between us.

"I thought if you were there, she'd back off, but she didn't. And she was so pathetic and old and vain—I just didn't know how to stop it. I was so afraid I'd lose my job."

"I never told Mom about it," I said, almost a whisper. "But not because EJ paid me to keep quiet. I thought if Mom didn't know, it would be like it never happened. And everything could go back to normal." I looked over at him. "Did *you* tell Mom? Is that why she was so mad at you? I mean, besides the accident?"

He nodded and swiped at his eyes with the back of his sleeve. "I told her about EJ and about the others. EJ wasn't the first. Mom knew already, though. When I first met your mother, I was involved with a woman that I didn't love or even like. We thought that once we got married and had you, it would change everything."

The air between us was thick and I could feel his shame. He dropped his head.

"Is it different now—I mean, with Skyla?"

Dad took a big breath, squeezed his nose. "Yeah. What happened to you and to your mom and me changed everything."

I bit down on my lip. "Why couldn't you just stay, then—with *us*?"

He was silent for the longest time, and I wondered if he would ever answer.

"Your mom couldn't forgive me, and I don't blame her. I couldn't forgive myself. We didn't want you to have to live in the aftermath of that."

"Maybe," I said, my voice breaking, "maybe somebody should

have asked me—asked me what I wanted. It was my life too."

Dad scrootched over toward me and pulled me close to him. He put his chin on the top of my head, and I could feel his whole body shake. His other arm stretched across me to pull me close. He cried into my hair—I could feel his tears running like little waterfalls over my head. And he just kept saying "sorry" over and over. And over.

We stayed like that, locked together, until the flames burned themselves out and all that was left was the smoky embers.

And that's how Skyla found us when she walked down to the beach to tell us that Kiki had called. He wanted me to know that Coach had stayed through the sunset, which he watched through the window in his room. And right before he died, he'd grunted like he always did when something really pleased him—but he didn't want you to know it had.

CHAPTER **THIRTY-NINE**

TURNS OUT THAT SKYLA WASN'T the only one who was loaded. Apparently, Coach was nearly Howard Hughes. He left his house and a small fortune to Kiki and his daughter. He'd been investing in beach real estate for years and had made a killing.

Kiki talked to Coach's doctor after he died. The doctor told him that Coach had been having heart problems for a while but hadn't been willing to do much about it. Even though he ate like a monk, he had high cholesterol—the kind you inherit. Plus he worked too hard, took things too seriously, held a grudge with an iron fist, and was pretty much a heart attack waiting to happen. Not only that. As I suspected, he was still was smoking a cigar most nights before bed.

I locked the door of Coach's house behind me and sat down on the porch. I'd ridden his bike back over and put it in the garage. And I'd needed to pick up some of my stuff I'd left there. Kiki lent me some keys. I sat in Coach's living room a long time, just being quiet and trying to absorb that he was really gone. His place was so much like him—quiet, no-frills, and everything there had a purpose. He didn't have any sentimental stuff around, unless you counted his stopwatch collection. He displayed those instead of pictures of his family and friends. I wished I'd asked him what made him start collecting them. A shrink would probably say he was trying to hold on to time or something like that. Or maybe he just thought they were great to look at. You could tell they were really important to him, even if you didn't understand why.

There was something else that was important to him, and I had promised that I would work on it. I needed to get Dad to stop fighting the public access stairway. I was scared to bring it up with him, though. What if he was a real jerk about it and said no? What might that do to our brand-new-paint-is-still-wet truce? Since the bonfire, he and I were both uncomfortable with each other. Things had been so intense between us that night. Now I didn't know what to say to him. I don't think he knew what to say to me either.

Skyla pulled up right on time in front of Coach's house and beeped her horn. I waved and hurried out to her car, hopping along on my crutch. We were having lunch, and then she was taking me over to her orthopedist for a fitting. She said I could argue all I wanted, but there was no way she was sending me home to mom without my leg. Said she'd get written up in the *Bad Stepmother Journal* for sure, and she'd never live it down. I told her Mom would understand since I was the one who had thrown my leg out into the deep blue sea, but she was adamant about it. She'd shown me some pictures on the web of this new leg she wanted me to try. It was totally high tech. It cost a fortune, but Skyla said she funded a lot of their research and they would just give it to her. Probably three or four if she wanted.

"Hi!" she said as I climbed into her car. "Did you get everything?"

"Yeah," I said, looking back over at his house. I rolled down the window and took a big, long breath. "I can't believe I'll never see him again."

She reached over and gave my arm a squeeze. We were both quiet for a few seconds, and then she asked, "Do you want to sit awhile longer?"

"No, we can go," I said.

"You hungry?" she asked. "What sounds good?"

"Burger?" I asked hopefully.

She turned to me and smiled. "Surf Burger coming up!" she said.

It was later in the afternoon, so we had the place nearly to ourselves. It was quiet, and an old fan whirled overhead. Kiki came out when he saw us and gave us both a big hug. Told the chef to fix us the best the house had to offer. I noticed he had a framed picture of Coach up by the cash register with a card that read:

IN MEMORIAM

PETER M. WITSAK "COACH"

MAY 3, 1933–AUGUST 28, 2005

"SEEING DEATH AS THE END OF LIFE IS LIKE SEEING

THE HORIZON AS THE END OF THE OCEAN."

—DAVID SEARLS

They were having a memorial for Coach in two weeks, but I'd already be gone by then. Kiki said a lot of his old buddies from all over wanted to come, and it was going to take a while to get everyone together. And maybe Coach's daughter would come too, but she was still thinking about it. When I heard stuff like that, it made me realize that I didn't want to go through my whole life that way.

I stirred a french fry in my cup of ketchup. "Can I ask you something?" I said.

Skyla paused behind her mountain of salad. "Sure!"

"Why is Dad so obsessed about keeping people off the stairs? I mean, he's generally a pretty laid-back guy. Not really stingy, or anything. But those stairs make him go crazy. I don't get it. You don't care if people use the stairs, do you?"

She sighed and laid her fork down. "No, it's one of the few areas that your dad and I ever argue about. We had some pretty big yelling matches over it until I finally figured out what it was all about for him."

I stopped chewing and raised my eyebrows. "What? What is it?"

"Think about it."

"I have! All summer! It makes no sense."

She gave me a long look, deciding, I think, if I was in a place to understand. "Your dad lost his whole family once—his wife, you, his house, everything. You're not the same after that, Stump. It shakes you to the foundation. When your dad came and moved in with me, he brought some of that fear with him. Our house became very important to him. I became very important. Jesse too. It was like he was being given another chance and he didn't want to blow it. Does that make sense to you?"

I looked down at my plate and nodded. "I guess so." It was probably why I first started drawing houses. Ones that no one could take away from me.

She went on. "People are curious about these big places. We'd get people hopping the stairs and showing up on our deck peeking in the windows. Now and then kids would jump in the pool after surfing or maybe have a drinking party on the lower deck. Ian would just ask them to leave and it was no big deal. But for your dad, it was a huge deal. He felt invaded. He felt his family was being threatened. Well, you remember how he was the night those surfers came and threw his signs at the house."

"Boy, do I!" I said.

"I know. I'm sorry," she said, putting her hand over mine. "When I see him behave like that, I just try to think about what's he's really doing, you know? He's acting out how devastated he was to lose you and your mom."

"You really think so?" I said.

"I know so, kiddo. He barely survived that. That's why I'm so glad you came this summer."

"Even after all that happened?"

"Absolutely," she said. "I wouldn't have missed this chance to know you for the world."

Kiki came by and gave me a soda refill. He threw a magazine on the tabletop. "Have you seen this one?"

I studied the cover of *Daytime Flash*, another soap magazine. Jesse had called and warned me about it. The headline read "CELEBRITY MIS-ADVENTURE RACE!" One side of the cover showed a picture of Jesse and Sergio on the *Orca*, obviously yelling at each other. The other side had a picture of me sitting on top of Coach in the water, waving my lifejacket. The caption read: "Heroic One-Legged Hunk Steals the Show." The article went on to say that I'd been the cause of the recent breakup between Sergio and Jesse. Oh, boy, that's a good one. I took some pleasure in thinking about how much that must tick off Sergio. And an anonymous race official had reported there'd been a knock-down, drag-out fight on the beach between me and Sergio over Jesse. Too bad they didn't have a shot of me throttling him in the water.

Coach and I also made the *LA Times*, the *Lumina Beach Press*, and the *Vendanta Tribune*. Famous once again.

"Can I keep this?" I asked Kiki, handing the magazine to Skyla for a look. "It'll save me some time when I write my how I spent my summer vacation report."

"Sure thing, sport," he said. He rubbed his hand over the top of my head. "Hair's growing out. Looks good."

"I'm sorry that they printed that picture," Skyla said after Kiki went back to the kitchen. "That must be hard to look at."

"It's okay, really," I said. "I tell you, if those reporters hadn't been there, who knows how long it might have taken for the Coast Guard to come? I was glad to see them."

I turned the cover over on the table, looked at Skyla, blurted, "I made a promise to Coach that I'd get Dad to stop trying to block the stairs. I feel bad. Like I didn't keep my word."

Skyla sat back against the old green leather booth. "You know, Stump?" she said. "This might be just the right time to ask him."

CHAPTER FORTY

MY LAST THREE DAYS IN Lumina Beach sped by. I had a couple more fittings on my new prosthetic. Dr. Rui had shown me this running attachment I could use that Skyla said I had to have. She also made me get a special one for biking and one for cross-country skiing too. Oh, boy, I was definitely going out for some sports this year. Those guys at school weren't going to know what hit them.

And before I knew it, the last night was here. And it looked a lot like my first night—except nothing was the same. The sunset outside the dining room window was still spectacular, the dinner table was being set with flowers and crystal things, millions of candles were lit, and Jesse still took my breath away. But I'd live through it.

She and I had come out on the deck until it was time for dinner. I'd talked to her on the phone a few times since the race, but we didn't really talk about anything important. Just small stuff. She'd called the day after the race to tell me that *Chicago Central* was the winning teen team. And that Skyla was still donating fifty grand to Challenged Athletes in our team's name because we'd all worked so hard. Somehow that didn't surprise me. Skyla was pretty cool all around.

"Are you excited about leaving tomorrow?" she asked me.

"Yeah! I can't wait to see my mom. I got to have a long talk with her today. She finished her program and sounds so good. But she'll go back to them in a month for a tune-up. And she has to go to AA meetings at home every day for a few months. I'm really proud of her."

"That's such great news! I know you've worried about her all summer."

"Yeah, and now she's like total hiker woman. Man, I hope she didn't stop shaving her legs. She and Aunt Clem are taking me camping for three days before school starts."

"You're lucky," Jesse said. "I'd give anything to go camping with my mom. She won't even garden, or let me. God forbid I get any dirt under my fingernails."

"So, are you ever going to quit the show?" I asked. "I bet Skyla would give your mom a job if she needed one."

She sighed and twirled a piece of hair. "I don't know if either of us could survive the real world. You know how they can never release zoo animals into the wild? They always say they've lost their survival instincts. I feel like that sometimes, you know?"

"You've got good instincts, Jesse. You'd be okay. "

She looked over at me. "Yeah? Do you think I could make it in public school without the kids thinking I was a total freak?"

"Are you kidding? They'd probably vote you student body president and homecoming queen the first week of school."

She didn't say anything for a minute, and then she just blurted it out like she'd been holding on to it way too long. "I'm really sorry about what happened at the race."

My face flushed, and I hoped she wasn't going to want to have a big long talk about this like they always did on *Splendor Town*. Savannah and Tye had the lamest conversations about stuff like this that went on for days. I couldn't take it. I shrugged. "No big deal."

"But I never meant to hurt—"

I cut her off at the pass. "Hey, it's okay, Jesse. You never even made it into my diary."

She swatted me, but her eyes warmed with gratitude. She smiled big then and bumped my shoulder. "Thanks, Jingle Boy."

It felt just right to have Kiki join us for my last dinner at Dad and Skyla's. Now that I knew Coach had been his dad, I could kind of see how they looked alike. Except Kiki looked like Coach would have looked if he hadn't been so mad at the world. Well, and if you subtracted the wild fried surfer hair and hula shirt.

Kiki looked around the table and I could tell he was feeling a bit like I did the first time I'd had dinner here. "Wow!" he said. "That was the probably the best meal I ever had. You folks eat like this every night?"

Jesse laughed. "Well, if they did, they'd weigh about three hundred pounds each," she said, lathering a big roll with butter.

Skyla looked around the table at everyone, then raised her glass. "Let's make a toast," she said. "To Stump and a memorable summer's end."

We all clinked glasses and Dad added, "And to our good health—"

"To all those we love," Jesse said.

Dad put his arm around Skyla at that, and I looked down at my plate. "To Coach," I said.

Kiki chimed in. "Yes, to Coach! One of a kind."

We raised our glasses together and drank to him. It grew quiet a moment after that.

Kiki cleared his throat. "I have something I want to give to Stump." He reached under his chair and pulled out a small box. He'd wrapped it up in a piece of a map and tied it off with twine.

I hesitated, and he nudged me. "Open it, kid."

I pulled off the wrapping and saw that the map was of California and the piece he used was Lumina Beach and the surrounding area. I took off the lid and sucked in a breath. It was one of Coach's fancy stopwatches.

"This one was from the '84 Olympics in LA," Kiki said. "Coach got a gig working with the swimmers. This was one of the official stopwatches that timed Matt Biondi's relay when he won the gold medal for the United States."

"Wow! Are you sure you don't want to keep this one?" I asked.

"Nope, none of them. I'm giving them all to you."

"All of them!" I said, shocked. "But there must be—"

"Sixty-two, according to his attorney," Kiki finished for me. "This is your first. You'll get the second one the next time you come visit and the third the visit after that. You want the others, well, you're going to have to keep coming back." He clapped me on the back.

I sat there, too stunned to say anything else.

"I didn't talk to my dad often," he said. "But he did tell me once this summer that he thought you had more guts than he'd seen from a kid and a whole lot of raw power. He'd want you coming back here to work on your swimming and stuff." Kiki gave me a look with the "stuff" part, and I had a feeling he meant stuff with me and Dad.

"Kiki talked to us earlier about this, Alastair. It's a very valuable collection," Dad said.

"It's probably a good thing you're not coming to the memorial service," Kiki said. "A lot of Coach's old buddies have been trying to get a piece of his collection for years. It's a relief for me not to have to deal with them."

"Uh, well, thanks *so* much! I really don't know what to say."

"Just say you plan on coming back and picking up every last one of them," Jesse said. "We're all going to miss you! Let's see, if you come visit *twice* a year, you'll have them all in about—what? Just thirty short years!"

I looked over at Skyla and Dad and wondered how they felt about me coming back. As far as houseguests go, I hadn't exactly been a walk in the park. Ian was probably counting the hours until I was gone. He'd have my room scoured and disinfected before my plane even went wheels up. I planned on leaving him at least one pair of hidden underpants, just for old times' sake.

Skyla read my mind. She was getting nearly as good as Mom. "You're part of this family, Stump," she said. "You don't ever need an invitation to come back."

My ears burned, and I couldn't think of a single clever thing to say.

Dad scooted his chair back. "I am completely stuffed. There's a full moon out there. Anyone up for a walk?"

Skyla and Jesse, Kiki, too, jumped at the suggestion. "Yes!" "Perfect!" "Excellent!"

"I'll get some sweatshirts for us," Dad said. "Go on ahead. I'll catch up."

I followed everyone out to the deck but stopped before the stairs. Jesse turned back to me. "Aren't you coming?"

"Nah, I think I'll just sit out here awhile. You guys go ahead."

As they clomped down the wooden steps, I went over to the pool and sat on its edge. Put my leg and stump into the water. I'd really miss this. I'd gotten spoiled being able to swim every day. But my life was with Mom. That was the life that made sense to me. This was still all so unreal.

I pulled Coach's stopwatch from my pocket. It was heavy and smooth. I really liked the feel of it. I fiddled with it until I got the time started and listened as the seconds pounded away. It was the sound track to Coach's life. Ticking. Ticking. Ticking. So *fast*.

Dad came around from the house with a load of sweatshirts. He didn't see me.

"Dad!" I called, and then wondered why I had.

He looked around. "Hey! Aren't you coming?"

I shook my head. "I'll pass. I thought I might swim in a while."

"Oh, okay," he said. "Everything all right? Need a sweatshirt?" he asked.

"I'm good," I said. "But thanks—"

"Guess I'll see you in a bit, then—" he said.

"Yeah—"

He hesitated, then started down the stairs. The seconds continued their frantic clacking. I pressed the stop button hard. "Dad!"

He turned.

"If I come back to visit, do you think you could teach me to surf?"

He paused, then smiled. "Absolutely."

"Cool," was all I said.

It was enough said for now.

ACKNOWLEDGMENTS

I am deeply grateful to my marvelous agent, Erin Murphy, for putting me together with Liesa Abrams and Razorbill for such an exciting and satisfying collaboration. And, I want to thank Diane Lingle for sharing a story from her childhood about a kid on a lift chair that nearly leapt to his death. His jump haunted me for years, and I had no choice but to follow his flight so he could tell me his story.